"You rem............... You kind of look like him."

Kendall almost laughed at her gross understatement. It felt too strange to tell Max the whole truth.

"Simon told me—" Max paused, shifting his gaze to his feet before peeking back at Kendall "—about his dad. I'm sorry for your loss."

The strain of the day, combined with the way Max's face messed with her head, left her speechless and overcome with emotion.

"Oh, man. I'm sorry." He gently wiped a tear from her cheek with his fingers. The physical contact caught her off guard. It was so familiar, yet not. It made her want to cry harder. "I didn't mean to—"

Kendall shook her head and stepped back, out of reach. She couldn't let him get too close. "I'm fine," she lied. She hadn't been fine in a long time. "I better get home. Have a good night."

He didn't stop her from going, but he looked like he wanted to.

Dear Reader,

My career in social work has placed me in the lives of many children and families in the middle of crisis. I've worked with children, like Simon in *The Better Man,* dealing with the death of a parent or struggling with school anxiety. I've seen the toll it takes not only on the child but the entire family.

The Better Man is a story about parents trying to do right by their children and ultimately themselves. Kendall and Max both feel lost and are afraid to trust. The pain their kids feel is their pain, as well. It's not until they open their hearts that the real healing can begin.

Time and time again, I have witnessed people find their way out of the darkness. I wanted to write a story about characters who do just that. Overcome. Persevere. Start again. Kendall and Max aren't perfect. They're flawed just like the rest of us. But by trusting one another, they find a way to be better than they were.

Thank you for joining me on their journey of love and self-acceptance. I hope you enjoy the story and come visit me at www.amyvastine.com!

Amy Vastine

HEARTWARMING

The Better Man

—

Amy Vastine

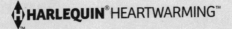
HARLEQUIN® HEARTWARMING™

Recycling programs
for this product may
not exist in your area.

ISBN-13: 978-0-373-36693-4

The Better Man

Printed in U.S.A.

HARLEQUIN®
www.Harlequin.com

AMY VASTINE

has been plotting stories in her head for as long as she can remember. An eternal optimist, she studied social work, hoping to teach others how to find their silver lining. Now she enjoys creating happily-ever-afters for all to read. Amy lives outside Chicago with her high school sweetheart turned husband, three fun-loving children and their sweet but mischievous puppy. Visit her at www.amyvastine.com.

Books by Amy Vastine

HARLEQUIN HEARTWARMING

29—THE WEATHER GIRL

Dedication

To my husband and my dad. Forget about the better man, you two are the best! Jerry, I'm a lucky girl to have someone who supports me and loves me unconditionally. I will love you forever. Dad, you've always been my hero. Your big heart and generous spirit are a gift to everyone who knows you.

Acknowledgments

I would like to thank everyone at Harlequin for their hard work and dedication to making this book everything it could be, especially Victoria Curran for taking a chance on me, and Claire Caldwell for being an amazing editor. Claire, your encouragement and keen eye make this such a painless process. Thank you for making me look good!

Thanks to my dear friend Jo for her constant support and willingness to hold my hand whenever I need it. I am so fortunate to have you in my corner!

A big thanks to Eden, Lisa, Suzanne and Jen for the friendship and laughter you bring to my life. It also helps that you are so awesome at brainstorming character names! I'm sure I'll use one of your suggestions...someday.

To Christine for being my friend even though I feed my kids Cheetos and refuse to try kale. Lucy wouldn't be who she is in this series if it wasn't for you!

To all of you who have encouraged me. My family and friends, my MSN family, my FIPsters, and every reader, blogger and writer who has supported me and my writing career. I couldn't do it without you.

CHAPTER ONE

A CONSISTENT MORNING routine was the key to a successful day. Toast popped up and the tea kettle whistled. Kendall Montgomery carefully ripped open the instant oatmeal pouch and dumped the contents into a bowl before adding the hot water. Brown-sugar-and-maple was Simon's favorite. The time Kendall bought strawberries-and-cream had been a disaster. It was a mistake she would not repeat.

"You want to stir this time?" She offered the spoon to her sleepy-eyed six-year-old. He nodded and took it from her as she turned her attention to buttering the toast. They had fifteen minutes to spare before they needed to leave for school. If they weren't the first ones there, Simon wouldn't go in. Kendall had a busy day ahead of her; she needed him to go to school today.

"What two things are you worried about today?" she asked, taking the seat next to him and pushing the plate of toast his way. It was the same question she asked every school day.

Her son's frail shoulders, which always carried more weight than necessary, lifted and fell. Nothing was said. The only sound in the room was the hum of the refrigerator. It was the single most irritating sound in the world some mornings.

Kendall didn't fill the silence, even though she wanted to do nothing else. Experience had taught her that if she waited him out, he would answer. If she spoke first, he'd hold it all in.

"Calendar and free time." The whispered words were spoken to the bowl of oatmeal in front of him but were spoken nonetheless.

"Calendar and free time," she repeated. These were typical, easy ones. *Thank God.* "Let's remember Mrs. Taylor promised that she wouldn't call on you during calendar unless you raise your hand, right?" Simon nodded, spooning in another mouthful of oatmeal. "And free time is free time. You get to choose your activity. If you want to listen to a book with the headphones, you can do that. Or maybe you'll want to play with the blocks today. Remember when you made that tower almost as tall as you last week?"

Simon's slate-blue eyes met hers and stared.

They were the same color as his father's and always caused that familiar ache in her chest to flare up. Simon nodded again. No protest was a good sign. His shaggy brown hair covered his eyes as he glanced back down at his breakfast.

"Two things you're looking forward to today," she prompted. It was Psychologist #4 who helped her realize that if she could get him to focus on the positives, even if it was going home at the end of the day, he would have a better shot at making it through the day.

"When Nana comes to get me." These words were a tiny bit louder than the last. Kendall smiled at both his volume and the choice. Her mother had a way with Simon, brought out the spirit that sometimes dwelled too deep.

"I bet Nana is looking forward to that part of the day, too. She told me last night that you guys get to take Zoe for a haircut." Zoe was Nana and Papa's dog, a feisty Bichon with a gentle heart and an endless need for affection. Simon loved the dog almost as much as he loved his grandparents.

The little boy perked up significantly. He snatched a slice of toast from the plate and began tearing off the crust. Kendall resisted the urge to remind him how wasteful it was to not eat the whole piece.

"Zoe gets haircuts? Like me?"

Taking the crust for herself, Kendall nodded. "Just like me and you, but she has to go to a special place for dogs. She can't go to Supercuts like you."

"Number two is seeing Zoe get a haircut." Simon was bouncing in his seat, making his mother happier than she expected this Monday morning. She kissed him on the head as she got up to get her coffee. Today had potential. Great potential.

Hand in hand, they walked along the shaded sidewalk. Simon's green camouflage backpack gently bounced up and down in time with their steps. Fall was quickly making its move on summer's final days. It wouldn't be long before Kendall would have to drive the three blocks to Wilder Elementary. Chicago was just too cold in the winter for walking.

The closer they got to school, the more Simon reverted into his shell. The term selective mutism was so deceiving. Silence was not something he selected, but rather was what held him prisoner. His hand tightened around his mother's, squeezed it like it was a lifeline. It broke her already battered heart.

"It's going to be a great day, buddy. I can

tell," she tried to reassure him as her cell phone rang in her bag. Without letting go of Simon's hand, she fumbled and struggled to get hold of her phone. "Good morning," she answered, trying to believe in the power of positive thinking and all.

"I'm stopping at Starbucks. What do you want?"

"Nothing, Owen. I'm good."

"Nothing?" he screeched. "We have a presentation in less than two hours that will make or break us in the Chicago interior design world, and you're willing to go in there not jacked up on something with an obscene amount of caffeine? Am I hearing you correctly?"

"I don't want to be a jittery mess. We need to give off an aura of calm and Zen, my friend."

"I'm Asian, sweetheart. People see me and can't *not* think Zen."

Kendall laughed. "That's funny, I see you and automatically think crab rangoon."

"For the love…" Owen let out a dramatic sigh. "How many times do I have to remind you that I'm Korean, not Chinese."

"Well, the term Zen is Japanese, so don't start with me."

"Okay, no coffee for you. How's the kiddo?"

The levity of the first part of the conversation was immediately weighed down like a lead balloon.

Kendall gave Simon's hand a loving squeeze as they crossed the street. He didn't look up at her but kept his eyes on his feet. "I'll tell you in about ten minutes."

Owen switched her to speaker. She could hear more of the background noise around him. "My fortune cookie app says...you are in for a pleasant surprise. That sounds promising."

"Let's hope so, Mr. I-Thought-You-Were-Korean-Not-Chinese." They were close to the school. Simon's steps grew slower. Kendall had to pull him along. "I'll see you in a few."

"In a few, K."

Dropping her phone back in her bag, Kendall stopped and crouched down so when Simon chose to look up, they would be eye to eye. "Owen says good things are going to happen today. He said we're in for a good surprise. Can you try to remember that when the yucks come?"

Uncertain eyes rose to meet hers, while his small mouth twisted. Yucks were what Simon called the anxiety. He gave her the tiniest nod, allowing her to stand and start for the school steps.

They were the first ones in class, as usual. Mrs. Taylor welcomed mother and son warmly. The woman was a godsend. She was a million times better than last year's teacher, who thought Kendall was a coddling helicopter parent.

"His grandmother will be picking him up today. They're taking Nana's dog to the groomer this afternoon. He's very excited. Right, bud?" Simon didn't speak but moved his head affirmatively. Again, Kendall bent down, gripping her son's upper arms. "I love you and I'll see you tonight. Keep an eye out for that surprise, okay?"

The little boy who existed before his father died pushed his way to the surface for a moment. He smiled and hoped. "Okay," he whispered so quietly Mrs. Taylor couldn't hear, but Kendall certainly did.

He spoke. He spoke in the classroom.

Kendall tried not to react too emotionally, but she wanted to squeal and cry and hug him. Instead, she kissed his cheek and gave his arms a firm squeeze. "I love you, baby." She bit down on her bottom lip and held back the tears until she made it into the hallway. If that was her pleasant surprise, she'd take it.

"So, MY COUSIN has a friend. Works for Abbott. Good-looking, great hair, super nice guy."

"Don't start with that today. I am not in the mood to discuss men. We have one hour before we sell this design to Mr. Sato." Kendall stood in front of the presentation boards with her arms folded in front of her. She had spent the last month putting them together and was now sixty minutes away from sharing them with their potential client.

"You're never in the mood to discuss men, which is what concerns me more than anything," Owen said. "I mean, I'm not an expert in selective mutism, but I have to believe if Simon saw you living a life, he would realize that it's okay to live his."

He was lucky he wasn't in arm's reach because she would have hit him. Hard. She was much too stressed to be having this conversation.

"Trevor's been gone just over a year," she said wearily. The anniversary of his death had led to Simon's regression. It seemed every time Kendall thought they were making some good progress, something would set him back. She was not going to give her son another reason to worry. "Simon does not need to see me running around with men on dates. He needs me home. He needs to know I'm not ever going to leave him."

His father had left. His father had left them both.

"Avoiding a date here and there isn't going to make him better."

"He spoke in the classroom this morning. He whispered to me when we were standing *in* his classroom."

Owen wrapped his arms around her from behind and rested his chin on her shoulder. "That's so great, K. He's doing better. Before you know it, he'll be like me and the teacher will be calling you because he won't shut up." He hugged her tightly.

Kendall leaned against her business partner and friend and smiled. "I would give anything to get that call."

"As much as it kills you to see him close himself off to the world, it kills me to see you do the same. Trevor didn't just leave Simon. He left you, too. Simon stopped talking and you stopped believing you deserve good things."

Kendall patted Owen's arms. "Trevor was the only guy I've ever truly been in love with. I can't imagine feeling that way about anyone else."

"People do it all the time. Hell, I've been in

love more times than I can count." Owen let go of his friend and threw his hands in the air.

"Love and lust are not the same," Kendall corrected him.

He winked. "I know. I know. Lust was Brian, Greg and Manuel. Love was Hector, Johnny, Gil, Milo…oh, and Dylan. Wait, Dylan was lust *and* love. A lot of lust. A little love."

Kendall shook her head. It was so easy for him. She couldn't afford to be so careless with her heart. She had to be careful and cautious for Simon's sake. Simon had to and would always come first.

Mr. Sato sat like a statue. He didn't smile, didn't comment, didn't give any indication of loving or hating their design. When Kendall finished, the only sign of life he showed was the gentle tug he gave to the cuff of his shirt.

"We would love the opportunity to work with you," Owen said.

Kendall's rapidly beating heart was becoming a distraction. She unclasped her hands and tried to stand tall in front of her unreceptive audience, reminding herself that Mr. Sato never displayed emotion. The outside might scream apathy, but inside he could love it.

Mr. Sato leaned to his left and whispered to his son sitting beside him.

"We have a few questions," the younger Sato said. Kendall felt her confidence surge. Questions were promising. She welcomed any and all questions. "And it's likely Mr. Jordan will have some as well. We expect him any minute."

Mr. Jordan was the restaurant manager who was already twenty minutes late. Kendall had no problem waiting.

Until her phone vibrated in her pocket.

She knew immediately that it was the school. Her family, Owen and the school were the only ones who called her. Her family knew not to call right now and Owen stood next to her.

"Excuse me." She faked a smile for the Satos and looked to her partner for reassurance that he could handle this on his own.

"I got it. Go."

She grabbed her bag and pulled out her phone as she headed out of the room to take the call. *Not today. Not today.*

"Kendall Montgomery," she answered on the fourth and final ring.

"Mrs. Montgomery, it's Lisa Warner."

"Hi, Lisa." Kendall sucked in a deep breath. Lisa was the social worker at Simon's school. Lisa was always the one to call with the bad news.

"We need you to come in."

"I'm in a meeting. Is he with you? Can I give him a pep talk over the phone?" She hoped but knew the answer would disappoint.

"No, he won't come out of the bathroom."

Kendall pinched the bridge of her nose as she made her way outside and prayed for a taxi. "I'll be there as soon as I can. What happened?"

"We had a dad volunteer in class today," Lisa said solemnly. The word dad was all Kendall needed to hear. She hung up and texted Owen, feeling every bit like the burden she had warned him she would be when he'd asked her to go into business with him.

The drive to Wilder seemed long, longer than it should have been. Kendall shoved money at the driver and jumped out of the cab. Her feet moved swiftly across the pavement, up the steps and into the building. Deep breathing did nothing to ease the knot in her stomach or the pain in her chest.

Trevor would have had mixed feelings about this school. He would have liked that the children wore uniforms, and not just because he was a military man. He had loved the simplicity of them. "No nonsense" had been his middle name. Trevor believed time should not be wasted worrying about things like "What color should I wear today?"

Trevor would have wanted a school with a male administrator, however. Not because he was sexist, although it might have come off that way, but because he felt more men should show interest in the development of young minds. Trevor, like his own father, took the role of father seriously and believed boys needed a strong male presence in their lives to survive in today's world.

Familiar faces greeted her in the main office. Her welcoming committee consisted of Lisa, the social worker, the principal, and the school nurse. They quickly ushered her to the first grade hallway, into the small boys' bathroom with blue-and-white tiles on the wall and worn-out linoleum on the floor.

"Simon, it's Mommy."

Black sneakers with neon green striping poked out from under the one closed door. He knocked as if she was the one who needed to open up for him.

"Can you unlock the door for me? We can go back to class together."

His little feet shuffled back, recoiling from the suggestion of going to his classroom. Avoidance, escape—these were his friends.

These were his comfort when the anxiety took over.

"I talked to Nana and she said you can hold Zoe's leash when you go to the groomer, but you have to make it through the school day. If you don't make it through the day, then there's no playtime with Zoe." It was a bribe, plain and simple, but sometimes that was the only thing that worked.

Silence.

Kendall hated the silence. She wished it was a tangible entity that she could strangle and put out of its misery. Her hand rested on the stall handle.

"Come on, Simon. Open up, honey." She resisted the urge to say she would take him home. As soon as she made that promise, she was done for. One thing she learned from Psychologist #1 was that she couldn't make a promise in the middle of one of these episodes and not follow through. His trust was essential. He had to be able to rely on what she said.

She wanted him to stay and finish his day of school. She wanted to try to save the mess she might have made of the Sato project. Yet what she wanted was of little importance when the anxiety was in charge.

"I'll stay for lunch. We can have lunch together. Then you can tell the yucks to take a hike and finish your day. I know you can do this. I know you can."

Silence.

Sometimes she wished the silence would finish her off. It was good at choking her, but she always survived its evil games. Survived but never won. No, the silence was always the victor.

Kendall could feel the three pairs of eyes watching her. Watching. Judging. Pitying. She hated that the most. The pity. Pity and sympathy made her almost as angry as silence. Almost.

Everyone at school knew why the boy didn't talk. Kendall had sat in the principal's office on more than one occasion to discuss the difficulties Simon was having at school, at home, in life. She had accepted their referrals for counselors and behavioral specialists. They had done the charts and incentives. She had taken him to Rainbows grief support groups, which ended up being filled with more children dealing with divorce than the death of a parent. She had read every book written on both grief and selective mutism. Still, she felt lost. She refused the medication because he didn't need medication. He needed his father. There was no pill to cure a broken heart. She would have taken it a long, long time ago if there was.

"I'm going to count to ten and then I want you to open the door for me. Ready? One, two…" she counted slowly, each number that went unacknowledged by the boy on the other side of the door tearing at her paper heart. "Ten."

Silence.

In an alternate universe, she pounded on the door with both fists, making it quiver and rattle. She screamed at the top of her lungs, "Knock it off! Stop being afraid!! It's just school!" In her fantasy, she stormed off and back to her meeting with Mr. Sato.

But in the real world where she had to live, Kendall dropped to her knees and pushed her pride and dignity aside. She buried her rage and her fear. She crawled under the door and into the stall with her son. She righted herself and pulled him into her arms. He melted against her.

"I love you. I don't know what to do. I don't know how to make the world okay for you and I'm sorry. I'm so sorry, baby." Kendall's tears fell on top of Simon's head as the weight of his world began to crush her.

He clung to his mother, not caring that her body had been in contact with an elementary school boys' bathroom floor. He hugged his mother like he wished he could make the world right for her, too. But the world would never be right because his dad was dead and he was never coming home. He was never going to help out at school or eat lunch with him. Dead was forever.

"Let's go home," she whispered. Resigned. Defeated.

The walk to the house offered much less promise than the one in the opposite direction a few hours earlier. Simon held tight to his mother's hand. Kendall's eyes were focused solely on the sidewalk ahead of her. She was a failure. A complete and utter failure.

Trevor would never have given in. He would have made the boy tough it out. Told him to man up. Trevor wouldn't have given in to the silence. He would have filled it with a firm voice and a confidence that couldn't be ignored. Trevor would never have surrendered.

At the last stoplight, they had to wait for the signal before crossing the street. A blur of colors went by as car after car moved past them. The city was alive. Her husband was not. The city roared, a myriad of noises— buses, people, machines, music. Her son was a mute.

Simon pulled on Kendall's arm. Tugging and tugging.

"Stop it, Simon!" she snapped.

"Dad! It's Dad!" he yelled over all the street noise. He pointed across the street to a man jogging toward a cab. Simon pulled on her arm again, almost taking them both into the busy road. "Dad! Wait! It's us!"

Kendall's whole body froze like it had that day, one year, two months and three days ago. The man looked up at the screaming boy and his mother. Eyes met. Her mouth fell open and she was sure her heart stopped.

"Trevor?"

CHAPTER TWO

Max Jordan was a punctual man. *Always* on time. *Never* late.

Except when meetings were scheduled before noon, that is. He tended to be a little tardy for those.

In his defense, he was still adjusting to the time change. It was only eight-thirty in Los Angeles, and the only time Max saw eight-thirty was if he was getting ready for bed after an extremely late night. In the restaurant and night club business, daytime was bedtime.

Even though the restaurant he was here to run wasn't open yet, it was difficult to change his sleep schedule. There were plenty of places for him to scope out, as competition in the restaurant business was tight in the Windy City. He wanted Sato's to be a success. He needed it to be.

Managing a successful restaurant would look good, and right now, Max needed to look good—in the eyes of the court, his ex and, most important, his son. Being late to his first meeting with the interior designers was not going to help.

The invitation to sit in on the presentation had been unexpected, especially since Max knew Mr. Sato had the only vote that counted. Sato was a shrewd businessman who only hired the best of the best. Whomever he chose to design the restaurant's dining area would be top-notch.

That didn't excuse Max's lack of punctuality, however. He should have been there. On time. How he was going to explain his late arrival was the only thing on his mind as he raced down the steps and out the door toward the cab he had called. Just as he reached for the car door handle, he heard a voice.

"Dad! Wait! It's us!"

Max stopped, looking up and across the street. Nobody called him Dad. Not even Aidan, his own son. It wasn't the name that captured his attention, but the desperation.

The boy across the street looked much older than Aidan, but they shared the same brown hair and strong lungs. Aidan's scream rivaled that of any horror movie leading lady. Max glanced around, searching for this other child's father. There wasn't anyone on his side of the street and the boy looked like he was about to dart into traffic.

Max felt his heart skip a beat until he noticed the boy held a woman's hand, his mother most likely. She'd keep him from getting hurt.

Their eyes met for the briefest of seconds and he could've sworn she recognized him. But that was impossible. There was one thing he hadn't made time for since he moved to Chicago and that was women. The only person he'd spoken more than a couple of words to was the nice—almost too nice—guy who owned the condo under his in their three-flat.

Max slid into the back of the cab and rattled off the address and a plea for haste. Rubbing his tired eyes with his thumb and forefinger, he tried to refocus on his excuse for being late. He had texted Mr. Sato's assistant that he'd be late the moment he'd woken up and realized the time. He hadn't, however, given a reason.

An accident. A boy ran into the street and was hit by a car. Max had to stop, wait for help to arrive.

Nah. Boys being hit by cars would probably make the news. He needed to think less dramatic.

Traffic? Traffic in Chicago was almost as

terrible as in L.A. Almost. Unfortunately, it wasn't bad enough to make him an hour late.

He could almost hear Katie now. His ex-wife would be reading him the riot act if she knew. *This is what you call being responsible? The only thing you're good at, Max, is lying. Doesn't this prove Aidan deserves better than you?*

Some days he hated her. Her, her sanctimonious attitude and her new attorney husband. Nothing bugged him more than the way she acted like a saint. As if he didn't know who she used to be. As if her life in L.A. never existed. Sadly for her, he did remember and she wasn't perfect.

Max took a deep breath and stared out the window as the buildings grew taller and the streets more crowded. He swore things would be different in Chicago. He would be different. He came here to prove something and he wasn't going to blow it. He was not going to be like his deadbeat father. Not if he could help it.

MR. SATO'S OFFICE was in the heart of the West Loop. Max knew they were close when they passed the Willis Tower. He threw in a couple of extra dollars of tip for the speedy service and jumped out of the cab.

With no excuse but the truth, he marched into the building and headed for the elevators. Hopefully he hadn't missed the entire presentation. Perhaps they'd waited for him. The designers were sure to be less than pleased with him if that was the case. That accident excuse felt less wrong for a minute until the elevator reached the correct floor.

The dark gray marble beneath his feet matched the color of the imaginary cloud above Max's head. He approached the receptionist seated behind a curved glass block desk, buttoning his jacket closed before smoothing down the lapels. He smiled, hoping the friendlier he was, the friendlier others would be in return. "Good morning. Max Jordan. I'm here for Mr. Sato's meeting with the interior designers."

The woman pushed her red glasses up her nose and tucked her jet black hair behind her ear. Everything about her was severe, from her hair color to the angle of her chin. "Mr. Sato's nine-thirty meeting?" she asked, lifting an eyebrow.

"That's the one. Better late than never, right?"

The woman's lips didn't even twitch. "Let me see if it's still happening," she said, her tone as judgmental as the look she gave him.

She picked up her phone and dialed. "I think the designer left," she told Max.

That figured. Max bounced on the balls of his feet and patted his pockets for the cigarettes that weren't there because he'd quit. He needed to figure out a way to make it up to Mr. Sato. Work harder. Do more promotion. Put in more hours when the place opened.

"Through those doors and to your right. The conference room is at the end of the hall." The receptionist glanced over her shoulder at the glass double doors.

"Thank you," Max said, trying to still appear professional while nearly sprinting to his meeting.

He ran a hand through his hair and rolled his neck around before pushing open the conference door. Mr. Sato's eyes were the only part of him that moved when Max entered the room. His son, Jin, wore a look of disapproval that spoke louder than any words could. A third man stared like he was seeing a ghost. He rubbed his eyes and shook his head.

"Mr. Jordan, how nice of you to join us," Jin said, without an ounce of sincerity in his tone.

The designer approached him cautiously and held out his hand. "Owen Sung, the O in KO Designs."

Max shook it firmly and apologized for being late.

Max turned to Mr. Sato. "I wish I had a better excuse than sleeping through my alarm. I will not let it happen again. I assure you, sir."

Mr. Sato's head bowed ever so slightly in acknowledgment.

"Shall I go over our design for Mr. Jordan?" Owen asked, handing Max a folder filled with the breakdown of the design elements and cost.

Mr. Sato whispered to Jin, who relayed the man's wishes. "Just a brief overview. Time is of the essence."

Max felt the sting but took a seat. Owen quickly outlined his firm's vision for the restaurant and Max listened with rapt attention. It was a beautiful, contemporary design. There was a hipness that would attract the younger crowd but a sophistication that would lure the more established money in the city.

"Where in the world are you going to find an artist to paint a mural of this size for nothing?" Max asked as he reviewed the price points, hoping to win back Mr. Sato's approval by finding a hidden cost.

Owen immediately squashed that dream. "My partner will be painting the mural, so her services are already paid for."

Mr. Sato whispered a few questions to Jin while Max asked about project management. Owen stated both he and his partner would be overseeing everything on a daily basis.

"Where is your partner today?" Max asked. His tardiness was troubling, but for the K in KO Designs to be missing seemed inexcusable.

Owen puffed out his chest, an offended tone coloring his words. "Kendall was here earlier, Mr. Jordan. She had a family emergency and couldn't wait on you any longer. I assure you, there is no need to worry about her dedication to this project. She put her heart and soul into this design."

Properly put in his place, Max decided to stay quiet for the rest of the meeting. There was little fault to be found in the design. He could see why Mr. Sato had solicited KO Designs to make a bid. At his father's whispered request, Jin called the meeting to an end and informed Owen they would be in contact soon. Escorting the designer out, Jin left Max and Mr. Sato alone.

A full minute passed before Mr. Sato broke the silence. "I hired you because I believe you are the best at what you do, Mr. Jordan." His voice was deep and gravelly. He was a man of few words, and when he spoke it sounded like he hadn't done so in years.

"Thank you, sir."

"As manager, I expect you to be a role model. Being late is unacceptable. Understand?" Max nodded and tried to swallow down the lump in his throat. "You will be at the site every day. Early. No excuses."

Mr. Sato's warning had magically tightened the tie around Max's neck. Slipping his fingers under his collar and giving it a tug, he promised, "I'll be there every day, sir. I won't let you down."

"I hope not." Mr. Sato stood, his stature not nearly as intimidating as his usual silence. At six foot two, Max was a giant in comparison. "I will accept the bid from KO later today and request we begin as soon as possible."

Max got on his feet. "That sounds perfect, sir. I've been scoping out the competition to ensure we'll be better than all the rest."

"Glad we have the same goal, Mr. Jordan." As if on cue, Jin opened the door as Mr. Sato made his exit.

Jin shut the door after his father left the room and began to circle Max like a lion stalking his prey. He had voiced his displeasure with his father's choice to hire Max from the beginning. Jin had been under the impression the job would be his simply because of his last name.

Jin wasn't exceptionally good at hiding his dislike for Max. The man was more of a boy, fresh out of college and overeager. His sense of entitlement was annoying. He believed himself worthy of the same respect his father had spent decades earning. He was child with a lot to learn.

"It won't take much for me to persuade him to let me run the restaurant if today is any indication of your work ethic," Jin said.

"It's not." The only job Max had ever handed over to someone else was parenting Aidan. He planned to earn that job back and prove himself worthy of this one.

"We'll see, won't we?" Jin said snidely. "For some reason, I have little faith in you, Mr. Jordan."

Get in line, Max wanted to reply. Instead, he smiled and wished the junior Sato a good day before leaving. He certainly wasn't going to prove anyone right or wrong standing in a conference room arguing with someone who had no idea what he was talking about.

MAX TIPPED HIS cab driver less generously on the ride home. Feeling deflated, he headed up to his condo with much less vigor than when he'd left. The guy from the second floor, who'd previously introduced himself as Charlie, was the hare to his turtle, nearly running Max over as he dashed down the stairs.

"Sorry about that, Floor Three." Dressed in jeans and a navy T-shirt with the Chicago Fire Department logo on the front, Charlie gave Max's arm a friendly punch. "I need to remember someone lives above me and might be on these stairs now and again."

"No problem," Max assured him, hoping for a quick escape.

"You home for lunch or something?"

"Or something." Max continued his ascent.

Charlie stopped him. "I'm grabbing lunch down the street. Best burgers on this side of the city, and as a good neighbor, I feel it's my duty to expose you to the finer things we have to offer around here. You have to come with me."

"Maybe another time." He didn't want to be rude, especially since Charlie was nicer than anyone he'd ever met in L.A., but right now, he wanted to be alone.

Charlie relented with a smile. "I'm gonna hold you to that."

Max didn't doubt he meant it. He retreated into his condo and loosed his tie, pulled it over his head and tossed it on the couch. Stepping around a stack of boxes, he made his way to the kitchen to grab a drink. He'd had big plans to unpack and make this place a home, but work was always his default. His apartment back in L.A. had been spotless because he was only there to sleep. This place was going to take a little more effort once Aidan started coming around.

Max bypassed the television and headed for his music. His records were the first thing he unpacked when he got to Chicago. The vinyl collection really belonged to his mother, but she had lost her love for it long ago and he had happily taken it over.

Joanna Jordan currently lived in Portland, where she was exploring her newest fascination—healthy living. Max couldn't complain. It was much better than her former love affair with alcohol or her cosmetic surgery phase. She'd traded her vodka in for kale shakes and did hot yoga instead of Botox injections. But Max knew it was only a matter of time before she moved on to something else. Another obsession. Another addiction. His mother re-created herself every couple of years. He never knew who she'd become, but he could always count on her to be different from the last time he saw her.

Max rarely benefitted from her frivolity, but the record collection was a wonderful exception. He had everything a music lover could want, from the Beatles to Buddy Guy. He slipped his favorite Pink Floyd album from its sleeve and set the record on the turntable. The music filled the room and Max lay down on the couch and closed his eyes, letting it take him away for a moment or two.

He patted his chest pocket, looking for something he knew wasn't there. Old habits died hard. As a teenager, Max spent more afternoons than he could remember blowing off class, listening to music and smoking his mother's cigarettes. It used to be what calmed him down, allowed him to escape his life.

Responsible parents didn't expose their children to secondhand smoke, however. And Max was determined to be a better parent than either one of his had been. He'd failed thus far, but that was going to change. Giving up cigarettes was step one.

Scrubbing his face, Max sat up. Step one of a hundred. Maybe a thousand. He got up and went to the kitchen for more water and something to eat to keep his mouth busy.

The catalyst for his reform was taped to the refrigerator. The single sheet of monogrammed stationery was wrinkled from being crumpled up into a ball and thrown across his apartment back in L.A.

A little over four years ago, Max met Katie, who was on the rebound from some guy who had failed miserably at giving her the attention she desired. She was the stereotypical wannabe actress working as a waitress. Max's nightclub was a favorite hangout for her and her friends.

Max, being Max, made her feel like the most important person he'd ever met. She was fun to be around when she wasn't partying too hard and didn't seem any more ready to settle down than he did. Neither one ever spoke of marriage or of moving things along too quickly. Not until she told him she was pregnant. Proposing was his first attempt at not being like his father, who hadn't bothered to stick around when his mom dropped the baby bomb.

The marriage lasted about as long as the pregnancy. They fought about everything— Max's work schedule, his friends, his cleaning habits or lack thereof. Things didn't get any better when the baby came along. Aidan was born with what Max thought had to be the worst case of colic in medical history. He cried and wailed day and night.

Katie warned Max she would move back to Chicago to be closer to her family if he didn't help out more, and he prayed she would.

Aidan was three months old when she made good on that threat, and he had shamefully felt nothing but relief. Katie and Aidan left California and Max went back to the way things were before he met her. For the next three years, he worked hard and made a name for himself in the restaurant business. Life was good.

Until the letter came.

She had handwritten it, which made it that much more personal, more real. Her words leaped off the page in attack like they had fired out of her mouth when they were together. Her low opinion hadn't changed over the years.

He was a deadbeat dad. He was an unfit parent. He was a pathetic human being. She wasn't looking for any more of his money. She didn't want anything from him except his signature.

Katie had remarried. She was Katie Michaels now. A swirly K and M were embossed in glossy black on the top of the heavy ivory paper. Her new husband was a brilliant attorney in Chicago. He was rich and well connected. He was the man Aidan called Daddy. He wanted to adopt Max's son and change his last name. All Max had to do was give up his rights. When he refused to do that, Katie filed for sole legal custody of Aidan with no visitation rights, effectively finding another way to cut Max out of Aidan's life forever.

It was the wake-up call of a lifetime. He had not only done what his own father had done, he'd let someone else be the father he had promised he was going to be.

He was Aidan's father and it was time he acted like it. Every decision he'd made since that letter arrived was made with Aidan in mind. Those decisions brought him here to Chicago, where he was going to do things right. Max and Katie weren't made for each other, but Aidan was made for them. Both of them. And no one was going to replace Max in his son's life. Not anymore.

Max made himself a sandwich and pulled the lid open on one of the boxes. A father needed a home for his son to visit. This would be that home for Aidan.

CHAPTER THREE

SIMON DIDN'T STOP talking about his dad all through lunch. He had a thousand theories about what Trevor was doing on their street that morning. Kendall knew she should stop her son from fantasizing about his father being alive, but she couldn't deny what she had seen with her own eyes.

The experience may have made Simon a chatterbox, but the shock of it all had left Kendall speechless. She was still trying to make sense of it long after they ate lunch. She didn't even bother reminding him not to speak with food in his mouth as he hypothesized his father was a guardian angel and couldn't stop for them because he had to save someone.

Kendall had no explanation as to why Trevor didn't come home first to tell them he was an angel or why he might not have heard Simon yelling for him, especially since the little boy was fairly certain angels had better hearing than humans. She couldn't bring herself to answer any of Simon's questions. Mainly because she had no answers.

After cleaning up lunch, she sat on her overstuffed sofa lost in her own thoughts. She twirled her hair around her finger while Simon pondered if they should go looking for Trevor or wait for him to come to them. Her phone rang, bringing her out of her head. It was Owen.

"Please don't dissolve our partnership," she pleaded.

"Are you joking?" he replied with a laugh. "How would I ever explain to Mr. Sato that he only hired the O in KO Designs?"

Kendall jumped up, a huge weight lifted. "Hired? He hired us even after I disappeared?"

"He hired us because we came up with the most amazing design concept he's ever seen, and he knew he'd be a fool not to hire us."

Kendall hopped up and down like a child. At least one thing had gone right today. They had needed this account, not only for the money but also for the new business it would bring in after the restaurant was done.

"Thank you for covering for me, for answering all the questions, for being the best business partner in the world."

Owen laughed on the other end of the

line. "We all know I'm the lucky one. How's Simon?"

Kendall glanced at her son, who had moved on to drawing pictures of his dad with the scented markers his grandmother bought him last Friday as a reward for making it to school on time for one whole week. The joy she felt in getting the job quickly dissipated. Trevor wasn't running around the city playing guardian angel. There was no chance of him showing up on their doorstep later tonight. Whoever they saw today was not who they thought he was, and the reality of that would certainly hit Simon hard.

"He's good." She left the room so little ears wouldn't overhear. "But something tells me the worst is yet to come and there's nothing I can do to stop it. I stink at being his mom, O. I have no idea what I'm doing."

"Stop it," Owen scolded her. "You are the best thing that kid could ever ask for. You have the patience of a saint and always have his best interest at heart. The only thing that stinks is that your husband died, which wasn't your fault, either."

Kendall sank into a kitchen chair, already physically and emotionally exhausted at three in the afternoon. "My patience isn't what it used to be. I may want the best for him, but

I'm beginning to wonder if I know what that is anymore."

"You'll figure it out. If anyone can figure it out, it's you."

She appreciated his faith in her, but she knew herself better than he did. Kendall was losing her grip. It wouldn't take much to push her off the edge. She thought she'd seen Trevor today. Nothing said losing your mind like seeing ghosts.

"Thank you. And I promise to carry my weight on the job. In fact, I can make some calls and start ordering materials."

"Take care of Simon and worry about Sato's tomorrow. We'll split up the responsibilities and start filling out purchase orders then."

As she said goodbye, someone knocked on the front door and opened it at the same time. "Anybody home?" The sound of Kendall's mother's voice reminded her that she'd neglected to call about taking Simon home early and there being no need for her mother to pick him up.

"Nana!" Simon burst into the foyer, his drawing clenched in his hand. "You won't believe it! You'll never believe who we saw today!"

Kendall gave her mother an apologetic grimace, but Nana was too startled by Simon's verbosity to notice. "Who? Who did you see?" she asked, crouching down to his level. He handed her the picture he'd drawn.

"My dad! We saw my dad right down the street!"

Kendall's mother looked to her for confirmation. "We saw someone who looked like him," Kendall explained. "I know you want to believe it was Daddy, Simon, but we know he's in heaven, right?"

"Mom," Simon said, exasperated. "You *saw*. It was Dad. I prayed he would come back and he did. You should have seen him, Nana. He was for real and he got in a cab by the park. I can show you." He took his grandmother's hand and tried to pull her out of the house.

"Hold on," Kendall said, placing a hand on the door as he tried to pull it open. "Why don't you go clean up your markers and let me talk to Nana a minute. Then you can take her to the park, okay?"

"Moooom," he whined.

"It'll only take you a couple of minutes."

"I don't wanna."

The whining was much easier to fight than the silence. "Go." She pointed back at the family room.

Snatching his drawing back from his nana,

Simon spun around and stomped all the way down the hall. He was lucky he was cute when he was mad.

"I forgot to call you back and tell you I had to bring him home," Kendall said when the two women were alone. "I'm so sorry."

"What in the world is going on? Did he see this Trevor look-alike on the way to school? Is that what set him off?"

Kendall sighed. "They had a helper dad in the classroom today. That's what set him off. We were walking home when we saw... Trevor." Saying his name brought back her own version of the yucks.

Maureen Everhart knew her daughter better than anyone. The look she gave her daughter as she pulled her back into the kitchen told Kendall she understood today had taken its toll. "It wasn't Trevor."

Kendall leaned against the counter and wrapped her arms around herself, shaking her head. Her mom was right. It wasn't. Trevor was dead. He had left and now he was dead.

"Was it a soldier in uniform?"

"Oh, my gosh, Mom. Trevor was a marine. Never call a marine a soldier. That's like... blasphemy."

Maureen rolled her eyes. "Apologies, dear

daughter. Was it a *marine?* A man in uniform? Is that why he thought he saw his dad?"

Kendall shook her head again. "I know it sounds crazy, but the man we saw looked exactly like Trevor. I mean, he was across the street and we only saw him for a second or two, but...Mom, he looked *exactly* like Trevor." The tears she'd gotten so good at holding back fell for a second time today.

"Nana!" Simon called. He ran into the kitchen. "Come on, let's go to the park. Maybe he'll be there and we can see him again. Mom, can you come, too?"

Kendall wiped her cheeks and pushed all the emotion away. She knelt down so she and her son would be eye to eye and gripped his arms with both hands. "I know how badly you want that man we saw today to be your dad, baby. But that wasn't Dad. Dad is not coming back."

"It was," Simon argued.

"No, it wasn't."

"It was," he said more softly.

She could feel the silence creeping back in. "It looked like him, but it wasn't him." Simon sealed his lips shut, splitting Kendall's heart in two. "But we can still take a walk with Nana," she tried. "Or maybe we can go to Nana and Papa's and see Zoe." Kendall looked to her mom for help.

"You know how much Zoe loves it when you come over to play. What do you say? Let's go, huh?" She held out her hand, but Simon didn't take it. Instead, he pulled out of his mother's grasp and ran out of the kitchen and up the stairs, slamming his bedroom door behind him.

Kendall was grateful she was on her knees because her legs most certainly would have given out if she'd been standing. Her mother wrapped her arms around her.

"Why does this have to be so hard? When is it going to get easier? Isn't it supposed to get easier?" Kendall cried on her mother's shoulder.

"The Lord never gives us more than we can handle. You have to believe you're strong enough to get through this."

"I don't feel very strong. I feel tired, Mom. I'm so tired."

The two women clung to one another. Kendall's mom stroked her daughter's long chestnut hair. "Lean on me, honey. Lean on your father, your sisters. That's why you moved back, so we could be here for you."

Kendall and Trevor had met in Chicago, but his military career took them away soon after they married. After he died, Kendall returned, needing to come home so Simon would be surrounded by family. Her parents and both of her sisters were in the city, and Trevor's parents were less than an hour away in the northern suburbs.

She loved her two sisters and they had been nothing but helpful, picking up Simon from school when their mother couldn't, stocking her pantry with food when she didn't have time to run to the grocery store, offering to listen when she needed to talk. Kendall didn't take advantage. She had always been the quiet one and hated to burden people with her problems. She tended to bury them instead.

"I'm sorry for falling apart. I hate whining." Kendall let go and ran her hands over her face until the only sign she'd been crying was her red eyes. No one's life was easy, and people like her mother knew the true meaning of being tired. In remission for five years this winter, her mom had endured a double mastectomy and a year of chemotherapy. She still wore her gray hair short and spiky, never letting it get as long as it had been before she was sick.

Maureen held her daughter's chin gently but firmly enough that she had to maintain eye contact. "You have a right to your feelings, Kendall Marie. Never apologize to me for crying. Or whining, which, by the way, wasn't what you were doing." Kendall nodded, and her mother continued. "We're going to get through this together. Stop thinking you're alone."

She did feel alone. She'd felt alone for much longer than anyone knew, really.

"You want me to bring Zoe over here after I take her to the groomer? Maybe Simon will perk back up if he can play with the dog."

If only it was that easy. Kendall feared just how far today was going to set him back. "He needs time to process what he thought he saw. I'm just going to leave him alone for a little bit." She wrapped her mom up in another hug, this one full of appreciation. "Thank you, though."

"Call me tomorrow," her mom said as she squeezed Kendall a little tighter.

As soon as the door closed behind her mother, the phone rang. Kendall was relieved that she didn't have to experience the silence she knew was waiting to greet her until she looked at the caller ID. Trevor's father never called when he was anything other than miserable. Kendall almost wished for the quiet.

With a deep breath, she pushed the talk button on the phone. "Hi, Paul."

"Oh good! You're home. I planned to leave a message since Simon is usually being shuffled all over the city because of your schedule."

In the year since Trevor died, his father had gone from the man who believed his son could do no wrong to the depressed and delusional man who believed that his daughter-in-law could do no right now that his son was dead. Paul once had the audacity to suggest Simon's selective mutism was related to Kendall's "selfish need to work." His wife, Nancy, had been a stay-at-home mother and, according to Paul, that was the reason Trevor turned out the way he did.

However, unlike Paul, Trevor hadn't made millions of dollars for Kendall and Simon to live off for the rest of their lives. Military pensions and dependent compensation weren't nearly enough to pay off the debts Trevor had left behind or provide the life Kendall wanted for Simon. Taking the leap and partnering up with Owen had definitely provided her with a much-needed artistic outlet, but it was far from a selfish decision.

"I'm working from home this afternoon." It was a small lie. Kendall planned on doing some work. Plus, telling Paul that Simon had to leave school would only lead to some condescending comments for which Kendall had no patience today. "What's up?" she asked, keeping her voice light and upbeat.

Paul was the complete opposite of light and upbeat. She could hear the clinking of ice in an empty glass. "Can I talk to Simon? I really need to talk to my boy."

"Oh...I'm sorry. He crashed after school. Fell asleep watching some TV. Long day and all." This was a bigger lie than the last. And part of her felt terrible about it. The man had lost his wife and his son within a year of each other. He was lonely. On the other hand, Kendall felt justified. Without Trevor to dote on, Paul had become bitter and fixated on Simon. The little boy represented everything he'd lost when Trevor died, and Paul was bound and determined to hold on to him with both hands.

Simon, however, found his grandfather a little overwhelming. So much so that he never spoke around him and begged his mother not to leave them alone. He told Kendall that Grandpa Montgomery only wanted to talk about his dad and it made him too sad.

"Well, go wake him up," Paul said. "It's not good for him to sleep in the afternoon at his age. You won't be able to get him to bed tonight, and then you'll wonder why you have trouble getting him up in the morning. This is half your problem, Kendall. Trevor would have made sure Simon kept a consistent routine. Children need a consistent routine."

Apparently a lecture was unavoidable. Kendall plucked a pencil from the holder by the phone and began doodling on a notepad while her father-in-law enlightened her for the hundredth time about the way to perfectly parent a boy. This was something Paul didn't feel Kendall's parents could properly teach her because they only had daughters. Raising sons was not the same as raising daughters, said the man who had one son and *no* daughters.

"Trevor was such a good boy when he was Simon's age. That's what proper parenting accomplishes. When you're in charge—more importantly, when you're present—boys respond. Of course, a boy needs a father. I always said that." Paul's voice began to crack. Whatever he was drinking was only making him weepy. "It's so unfair. Poor Simon had the best role model a child could ask for. And now…now he has no one."

Kendall shaded in the fire she had drawn coming from a dragon's mouth. Talking to Paul used to make her cry. Now she only felt exhausted. She knew what her father-in-law wanted to hear.

"Trevor was an amazing father and husband," Kendall said. It was the truth.

Mostly.

"He was, wasn't he? He really was." He said before blowing his nose loudly. "And a hero, too."

Kendall crumpled up the sheet of paper into a ball and tossed it into the garbage. "Maybe Simon and I can drive out to Lake Forest this weekend. Are you going to be home Sunday night?" She was going to regret this later.

Trevor's father was a partner at one of the bigger investment banking firms in the city. When she first met them, Kendall thought the Montgomerys had more money than anyone she'd ever known. Trevor's mother had had a closet full of designer clothes and another one just for her shoes and purses. Besides the mansion in Lake Forest, they had a summer house in Michigan and a winter home in Naples. There were also several rental properties, including the house she and Simon currently lived in. There was no way Kendall could afford to live in Lincoln Park otherwise. As much as she hated needing Paul's help, she loved being close to her family.

Kendall heard him capping the crystal decanter in the background. "I fly out west Sunday afternoon. You could come for lunch on Saturday. If the weather's nice, Simon could ride the horse."

"We'll see. I'll call you later this week, all right?"

"Sounds good. Tell Simon I called. And that I love him, okay?"

The familiar guilt poked Kendall in the gut. She should have tried to get Simon on the phone. He wouldn't have said a word, but at least Paul could have spoken to him. "I will."

She hung up and climbed the stairs to Simon's bedroom like she was hiking up Mount Everest. Slow and steady, trying to ignore the pain in her chest. She hated when he wouldn't talk in front of other people, but when he refused to speak to her, it was torture. She feared they'd soon be eaten up by the silence.

She knocked softly on his door, giving him a chance to let her in. He didn't answer. Her hand gripped the doorknob as her forehead rested against the wood. "Simon."

No answer.

She twisted the knob and pushed the door open. From the other side of Simon's twin bed, she could see the top of his head, his cowlick stuck up like it wanted to make sure she didn't miss him sitting there.

Kendall walked around the bed and joined him on the floor. He had all of his Hot Wheels lined up in front of him. Cars were his passion, something he shared with his father. He had over a hundred little cars in his collection and used to play with them every day. Anything could be turned into a roadway or racetrack. Nowadays, the cars were stored in boxes under his bed. Simon only brought them out when he was missing Trevor the most.

"Remember when Daddy came home with that bright yellow Mustang?" Kendall picked up a toy car that looked much like it. Simon had a photo of it taped to the mirror above his dresser. "I thought he was crazy. Until I saw your face. Your eyes got so big, I thought they were going to pop out like they do in the cartoons."

She smiled at the memory. She hadn't only thought Trevor was crazy, she had been so angry. He'd spent way too much money on a car they didn't need, but he promised her it was no big deal and the expression on their son's face made her want to believe him. Trevor had a way of making her forget her head. With him, her heart made all the decisions.

Simon took the car out of her hands and turned it around and around in his.

"Your dad loved you so much," Kendall said. "He would have done anything for you. If he could come back from heaven, I don't doubt for a second he'd do it."

"But you can't come back from heaven," Simon whispered.

Kendall put an arm around him and pulled him against her. The words pushed their way through the emotion. "No, you can't."

Simon tossed the car aside and wrapped both arms around his mom. He buried his face into her chest. "Don't ever go to heaven, Mommy."

In that moment, Kendall knew exactly how it felt when Trevor set off that roadside bomb —destroyed.

SIMON REFUSED TO go to school the rest of the week and Kendall didn't have any fight left. She had to bring him to her office twice, and her mom stayed with him the other days. She cancelled her plans to take him to Lake Forest, claiming he was under the weather. Paul wasn't too happy about it, but Kendall wasn't up for the million questions and couldn't deal with the disappointment she'd certainly see on Paul's face when Simon couldn't talk to his grandfather.

Monday meant going to Sato's to meet with the contractors. She couldn't have a tagalong, and Kendall's mom had a doctor's appointment. Simon needed to go to school. They had talked about it several times on Sunday. He knew the expectations.

Kendall woke him up on time and left him to get dressed in the clothes they had laid out the night before. She turned on the stove and heated up the water for oatmeal while she waited for him. Sleepy-eyed, Simon shuffled into the kitchen looking none too happy about going anywhere.

"What two things are you worried about today?" she asked as she set a glass of orange juice in front of him, ignoring the frown.

He shrugged.

She waited him out, making his lunch instead of talking for him. He finished his juice and watched her cut the crusts off his peanut butter and jelly sandwich.

"Seeing Dad and it not being Dad," he said softly.

Kendall held her breath for a second then spun around. "We aren't going to see Dad." She quickly corrected herself. "I mean, it's highly unlikely we'll see that man again. If we do, maybe we'll walk up to him and introduce ourselves. That way, it won't be weird anymore."

She prayed they wouldn't see the man now that she'd promised to speak to him. She could only imagine how embarrassing it would be to approach a stranger on the street.

Hi, my name is Kendall and this is my son, Simon. We just wanted to say hello because you look exactly like my dead husband and my son thought you were him and now hasn't gone to school for four days. Beautiful morning we're having, huh?

Nope, not awkward at all.

The teakettle whistled. She poured some water into the oatmeal and set the bowl in front of Simon, handing him the spoon. "What two things are you looking forward to today?"

Simon took the spoon but set it down. With his elbow on the table, he rested his head on his hand. "My tummy hurts. I want to go to work with you."

It was disappointing but not unexpected. Stomachaches were a sure sign of the yucks. "We talked about this yesterday. Mommy has to go to the restaurant today, and you can't come with. School is your job. You need to go to your job and Mommy needs to go to hers."

"It hurts too bad. I can't go," he protested, shoving the oatmeal away.

Kendall stirred his oatmeal and pushed the bowl back in front of him. "Eat. It will make your stomach feel better. It hurts because it's empty." He frowned but picked up the spoon and took a bite. "What two things are you looking forward to today?" she asked as he ate.

He finished the whole bowl before answering. "Coming home and seeing Aunt Lucy."

Kendall's sister was picking him up from school today. Lucy swore she was never getting married or having children, so she reasoned that spoiling Simon was her God-given right.

"I'm sure Aunt Lucy is looking forward to seeing you, too. She told me on the phone that she's bringing something very special for any boy named Simon who makes it through the whole school day."

Simon's mouth twisted then fell back into a frown. "My tummy still hurts."

Kendall sat down next to him. "Mine, too. I've got the yucks about this new job. It's going to be a lot of work."

"You have the yucks?"

She nodded and put a hand on her stomach. "Everybody gets the yucks sometimes.

But we still have to go to work. I'll tell your yucks to beat it if you tell mine, okay?"

Simon almost smiled. "Okay. Beat it, yucks!" he said to her stomach.

Kendall jumped in her seat. "Whoa! I felt them run away. Good work, mister. My turn." She held on to his waist and whispered, "Beat it, yucks."

"Mom. They can't hear you when you talk so soft."

"They can't?"

He shook his head. Kendall put on a determined face and bent closer to his belly. "Beat it, yucks!" she said firmly. She glanced up into those big, blue eyes. "How was that?"

Simon looked down at his stomach. "I'm not sure."

Kendall sat back and surveyed the room like she might spot the yucks running away. "Let's try this," she said, before tickling his sides. "Beat it, yucks!"

Simon giggled and squirmed. It was the best sound she'd heard in a week. "Stop, Mom. They're gone. Stop!"

Kendall obliged and stood up. She held out a hand. "Let's get out of here before they come back, huh?"

With only a moment's hesitation, Simon took his mom's hand.

KENDALL REALLY DID feel the yucks coming on as she got out of the cab in front of Sato's. The restaurant was located in a great spot not far from the Mag Mile and just a couple of blocks from Ontario. She couldn't remember what used to occupy this space, but she was going to make sure no one forgot Sato's.

Owen was waiting outside for her. With coffee, because he was the best partner anyone could ask for. "He made it to school?" he asked, handing her the Starbucks cup.

"He made it. Let's hope he makes it all day." She sipped the warm, caffeinated goodness and thanked him.

"Let's get to work." Owen held the door open for her. "Oh, K…" He gestured with his head for her to come back outside. Her brow furrowed, and Owen glanced around nervously. "I meant to mention this to you earlier but with all the stuff with Simon, I didn't want to freak you out."

The yucks danced in her gut. "What?"

"Don't panic," he said, giving her arm a squeeze. "I forgot to tell you something about Mr. Jordan, the restaurant manager."

Kendall relaxed immediately. She was sure Owen was going to confess being in love or lust or whatever he felt. She hoped this wasn't about wanting to set her up again because she had no time for men.

"When he finally showed up for the meeting last week…this is going to sound strange…but he sort of looks like…"

Kendall stopped listening because behind Owen, Trevor was stepping out of a cab. Even though her brain told her it couldn't be Trevor because Trevor was dead, she watched as this Trevor ran a hand through hair that was much too long. Her Trevor always wore his hair short—military short. This Trevor patted his pockets then shook his head like he should have known there was nothing there.

It wasn't until he looked up and right at Kendall that she noticed the world around her had gone fuzzy, not just the sights but the sounds, too. It was like she was underwater. Owen seemed so far away. Did he see Trevor, too, or was she the only one? Owen's voice as well as the street noise was muffled. The only thing that wasn't blurry was this Trevor, who was smiling as he glided over to her.

He was beautiful, dressed in dark gray slacks and a light purple button-down. Her Trevor never would have worn purple. Ever. But it looked so good on him. The sleeves were rolled up like he was ready to do some work. His arms were as tan as the first time he came back from Afghanistan.

She wanted to touch him. Hold him. Cry on his shoulder. Beg him to be real. Then let him have it for leaving her, for not choosing her and Simon. She would have done all of that if her arms and legs weren't numb. There was a tremendous burning in her chest, but the rest of her was frozen.

Trevor's eyes never left her and his grin widened as he got closer. He was right in front of her, and she wasn't sure how she was still standing, or breathing for that matter. "You must be the K in KO Designs," he said in a voice that wasn't at all like her Trevor's. It was deeper, rougher.

Before she could say anything or hold his hand like she wanted, the world went from fuzzy straight to black.

CHAPTER FOUR

"SIT HER DOWN over here," Owen said, clearing some junk off a dusty chair. The poor guy was almost as pale as the woman in Max's arms.

"Does she have low blood sugar or some kind of medical condition I should know about?" Max asked. He wasn't sure how she was going to hold herself up when she was unconscious, so he held on to her.

"Not that I know of." Her business partner was flustered. "You should put her down. She'll pass out again if she wakes up and you're holding her."

Max's eyebrows pinched together. There was no way he was blaming him for this. Who passed out at the sight of someone? *Although…* His mother had always teased him about being a knockout. Kendall Montgomery was indeed out cold, and all he had done was smile and attempt to introduce himself. Maybe he had KO'd the K in KO Designs with his devilish good looks. He fought a smile. It was funny, even though it wasn't.

Her eyes began to flutter open and, though it was absurd to think he had anything to do with her passing out, Max wanted to set her down before she came to. She looked up at him as he set her on the chair.

"Oh, God, did I die?" She was horror-stricken. Her eyes were wide and wild. "I can't die. What about Simon!" Her hand covered her mouth.

"No, no, no, K. You're fine. You're alive," Owen said, pushing Max aside and helping her sit up straight. "Mr. *Jordan,* here, brought you inside."

"Mr. Jordan?"

The beautiful but somewhat strange designer rubbed her forehead and stared at Max. She was pretty enough to be forgiven for spilling her coffee all over his shoes. This time.

"Please, call me Max," he said to both of them. This Mr. Jordan stuff made him feel uncomfortable. The only Mr. Jordan that Max ever knew was his grandfather, and his mother's father was nothing but a mean, old man. He scanned the room. "Let me find you some water."

The restaurant was a big, torn-apart space

with nothing to offer but broken furniture and an empty bar. He decided to duck outside and spotted a Dunkin' Donuts on the corner, down the street.

He bought Kendall water and a glazed doughnut, just in case low blood sugar really was the culprit. When he returned to the future home of Sato's, the two designers were hugging. This was not how he expected day one to start. He waited for them to break apart before he handed over the food and drink.

The biggest, softest brown eyes stared up at him. This woman was the knockout. Her dark brown hair was pulled into a ponytail that fell halfway down her back. The navy V-neck shirt she wore accentuated the length of her neck, and her skin was the color of the cream he put in his coffee.

"I figured everyone likes glazed doughnuts. I'm a Boston cream fan myself, but some people don't like stuff inside their doughnuts. I love vanilla pudding but hate jelly. I mean, if I want jelly, I'm going to put it on toast, not in my doughnut."

Both designers stared and blinked, blinked and stared. They were beginning to make him self-conscious. He hadn't had a pimple since the twelfth grade, but all their gaping had him wondering if he didn't have a giant red bump on his nose.

"You should probably eat something," he said, filling the awkward silence. "I bet you skipped breakfast this morning. Am I right?"

Kendall glanced at Owen, then nodded her head. "Yeah. I was in such a rush, I totally forgot to grab something. Thank you...*Max*." She said his name like she was testing the way it sounded. As if he might correct her and tell her it was something else.

"You're welcome," he said with a wink. "Eat up so we can get to work."

Kendall pulled out the doughnut and took a bite, humming in appreciation. She ate and she drank. She smiled and she blushed. She was even prettier with a little color in her cheeks. She wiped her mouth with the back of her hand instead of the napkin he had stuffed in the small paper bag, and she never stopped staring.

MAX WAS HOPEFUL things would be less awkward as the day progressed, but he couldn't shake the feeling he was under a microscope. During the morning meeting with the contractor, he caught her studying his shoes. When he was pointing out some issues in the blueprints, she seemed completely distracted by his hands. Not to mention the five minutes she spent fixated on his chin. Max had to go the bathroom to make sure there wasn't something there.

Getting a woman's attention was nothing new. One of Max's favorite things about his job was working the room, sparing no one from his charm. He was used to women watching him, flirting with crooked smiles and batted eyelashes. Those looks fueled his ego nicely.

This was not that.

Kendall was currently talking on the phone, but she was also watching Max tour the room with one of the subcontractors. The crease between her eyebrows was the dead giveaway that she wasn't flirting. She was judging. Why was she judging him? All day he felt like he wasn't meeting some standard.

As soon as she got off her phone, he intended to find out what her problem was. He finished with Joe the subcontractor and strode over to Kendall, who, even though she was looking right at him, didn't seem to notice he was headed her way.

"I bought you breakfast and still I feel like you're holding the whole fainting spell against me."

She startled when he spoke. "What?"

"Is there a problem I should know about?"

She leaned forward and narrowed her eyes as she peered at his. "Brown," she said, barely loud enough for him to hear. She was officially odd.

"What?"

"What?" She pulled her head back and folded her arms across her chest.

"You've been staring at me all day," he said, trying his best not to seem confrontational. "I'd be flattered if I thought you were simply appreciating my awesomeness, but I don't think that's it."

Kendall's gaze fell to the floor. "Sorry. You remind me of…someone." She shook her head and made eye contact again. "I didn't mean to make you uncomfortable."

"Apology accepted. It's actually good to know there's somebody out there who looks like me. Especially the next time I get picked out of a lineup for robbing a bank. I mean, the last time, they wouldn't take my word for it when I said it must have been my evil twin," he joked, but she didn't laugh. In fact, she may have thought he was being serious. "I'm kidding."

She exhaled like she'd been holding her breath the whole time he was talking. "Okay, well, I'm heading out to make sure our flooring gets delivered on time."

"Well, until tomorrow, then," Max said, stepping out of her way. "Don't forget to eat something for breakfast."

Confusion clouded her face for a moment before the light came on. She smiled and laughed at herself. It was the kind of smile that gave her lines that bracketed her mouth. She had full lips and lots of white teeth that had to have spent some time in braces when she was younger. "I will definitely eat something so you don't have to pick me up off the floor, Mr. Jordan."

"Max," he corrected.

"Right." Her smile faded for some reason. "Max."

MAX HAD THIRTY minutes to get from the Loop to the corner of North Avenue and Milwaukee Avenue. Joe, the helpful subcontractor, told him to jump on the Blue Line because a cab would cost him a bundle and take too long this time of day. Max was used to getting around in the safety of his own car. Everyone in L.A. had a car, hence the massive traffic problems. Chicago had its issues, but many of the people behind the wheel were making money doing so or commuting from the suburbs. True Chicagoans, Max had been told, walked, got around on bikes, or unlike everyone he knew back in L.A., they used public transportation.

The CTA station was crowded and smelled like a dirty bathroom. A man in a stained shirt and muddied khakis wove his way through the waiting commuters. He held out a paper cup that contained maybe a buck in change if he was lucky. "Spare somethin'?"

Max dug in his pocket for his wallet and pulled out a twenty-dollar bill. He pushed it into the cup. "Get a good meal tonight," he said.

The man's face broke into a grin of appreciation. "God bless."

Max tipped his head and smiled back as the man moved on.

The woman next to him snorted. "He's just gonna buy some booze with that money, you know." Dressed in a navy suit and flashy running shoes, she held on tightly to her humongous designer purse with one hand while the other scrolled through something on her phone. Neither the diamonds in her ears nor the rings on her fingers looked like they came from a Cracker Jack box. She could have easily spared a dime.

"Maybe. Maybe not. You never know

someone's story until you ask them to tell it," Max said as the train pulled up.

"Pfft." The woman rolled her eyes and made her way toward the train.

She was probably right. It was very likely the guy would use the money for some vice rather than food. Still, there was also a possibility he'd buy dinner with it. That was enough for Max. Things happened. Sometimes life threw people a curve ball they weren't expecting and all they needed was a hand up. Max had no problem offering help to others, though he had trouble asking for or accepting it himself.

When Max was twenty-two, he found out his mother was panhandling after she had lost her job working as a blackjack dealer in a Las Vegas casino. He was thankful for the people who offered her help. Who knew what else she would have been willing to do to keep from starving. But he hated that she'd hidden her desperation from him, opting to beg strangers for help instead.

He had taken her in after that, even though he was living in the tiniest apartment in all of California. She stayed for about two months, then she met some guy who persuaded her to follow him to Denver to start a church. Thus began her "religious" period.

Max's mom made him look at everyone a little differently. Her weaknesses taught him to trust no one to take care of him but himself. Her quirky strengths reminded him that people were interesting creatures, capable of both good and bad, depending on the day. To keep his faith in her, he had to have some in everyone else. Everyone except his father. His father lacked any redeeming qualities, he was sure of it. Anyone who would walk away from a pregnant woman and lay no claim to his son didn't deserve forgiveness or understanding.

Max wasn't going to be that kind of man. He was going to be a better man than his father. That was what he told himself as he rode the Blue Line to meet his lawyer. He had to believe that if he had any shot at winning joint custody of Aidan.

Wayne Faraday's office was three blocks from the CTA station. Max managed to walk there and still be on time. The temperature had begun to drop as the sun set. Chicago weather in early fall was unpredictable. Sometimes it felt like summer wasn't ready to go, and the next day it was rainy and forty degrees. Max dreaded his first Midwestern winter.

Wayne's administrative assistant was a

young guy with blond hair and black hipster glasses who always wore a bow tie and skinny pants. Max imagined he spent his free time in offbeat coffee shops where people drank lattes, ate organic muffins and competed in poetry slams. "Mr. Jordan. Right on time. Mr. Faraday will be with you in just a minute. He got a call right before you walked in."

"No problem," Max said, taking a seat—the only seat—in the reception area. The law firm of Faraday and Associates was small. In fact, the name was a bit deceiving. There actually weren't any associates. Wayne worked alone, but he had a passion for fathers' rights, which made him the man for this job. Max needed someone who knew what he was doing and was willing to take him on as a client, given the fact that Max's case wasn't particularly strong. At least not yet.

Picking up a copy of *Men's Fitness* magazine, Max tried to occupy his thoughts with something other than his crazy day. He still struggled to shake the strange feelings Kendall Montgomery had stirred in him. It had been a relief when she'd explained he simply reminded her of someone else. Hopefully that meant the constant staring would come to an end. Of course, it was the *way* she looked at him that was unnerving. Even when she smiled, there was this sadness about her. Like it made her sad to see him. That was an unpleasant thought.

Maybe he reminded her of some horrible ex-boyfriend or a bully from high school. Whoever it was, it distracted her all day and distractions led to mistakes. Max couldn't afford any mistakes on this job. Sato's needed to open on schedule. The restaurant and Max's success depended on it.

"Max." Wayne Faraday strode out of his office and extended a hand. "Sorry to keep you waiting. Come on back." They shook hands and Wayne turned to his assistant. "Feel free to take off, Jake. I'll lock up when I'm done with Mr. Jordan."

Jake nodded and wished them both a good night. Wayne ushered Max into his office, which was just big enough to hold a desk, one file cabinet, a bookcase filled with dozens of law texts, and two small office chairs. Max stepped over a pile of manila folders and sat down in one of the chairs. Wayne bent over to pick up the files, but set them down when he realized there was no room on his desk for anything else.

"Sorry. I think I need to hire one of those companies that help people maximize their small spaces," Wayne said, taking his seat on the other side of the desk. He didn't look like the kind of lawyer who'd be crammed into a tiny, disorganized space. In contrast to his office, Wayne was completely put together. He wore a designer suit and a TAG Heuer watch. The diploma that hung on the wall was from the University of Chicago and the picture that sat on his desk was of him and a happy bride and groom at a wedding in Paris.

Max had no idea what a guy like Wayne was doing in this dinky office instead of some corner office in a shiny building overlooking Lake Michigan, but he knew the lawyer's track record with these kinds of custody cases, and that was all that mattered.

"Okay," Wayne said, opening the file that lay in front of him. "We need to talk about a couple of things before we have our first appearance before the judge. The good news is you've consistently paid your child support."

Max had been willing to pay whatever Katie needed to care for Aidan. The divorce was easy. They'd had little money at the time, so they shared a lawyer. They'd agreed on joint custody, but Katie was the custodial parent. Max was granted visitation, but that hadn't really happened. As soon as everything was finalized, Katie moved Aidan to Chicago.

Max could have fought her, could have forced her to stay in California, but he hadn't. Sadly, his only excuse was that it was easier for him to have her gone. He made plans to fly out for visits, but work picked up and he kept pushing the trips back. Weeks turned into months, months turned into years.

Max's biggest regret was that he had thought his name was on the birth certificate and the money he put in Katie's bank account made him a better father than his own. There was so much more he could have done and so much time had been wasted.

"I'm fairly certain we can get a judge to consider some form of visitation between appearances even if Mrs. Michaels fights us on it. It would be even better if you two would agree to arbitration or mediation."

"I'll do whatever. I don't think Katie will agree to mediation, though."

"We'll ask for that first. I need confirmation from you that her moving was the reason your visitation agreement was not followed. Then we need something to go to the judge with that will cast you in a better light. It also wouldn't hurt if we had some character witnesses. Friends, family, people who will testify that you're a good man with every intention of being a good father."

Character witnesses? His mom was the only family he had, and she was unreliable at best. Friends were a luxury he couldn't afford. He was always friendly, of course—it was required in his profession. Max made it his job to know his patrons and keep regulars coming back by getting personal. He knew details about their lives only a friend would know, but they knew nothing about him. Did they like him? Everyone liked him. But no one really knew him.

"What if all my character witnesses live too far away?"

Wayne took a breath and held it for a second before exhaling. He held his hands out, palms up. "Then I need you to make some friends. And fast. Because right now, she's making a fairly strong case that your lack of involvement in your son's life is because you're negligent. We need people to tell the judge they know you as someone other than a guy who deserted his kid."

It felt like a ball of fire exploded in Max's chest. "I never deserted my son! Katie moved. What was I supposed to do? I had a job and a life in California."

"Okay, that, right there, you *cannot* do that

in front of the judge or the arbitrator," Wayne said firmly. "But what I'm hearing you say is, had Mrs. Michaels not left the state, you would have continued visits with your son. Am I right?"

Max wanted to say yes, but the truth wasn't that simple. Even if she'd stayed, it probably wouldn't have changed how much time he'd spent—or not spent—with Aidan. He hadn't deserted his son. He'd let them walk away from him and chosen not to follow.

"I'm sure I would have spent more time with him if he'd lived closer," Max answered, the heat of his earlier anger slowly fading.

"But was her moving out of state the major obstacle?" Wayne prompted him with a nod of his head.

"Yes?"

"Is that an answer or a question?"

"An answer?"

Wayne sat back in his chair, his lips turned slightly upward. "Don't do that in court, either. When you answer a question, you need to answer decisively. There can be no doubt. The judge isn't going to believe someone who sounds like he doesn't believe himself."

Max scrubbed his face with his hands. This was going to be tougher than he thought. "I'll work on that."

"That's all I can ask." Wayne unleashed his full smile. Two rows of perfect, white teeth. "Well, that and make some friends, Max. Quickly."

IT WAS A short cab ride back to his condo. The sun had set and the streetlights cast an orange glow on the pavement. It was only a little after seven, but Max was tired. And hungry.

He pulled out his keys and searched for the right one to open the main entrance. Before he figured it out, the door opened and Charlie nearly bowled him over.

"Oh, man, sorry about that!" His hulk of a neighbor stepped back. "Seems like every time our paths cross, I'm running you over. I swear I make my living saving lives, not taking them."

Max waved off the apology. "Don't sweat it. It's my ninja skills. They make it impossible for you to see me coming."

Charlie's caterpillar eyebrows scrunched together before lifting along with one side of his mouth. "You're funny, Floor Three. Ninja skills. That's a good one."

Max shrugged and reached for the door.

"Hey, I'm meeting a couple of guys for some dinner and the Hawks game, you wanna tag along?" Charlie offered.

As much as Max wanted to climb those stairs and lock himself inside his condo for the night, Wayne's voice played in his head. *Make friends, Max.* Charlie was a nice, up-standing citizen who worked for the city and saved lives daily. Who wouldn't want some-one like that as a character witness?

"Sure. Thanks, man." Max let the door close and followed a grinning Charlie down the steps.

Make friends, Max. Quickly.

CHAPTER FIVE

KENDALL POURED TWO glasses of wine with shaky hands as her sister sat at the kitchen table, watching and wondering. Lucy had no idea what kind of bomb Kendall was about to drop. Kendall's older sister was a realist. She didn't believe in things like fate or miracles, ghosts or doppelgängers. She was also the rock in Kendall's life. Strong and sure. It was six-year-old Lucy who told four-year-old Kendall that the tooth fairy wasn't real, but Lucy was also the first one to drop everything and fly to North Carolina the day the two marines showed up at Kendall's door to inform her of Trevor's untimely death.

Lucy plucked the wine glass from her sister's hand. "Okay, dish. What's going on with you?"

Kendall stepped out of the kitchen and tiptoed down the narrow hallway, allowing her a clear view of Simon on the couch in the family room, snuggling the snowy white stuffed seal his aunt had given him for making it through the entire school day. The television was a tad too loud, but she didn't ask him to turn it down since what she had to say wasn't for his ears, anyway. The little boy giggled at the antics of the cartoon puppies. It made Kendall smile to see him so content. His moments of peace were hers, as well.

That warm fuzzy feeling didn't last, though. As soon as she sat down across from her older sister, the ball of anxiety inside her chest pushed against her ribs and made it hard to breathe. "So, the guy Simon and I saw last week..." she whispered.

Lucy leaned in. "The one who looked like Trevor?"

Kendall nodded and took a sip of wine. "I saw him today."

"This is about seeing Trevor's freaky clone?"

The sound of his name scratched Kendall's skin, leaving her feeling raw and vulnerable. *Trevor, Trevor, Trevor.* His name had run through her head all day, a distraction she couldn't afford. "He works for Sato."

Lucy choked on her drink. She coughed, wiping her mouth with the back of her hand. "What?"

Kendall wished her thoughts weren't so scrambled. It wasn't Trevor. It was Max. *Max,*

Max, Max. That name, associated with that face, felt so strange as it bounced around her head. "He's the restaurant manager. I spent the whole day with him."

"Oh, honey." Lucy grabbed and squeezed Kendall's hand. "No wonder you were ready to fall apart when you got home."

Snatching her hand away, Kendall sat back in her chair. "I'm not falling apart. I can't fall apart. This is the biggest job of my career. I can't mess it up because this guy reminds me of…" She shook her head, unable to say his name aloud.

Lucy frowned at her sister before getting up and grabbing the wine bottle off the counter. "How Trevor-like are we talking here?"

"Very," Kendall said. Almost identical from a distance. Up close, she noticed the subtle differences—his nose had a small bump, there was no scar on his chin, and his eyes definitely belonged to another soul. Max had brown eyes like hers. Brown with little flecks of gold. They were so warm compared to Trevor's icy blue.

"You freaked out when you saw him, didn't you? Did you faint? Please tell me you didn't faint. That's so cliché." Kendall didn't answer, but gave a little shrug. Lucy's mouth dropped open before she began laughing. "Oh, my God, you totally fainted!"

Kendall's foot connected with Lucy's shin. "You have no idea what this is like."

Her big sister shook her head. "Oh, K. What am I going to do with you?"

"Tell me I can do this. Tell me I'll get this job done and not feel like I'm being haunted." Haunted was exactly how Kendall felt. Her heart pounded in her chest. Had it always been this relentless? Maybe she *was* falling apart. This felt like some sort of sick cosmic joke. She had no idea how she was going to survive working side by side with Trevor's double. It didn't matter that it wasn't him. This man would always be a ghost.

Lucy moved her chair so it was butted up against Kendall's. "You can do this. This guy is going to be in and out of your life faster than you think. Not to mention, the more you're around him, the less he'll seem like Trevor. What's his name?"

"Max," Kendall replied, still testing the name as it came out of her mouth. It was still strange no matter how many times she said it.

"Max is just some guy. No different than the mailman or the guy at the art store you love to go to."

Kendall dropped her chin. "The mailman

doesn't remind me of my dead husband. The guy at the art store is close to Dad's age. Max, on the other hand, could fool Trevor's father into thinking his son was still alive."

Lucy blew her blond bangs out of her green eyes. "Any chance the Montgomerys had twins and gave one up for adoption?"

"I seriously doubt it. There was no way Paul would give up anything that belonged to him." Trevor was gone only because he had been taken. Kendall rested her head on her sister's shoulder. "Every time I think I'm getting better, something like this knocks me back down."

"Stop it," Lucy said sternly. "You are strong and you are my sister. This is nothing. There are setbacks, and there's this. This is some weird coincidence, not some terrible twist of fate. Keep your distance from this Max, do your job and keep moving forward."

Lucy was right. This was why Kendall confided in Lucy. Her level head came in handy.

Shuffling feet alerted the two women to Simon's presence. The head of his stuffed seal was nestled in the crook of the little boy's elbow. He gave them a closed-mouth smile and scurried around Lucy to Kendall's other side.

"I'm hungry," he whispered in his mother's

ear. Simon didn't speak aloud in front of Lucy or their other sister, Emma. He talked to Kendall's mother, but not to her dad, and when everyone was around, he didn't make a peep.

"I'll start dinner in a minute. Did you think of a name for your seal yet?"

Simon shook his head.

"Her name should be Lucy, don't you think?" Lucy asked, petting the seal's head.

"How do you know it's a girl?" Kendall questioned.

"I adopted the real harp seal. I think I get to choose if the stuffed version is a boy or girl."

Kendall shook her head and stood up to start dinner. Of course the seal was part of some bigger cause. Lucy never did things the easy way, like go to a big box store and pick out something from their enormous toy section. In fact, Lucy refused to shop at most chains. She'd even participated in some big rally a couple of weeks ago, protesting against one company's employment practices. Lucy loved a fight, regardless of whether it was hers or not.

Simon pulled on his mom's shirt, and she bent down so he could whisper in her ear. "I want to name him Seal Lo Green." CeeLo Green, his cat and *The Voice* had been a big hit in the Montgomery house not too long ago.

Kendall smiled. "Sorry, sis," she said, patting Lucy on the shoulder. "Looks like it's a boy!"

Lucy scrunched up her nose and pouted. She playfully tugged on Simon's arm. "You were the last hope I had for your gender, buddy, and you blew it."

Simon gave her a confused smile before darting back out into the family room. "I love you, Aunt Lulu," he said when he was out of sight.

Kendall's eyes flew to Lucy's. He spoke! He wasn't in the same room with Lucy when he did it, but he spoke. Kendall was going to put that little nugget of positivity in her pocket and keep it. Any good that could come from today was priceless.

"He is so lucky I love him," Lucy said before downing the last of her wine. "Anyone else who called me that would be dead right now." She wasn't a fan of that particular nickname, even though Simon had been the one to give it to her. It was taboo because someone else used to call her Lulu and that someone was no longer allowed to call Lucy *anything*.

"Oh, I see how it is," Kendall said, pulling some chicken from the refrigerator. "You say I need to suck it up and deal with the fact that I'm working with a man who strongly resembles my dead husband, but you'll kill anyone who uses the nickname your ex-boyfriend stole from my son."

As strong as Lucy appeared, this subject always did something to her. Made her look more vulnerable than she ever allowed. Her arms crossed her chest and created a shield over her heart. "Your husband left you involuntarily. My ex had a choice, and he chose to walk away. I get to kill."

"I love you, but I'm not sure anyone has a choice once Lucy Everhart makes up her mind about how things are going to go down."

Lucy frowned. "Everyone has a choice."

Kendall couldn't argue with that. Everyone did have a choice. Trevor had one. He'd made several before he even left for Afghanistan. "Well, be that as it may, I'm pretty sure I won't have enough money to bail you out if you commit murder," Kendall teased. "So don't."

When Lucy gave in and cracked a smile, Kendall invited her to stay for dinner.

"Is that free-range chicken?"

"No."

Lucy got up and opened the refrigerator. She pulled out the gallon of milk. "What did I tell you about this stuff? It's chock-full of hormones, pesticides, antibiotics and pus.

Plus, do you have any idea how they treat the cows on these dairy farms? It's horrific. And what is this?" She pulled out a package of pudding in a cup. "Don't you know what the preservatives in this stuff are doing to Simon's growing body?"

Kendall snatched them away. After their mother's breast cancer diagnosis, all three girls had been forced to pay closer attention to their bodies. Lucy was the most diligent of all three of them, yet she was the one who'd found a lump in her breast two years ago. That should have pushed Kendall to make better decisions about what she ate, but buying and cooking all-organic was also another luxury this single, working mom couldn't afford. Not to mention that some things were just too tempting. Comfort food was all she had to make her feel better some days.

"Those are for me, thank you very much. Preservatives hopefully won't hurt my already-grown body. The worst these can do is make my pants tight, but I'm fine with the fact that I don't have a size 4 butt like *some* people."

Lucy rolled her eyes and shut the refrigerator door. "I think I'll go home and treat my body, including my size 4 butt, like the temple it is." She pulled Kendall in for a tight hug. "You can do this," she said, then kissed her on the cheek.

It was exactly what Kendall needed to hear.

LUCY WAS RIGHT about one thing—the best plan of action over the next two weeks was to steer clear of Max Jordan. Not only did he physically resemble Trevor, but he also knew how to give orders like him. The man acted like his life depended on being the bossiest person in the room.

Kendall hadn't been a fan when her husband forgot he wasn't her sergeant. She certainly didn't like it when Max did the same. Every time she stepped foot in Sato's to check on the construction progress, he was telling her what to do.

"You need to call the flooring subcontractor and get him back out here," he said, blocking her path. "I asked him three times to fix the tile in the bathroom and he didn't do it."

This guy was quickly becoming a giant thorn in Kendall's side. He might be a great restaurant manager, but he had no idea how to manage a remodeling project. She took a deep, cleansing breath instead of pushing him out of her way. "Once we get the west room finished, we'll put together a punch list and the flooring guy will come back in and make everything right."

"I thought we agreed that your redesign in the west room took away necessary space for the waitstaff to get to and from the kitchen."

"I'm not sure *agreed* is the word I would use." They hadn't "agreed" on anything. In fact, she recalled telling him she'd change the design when she heard from Mr. Sato and only Mr. Sato. She stepped around him and set her laptop bag on the main bar. "You know what I remember? I remember discussing it wasn't necessary for you to be here every day."

Max followed her. "Well, I remember telling you Mr. Sato left me in charge of overseeing this remodel, and I *will* be here every day to make sure this restaurant opens on time."

Kendall placed both hands on the granite counter, letting the coolness of the stone combat the heat of her temper. Max stood behind her. His reflection in the mirrored wall across from her was glaring at the back of her head. His eyes were narrowed and his five o'clock shadow emphasized the tension in his jaw. Like Trevor, Max was all hard, sharp lines, a perfect contrast to her soft curves. The facial hair made it easier to think of him as Max instead of Trevor, who was always clean-shaven.

She turned to face him. The brown eyes were still hard to get used to. They always caught her off guard. She struggled to regain focus, blinking and probably looking a fool. When she regained her composure, she attempted to appease him. "I have every intention of making sure this restaurant opens on time. If you let me do my job, we won't have any trouble meeting our deadlines."

He mirrored her movement to keep her from escaping and put a hand on her arm when she tried once more to move around him. It was the first time he'd touched her since their disastrous introduction. Kendall couldn't stop the déjà vu that it prompted. The last time she saw Trevor alive, she'd been storming away and he'd tried to stop her. The memory jolted through her like an electrical shock.

"I'm not going anywhere," Max said firmly. "I will be here. Every day. Whether you want me here or not."

It was the exact opposite of what Trevor said in her memory, and what she had so badly wanted him to say back then. Hearing those words now, from this man with her husband's face, was too much. She bit her lip to keep it from trembling. Max seemed to pick up on her emotion and released her from his grasp. He apologized and dashed away.

Kendall took off for the restroom and locked herself in the first stall. Fat, round tears rolled down her cheeks. Was it wrong to be this angry at someone who was dead? Was it worse to resent someone who was alive simply because he looked like that person? She just wanted Max to go away, to stay clear of the restaurant until the remodel was finished. It would make things so much easier on her, not only because he was annoying, but also because her heart couldn't take much more abuse.

"K, you all right?" Since Kendall was the only woman in the restaurant while it was under construction, Owen had no qualms about walking right into the women's restroom.

She wiped her cheeks and turned the lock. "I'm fine," she lied, hoping Owen would at least pretend to believe her. She exited the stall and avoided eye contact until she could check her reflection in the mirror and be sure there was no sign of those tears.

"Why do you insist on getting here before me? Let me deal with Mr. I-Have-A-Million-

Issues Jordan," Owen said, holding out a paper towel for her while she washed her hands.

"My chairs are supposed to come in today and I wanted to see if they finished taping the new wall yesterday. I want to get started on the mural as soon as possible."

Owen's expression was full of nothing but concern. He was more than a business partner; he had been her friend since they met at the Art Institute. They were design soul mates, but their dreams of starting their own firm had been dashed when Kendall met Trevor one Christmas break.

Trevor had been a senior at the Naval Academy back then, and he'd swept her off her feet. When he asked her to move to Virginia after graduation to be close to him while he trained at Quantico, the decision had nearly torn her apart. Leaving her family and friends terrified her. In the end, she'd chosen Trevor. He had this way of making her question herself by being so sure they were meant to be together. His confidence had convinced her that the right thing to do was walk away from one dream and toward another.

Owen considered going with her, but it wasn't meant to be. He never lost touch, though. He knew the day would come when they would make KO Designs a reality. While she'd been off getting married and starting a family, Owen had spent the past eight years working hard to make a name for himself in the Chicago design world. When Trevor died, Owen had given her the courage to get back into a career she'd set aside.

The only reason KO Designs had any clients when they first started a year ago was because of Owen. She owed him so much, and here she was thanking him by having a breakdown on the job.

"He's getting to you."

"It's less about him and more about my issues with my husband." Kendall checked herself in the mirror one more time. "Stop looking at his face," she told her reflection, then turned to Owen. "Maybe if I stare at his shoes or the buttons on his fancy shirts when he makes ridiculous demands, I'll get less rattled. Trevor never wore shoes like that."

"He does have impeccable fashion sense, doesn't he?" It was a trait for which Owen had great respect. "Let me handle him, okay? You take care of the other details."

"Deal," she said thankfully.

Unfortunately, even without Max's interference, nothing went smoothly. The chairs were delivered, but instead of sending her forty chairs, the vendor sent her a *hundred* and forty chairs. The delivery guys kept unloading them even though she told them she hadn't ordered that many. The customer service representative from the furniture company put her on hold for fifteen minutes, then told her someone would have to call her back. To top it off, in their attempt to fit a hundred and forty chairs in a restaurant that only needed forty, one of the stacks of chairs fell over and damaged a freshly painted wall.

All the while, Max felt the need to remind Kendall over and over that Mr. Sato would not be covering the cost of her mistake. "If this sets the project back—"

"You need to stop talking," she snapped, finally pushed to her limit. His resemblance to Trevor actually made it easier to argue with him. "This is not going to set the project back. This is the vendor's error. They'll fix it as soon as someone gets back to me and we'll move forward."

"I'm just saying this is not an expense the restaurant should have to incur."

"No one said the restaurant would incur any extra expense."

He moved closer and Kendall became all too aware of the differences between Max and Trevor. He was a bit taller than Trevor, who stood a solid six feet tall, and leaner.

Trevor had always smelled like soap, while Max's cologne had a peppery spice and citrus scent. It was a pleasant difference, like his eyes, and it made Kendall feel slightly off balance.

"I just want to be sure," he said as her phone rang.

She gathered her wits about her. "This is probably them right now." She answered without looking at the number. "Hello?"

"Hi, Mrs. Montgomery. This is Lisa Warner, from school." The apology was in her tone.

Kendall felt her heart sink. *Not now.* She turned away from Max and made her way to the restaurant entrance. She needed to find Owen. "What happened?" she asked Lisa.

"We're going to need you to come in. Simon locked himself inside the nurse's bathroom."

Kendall spotted Owen talking to the delivery man, who was trying to leave. The sooner she went to deal with Simon, the sooner she could get back to handle this fiasco. "I'm on my way."

SIMON OPENED THE door for his mom but wouldn't tell her what the problem was while they were at school. Lisa let them use her office, but all Simon would say was his stomach hurt.

"I can't help you if you don't tell me why the yucks are so bad."

"I need to go home."

"We can't go home, Simon. We both have jobs to do. Your job is school and Mom's job is at the restaurant."

"My tummy hurts too bad."

"Baby, Mommy has a big problem at work. I need you to tell the yucks to go away. You can do it."

That was when the tantrum started. Kendall didn't have time to deal with this today, and as much as she hated to give in, she was left with no choice. She got up and opened the door. "Let's go."

Lisa and the principal, Mrs. Nigel, were waiting for the two of them in the main office. They were talking but stopped as soon as they saw Kendall.

"Can I go down with him to get his backpack? I'm going to have to take him with me."

Lisa and Mrs. Nigel exchanged a look. Kendall knew they were unhappy with her weakness. She'd already received a letter from the school regarding Simon's attendance record. Lisa smiled at Simon. "How about I take you to get your backpack so your mom can talk to Mrs. Nigel for a minute?"

The suggestion gave Kendall the yucks. Mrs. Nigel had always been supportive, but that understanding might have an expiration date.

Simon held tighter to her hand, and truthfully, she wanted nothing more than to stick together. Regardless, she encouraged him to go with Mrs. Warner.

His reluctance was clear in his eyes and the dragging of his feet. He left with the social worker, repeatedly glancing over his shoulder to make sure his mother didn't bolt out the doors.

Mrs. Nigel motioned for Kendall to follow her into her office. Kendall suddenly knew exactly how Simon felt—her own feet were cemented to the floor.

The principal's office was a decent size, with two large windows on the long wall opposite the door. Inspirational posters with quotes about success and believing in yourself hung on the walls. They were similar to the ones in the social work office, which suggested never giving up and declared the space a no-bullying zone.

"Mrs. Montgomery," Mrs. Nigel began.

"Please, call me Kendall."

First came the pity smile. "Kendall, I know the anniversary of…" She averted her eyes. "Of Simon's father's passing was difficult. Simon has had a hard time rebounding."

Mrs. Nigel had no idea. "If this was any other day, I would make him stick it out. But I'm in the middle of a crisis at work and—"

"Please, I understand. You're overwhelmed. I just want you to know that we've been discussing as a team how to best help Simon, and we've come to the conclusion that his needs may need to be supported differently."

Before Kendall could ask what that meant, her phone rang. The number was unfamiliar and likely the vendor who mixed up the chair order. She declined the call. "Differently how?"

"Well, we'd like to meet and discuss Simon's placement and services."

"He already sees Lisa and the speech pathologist. Mrs. Taylor has been following the suggestions the psychologist gave me. What other services does he need?"

The pity smile was back. Kendall hated the pity smile. "Well," Mrs. Nigel began.

Kendall's phone rang again. It was the same number as before. "I'm sorry, I need to take this." Kendall answered the call and quickly gave the perturbed man on the other end of the line Owen's number. She apologized to Mrs. Nigel again and asked her to continue.

"I guess what we're thinking is we're not sure Wilder is the best place for a boy like Simon. We think his needs might be better met in a more…therapeutic setting."

"You want to kick him out of school?" Kendall could feel the protective mama bear inside her rear up. There was no way she would let them kick her son out of school.

"No, Mrs. Montgomery. It wouldn't be like that at all. We simply aren't equipped to handle a student who doesn't talk. His avoidance of school is proof of that. Of course, meeting as a team to discuss his progress will give us a clearer picture and help us determine what's best."

"And you think it's best that he be put in some special school?"

"I think Simon needs help. I think *you* need help."

Kendall couldn't hear that right now. "He needs some time. That's all he needs. A little more time to feel comfortable here."

"We have a meeting scheduled in two weeks. That's when we're going to take a closer look at the progress he's been making. I think you need to understand that if his attendance doesn't improve and his behaviors continue to escalate here at Wilder, we'll have no choice but to take a more disciplinarian approach."

Kendall's face was so hot, she imagined smoke coming out of her ears. "So, if I don't let you send him to a special school, you'll punish him for not adjusting well to his father's death? Is that what you're telling me?"

"If that's the way you see it, that's the way you see it. We all have Simon's best interest at heart here. I hope you see that as well."

"*I* have Simon's best interest at heart." Kendall stood and made her way to the door. "And I guess I have two weeks to prove to you he doesn't need to be kicked out or punished."

Simon was anxiously waiting for her on the other side of the door. She grabbed his hand and led him out. She tried to give him a reassuring smile and probably failed at that, too. As they got into the cab she had paid to wait, she wondered what Simon did need, because she, like the school, had no clue.

CHAPTER SIX

MAX WAS LOSING PATIENCE. The designers never listened to him. Not to mention everything took longer than they said it would. And now, in the midst of a delivery nightmare, Kendall had gone MIA. The hundred and forty chairs were stacked all over the restaurant, making it impossible for anyone to do their job. The painters couldn't finish painting. The electrical guys couldn't finish wiring the ceiling lights. Most important, Max had ten potential employees coming in today for interviews, and Jin was threatening to show up for a visit.

Max's frustration made him unreasonable, and that led to more communication breakdowns. He was sorry for being such a pain, but running a restaurant was the one thing Max knew he could do well if he was given the opportunity to do so. This should be the one place his confidence soared. Given his current situation with Katie and Aidan, he needed at least one thing to feel good about.

"Did you tell him about you-know-who?" Owen asked someone on the phone. He'd been on that thing almost constantly for the last half hour. "Can you drop him off at your mom's?"

He was obviously done speaking to the furniture vendor and had moved on to personal business. Did he not understand what a disaster this day had become?

"What about Lucy?"

Who the heck is Lucy? Owen made eye contact as if he'd heard Max's thoughts. He smiled nervously, then disappeared among the stacks of chairs.

"Don't worry about it," Max overheard him say as he followed Owen into the maze. "Do what you have to do and I'll take care of things over here."

"Is that Kendall? Is she coming back sometime today?"

Owen stopped and spun around. He ended his call and slid his phone into his pocket. "You know what you and I should do?"

Max shook his head, prepared to reject whatever he suggested.

"We should head over to this art gallery on Michigan Avenue and look at these paintings Kendall's had her eye on for this place." Owen pushed Max towards the exit.

"Is that where Kendall is? An art gallery? Because she should be here, dealing with these chairs," Max said, holding his ground and feeling more frustrated by the minute. "I have people coming to be interviewed. My office is unusable and there's nowhere to sit out here because there are too many things to sit on!"

"The irony is sort of hilarious, no?" Owen's wide smile shrunk when he noticed Max's scowl remained. "I get it. This is not ideal. The vendor assures me they'll send someone to pick these back up...eventually."

"Eventually? What does that mean?"

Owen sighed and resumed his efforts to get Max out of the building, this time pulling instead of pushing. "It means we should get out of here. The gallery isn't too far. We could even walk there."

"I'm not leaving," Max asserted. "You and Kendall need to find a way to get rid of these chairs *today*." Yanking free from Owen's grasp, he headed for the kitchen. It was the only area undisturbed by the chaos today. He could conduct his interviews back here if he had to, he supposed. It was quieter and offered some privacy. Now, if only he could prevent Jin from showing up, he'd be a little bit ahead of the game.

Patting his pockets in search of the cigarettes that still weren't there, he cursed himself for being so weak. He hadn't bought any cigarettes but had been tempted more than once over the last few weeks. Things were not going as smoothly as he'd hoped. Remodeling was a bigger headache than he'd anticipated. Throw in his personal problems, and it was amazing he hadn't jumped out of this third-story window yet.

Katie had agreed to arbitration, apparently with some coaxing from her husband. Max could resume his visits with his son, but the lack of prior contact was cause for concern. This meant he got *supervised* visitation until the next arbitration meeting. A court-appointed woman had the honor of watching Max fail miserably at connecting with a little boy who wanted nothing to do with him.

Sitting in a playroom with a counselor who had the best poker face known to man and a three-year-old who cried for the first half of every visit was beginning to traumatize Max. It had become more of a punishment than an opportunity to prove he deserved to be in his son's life.

Max would be the first to admit he wasn't very good with little kids. Growing up an only child may have had something to do with that. He'd spent most of his life around adults. His mom changed her friends every time she redesigned herself. It made him good at first impressions, but terrible at really getting to know someone. Even worse at letting people get to know him.

Taking care of himself and making sure adults had a good time when they came to one of his restaurants or clubs were Max's strengths. Three-year-olds weren't as easy to please as his patrons. Little ones didn't care about getting a free drink from the bar or a half-priced appetizer special. Likewise, complimenting a toddler's wardrobe choices got him nowhere near Aidan's good graces.

Some days, it felt like a lost cause to fight to be Aidan's daddy when Katie's new husband had already taken his place. It made Max question what he was doing in this city. It was probably making him a bigger jerk at work than he really was. He saw the way Kendall searched for an escape every time he headed in her direction. He didn't miss the looks she gave her business partner when they were discussing the things Max thought weren't working or the sighs she let out when he finished asking a question.

He wasn't trying to be a pain. He simply needed her to do everything in her power to make this restaurant look perfect. He'd handle the rest. He'd hire the best staff and make sure they had the best menu. He'd fill the tables. Maybe not all the chairs, but definitely the tables.

"Mr. Jordan?" Jin poked his head through the door and pushed it all the way open when he saw Max was there. "What in the world is going on out there? Why do we have so many chairs?"

"Delivery error," Max answered. "They're coming back for the extras as soon as possible."

Jin had already stopped listening. His attention had shifted to the newly delivered and installed teppanyaki griddle. He turned knobs and ran his hand over the smooth griddle top. "What time do the staff interviews begin?" he asked, moving on to the box of soy sauce dishes.

"First one is scheduled in about a half hour." Max prayed Jin wasn't going to stay. The last thing he needed was for Jin to think he had input in Max's hiring decisions. A manager needed to pick his own staff to ensure a well-run restaurant.

"I have a busy afternoon, so I want to see the applications before you interview."

Max took that to mean he wasn't hanging

around long and breathed a sigh of relief. "I can do that."

Jin inspected one of the soy sauce bowls. "I don't like these," he announced before setting it back in the box. "Come show me what your issue is with the new sushi bar."

"Mr. Sato," Kendall greeted Jin when they stepped into the main dining area. The missing designer had finally returned. In her high-heeled boots, she was a good inch taller than Jin, and, for some reason, that made Max smile. Kendall was also smiling, but it seemed a little forced. "We apologize for the mix-up with the seating. I promise there will not be this many chairs when you open."

Jin's icy demeanor completely melted away at the sight of her. The boss's son had a crush. It was almost cute. "No problem, Kendall. I trust you to get it sorted out."

It took all of Max's self-restraint not to laugh. Kendall could mess up big, go missing for almost an hour, and Jin acted like it was nothing. Max, on the other hand, didn't choose the right soy-sauce dishes and got a look that could kill. This kid had his priorities all out of whack.

Max hated having to kowtow to Sato's son. Jin's ego did little to make up for his inexperience. Max had to work twice as hard to make sure Jin's callowness didn't mess with the restaurant's success. Sharing control was difficult when the person he was sharing it with wielded it without proper training. Jin had a lot to learn and it was unclear who was teaching him.

"Can we show you some of the updates?" Kendall offered, and Jin readily accepted. Her long hair was pinned up in front while the rest of it fell over her shoulders. It looked soft, like the rest of her. Max certainly couldn't fault Jin for finding her attractive.

Suddenly, a movement under one of the stacks of chairs caught his attention. Max bent down and tilted his head to get a better look. Two eyes peered out at him, wide as saucers. Quicker than he appeared, the little boy retreated like a turtle in his shell.

No one else seemed to notice there was a child hiding in the restaurant. Hopefully he wasn't delivered with the chairs. Max broke from the group to search for the young intruder. He didn't find him hiding under the chairs. Instead, the boy sat in the back corner at a table covered in colored pencils and a large sketchbook.

"Hey there," Max said with a wave. The kid was older than Aidan by a few years. Definitely old enough to be in school, but here instead of there. "What's your name, buddy?"

The boy's stare was discomforting. Frozen, with his mouth slightly agape, the little guy looked like he was face-to-face with his hero.

Max was no one's hero.

"My name's Max." He pointed to himself. Maybe the boy didn't speak English. Max pointed at him. "Whaaat's yooooour naaaaame?" he asked, drawing out each word as if that would help him understand better.

The boy picked up a pencil and went back to his drawing. It wasn't until he lifted up the paper that Max realized he had written his name. "Simon," Max read. "Hi, Simon."

Simon still gawked at him. "Hi," he mouthed without any sound.

"Do you belong to someone here?" Max asked, cautiously moving closer. The last thing he wanted was for the kid to bolt, or worse, cry.

Simon nodded and flipped back to the first page in the book. He pointed to a drawing of a woman with warm brown eyes and long, dark hair. The kid was pretty talented for someone so young. "My mom." His voice was barely a whisper.

Kendall. Her disappearing act was no longer a mystery. Max took a better look at the boy. With the exception of his eyes, he was very much his mother's son. Same round cheeks and little nose. His lips were full and pouty.

Picking up the sketchbook, Max admired the artwork. "That's a good picture of her. You didn't draw this, did you?" Simon nodded. "Are you sure?" The boy nodded again. "Wow," Max said in genuine awe.

Simon's smile revealed one missing tooth. He was cute and quiet, the perfect child. Max wondered what he was doing here instead of school. Not that it was any of his business. It must have been something important, though, if Kendall had to leave in the middle of the chair delivery from hell.

"No school today?"

Simon's cheeks flushed red. "I got the yucks. Mom had to pick me up."

The boy didn't seem sick, but what did Max know? He wouldn't know the first thing about how to tell if a kid was well enough to be in school or not. He had so much to learn about kids in order to be the best dad he could be for Aidan. In fact, thanks to Simon, he was going to buy a thermometer on his way home today.

"Did your mom tell you to sit back here and color?"

Simon nodded.

"Are you okay? Did you need your mom for something?"

Simon shook his head back and forth.

"All right, then. You stay put, okay? A guy could get lost in all these chairs." He gave him a wink. "It was nice to meet you, Simon." Max needed to catch up with the tour and make his case for not putting in the bar extension.

"Are you sure your name is Max?" Simon had gotten up from his seat and was following behind him.

"That's the name my mom gave me."

The boy's blue eyes peered up at him. "Is your mom's name Nancy?"

The oddly specific question caught Max off guard. "Nope. My mom's name is Joanna."

"My mom's name is Kendall."

"I knew that. I could tell from your picture of her."

"I don't have a dad," Simon confessed. His gaze quickly fell to the floor. "He's in heaven."

That was unexpected and terribly depressing. Max felt bad for both Simon and his mother. The sadness that sometimes radiated off Kendall made more sense now. The woman had her hands full, it seemed. "I'm sorry to hear that, buddy. If it makes you feel any better, I don't have a dad, either."

Simon looked back up. "Is your dad in heaven, too?"

The child's naivety almost made Max chuckle. Even if his father was no longer alive, he hoped the deadbeat wasn't living it up on the right side of the pearly gates. "I doubt it," he answered.

Confusion creased the youngster's forehead.

"You better go back to your table and finish your drawing." Max placed his hands on Simon's shoulders and turned him around. "Your mom and I have some work to do."

The kid wasn't so easy to escape. He took two steps before the questions began again. "Do you like cars?"

"I guess."

"What's your favorite color?"

"Blue."

"Do you have to fight in the war?"

That was a strange one. Max squatted down so he was eye to eye with his interrogator. "No."

"Do you drink milk?"

"Does drinking what's left in my cereal bowl count?"

"Mom says no." *Figures.* Moms were no

fun sometimes. Simon kept at it. "Do you like chocolate ice cream?"

"Absolutely."

"Do you like dogs?"

"That depends."

His answer slowed the questions down for a moment. Simon's head cocked to the side, his bangs sliding across his forehead. "Why does it depends?"

He was still cute, but forget about quiet. This kid was quickly becoming a motor mouth. "I got attacked by this giant Saint Bernard when I was about your size," Max explained. "I'm sure he was trying to be friendly, but he had a good hundred pounds on me and it pretty much scarred me for life. And when I was twelve, my mom rescued this sheltie and those things shed 24/7. The kids at school made fun of me because my clothes were always covered in dog hair. So, I guess you can say I like little dogs who don't shed as long as they aren't yippy."

"What's yippy mean?"

"It means it barks a lot."

Simon's mouth formed an O when he got it. "My nana and papa have a little dog. She's not yippy. Do you like kids?"

Max swallowed hard and nodded his head

until the words found their way out. "Most kids. I have a son."

At that answer, Simon eyes widened and a look of longing appeared. "What's his name?"

"His name is Aidan."

Simon's face fell. "Aidan," he repeated. He bit into his bottom lip.

"He's three. How old are you?"

Simon held up six fingers.

Max heard Jin say his name. As much as he wanted to answer all of Simon's questions, he needed to get back to work. He stood up and tousled the boy's hair. "I've got to go, buddy. You should go back where your mom told you to stay."

Jin complained loudly about him from the other side of the restaurant. Max glanced over his shoulder and tried to spot them through the chairs. He turned back to Simon. "I'll see you later, okay?"

"Okay." Simon didn't look or sound so sure.

Max emerged from the stacks of chairs not expecting a warm welcome. "Sorry. Someone needed my attention."

Jin rolled his eyes while Kendall scanned the room. He could almost hear her checking off each and every person she knew to be working in the restaurant at the moment. When she accounted for everyone, she glanced back at where he had come from. Her eyes met his, full of worry. Simon was the only one back there.

"We've decided the sushi bar will go in as planned," Jin said, pulling Max's attention away from the nervous mother.

"Can I explain my concern at least?" Max pleaded.

Jin checked his watch. "Kendall already shared your concerns, and I still side with her and Owen."

Max's face felt flush. "I'm not so sure she presented all of my concerns as clearly as I can."

"I told him exactly what you told me. Were there any other issues besides the ones you brought up with me a hundred times?" Kendall's arms folded across her chest and the challenge in her tone was enough to make him forget the sympathy he was feeling for her a minute ago.

He could admit she had excellent taste and an eye for beauty, but the functional aspect of her design was lacking whether she wanted to admit it or not. Max had worked in restaurants long enough to get a feel for how space needed to be organized. The flow of traffic would be slowed down because of the bar placement, and in the restaurant business, minutes were a precious commodity.

He rattled off his concerns. She nodded affirmatively to each and every one of them. How dare she play fair. It allowed her to be so smug.

"There you have it." Jin stepped in between them. "Like I said, I side with Kendall and Owen on this one. The new bar goes in where it was designed to go in. I need to see those applications if you can manage to get them without getting lost."

It didn't matter what Max said. Jin would side with Kendall regardless of the validity of the points he made. Jin's experience was so limited, he had no idea what he was saying. He was making decisions based on personal feelings, which was a mistake in business.

If only Mr. Sato had come himself instead of sending his son. Max went behind the bar to retrieve his briefcase with the applications inside. As he handed them to Jin, the doors to the restaurant flew open and a blonde bombshell stormed in.

Max pulled out his phone to check the time. He hoped this wasn't his first interviewee. Jin might stay longer to talk to someone who looked like that, and Max wanted him out the door before he had the chance to interfere with his hiring.

The blonde woman headed straight for them, but Max apparently wasn't her reason for being there. Her target was Kendall.

"Sorry, I got here as soon as I could," she said as Kendall led her back into the mountain of chairs. She must have been there for Simon. Jin was immersed in the applications, so Max let his curiosity get the best of him. He wandered back to Simon's table to see what was going on.

Kendall was helping her son with his jacket. He handed the other woman some papers before slipping his arms into the sleeves. Kendall zipped him up and gave him a kiss on the nose. "Be good for Aunt Lucy."

Ah, another mystery solved.

"He's always good for me. Right, little man?"

Max wondered if they were sisters. They didn't look alike. Lucy had high cheekbones and a model's body. They were currently the same height, but Kendall was wearing heels and Lucy sported moccasins. Both women were beautiful but for different reasons. Kendall was soft to Lucy's hard. Lucy radiated confidence while Kendall had a vulnerability about her that drew Max in.

"Time to go already?" Max asked. Three set of eyes shifted in his direction.

"You have *got* to be kidding me," Lucy said before her mouth fell open. Her eyes almost popped out of her head.

Kendall elbowed Lucy hard in the side while her other arm pulled Simon closer to her. "My sister is here to get him. There was a…thing…at school."

Regaining her senses, Lucy stood beside her sister. "Yeah," she said fiercely. She was definitely the protective big sister. "A thing."

"A thing?" Max repeated.

"A thing," Kendall said with a sharp nod.

"I hate it when a thing happens." Max's lips curled into a grin. He enjoyed her discomfort more than he should. He turned his attention to the boy. "It was fun talking to you, Simon. I hope you make it to school tomorrow without any 'things' happening."

Kendall pushed Simon behind her like she needed to protect him. "I'm not sure what you said to him when we were showing Mr. Sato around without you, but my son doesn't talk to strangers. He wasn't being rude."

It always felt like he and Kendall were on a different page. "I never said he was rude. Kind of a chatterbox, but not rude."

Lucy let out a derisive chortle. Kendall

didn't think it was funny. She poked Max's chest with an angry finger. "He has some anxiety issues that make it hard for him to talk to people. Don't you dare make fun."

Max was more confused than ever. Why was she jabbing him so sharply? Since when was calling the kid who asked a hundred questions a chatterbox a crime? And why was Kendall even more attractive when she was mad?

"Let's go, Simon." Lucy took the boy by the hand, but he grabbed the papers he had given her instead.

"Wait," he said, searching through the pile. He pulled one drawing out and offered it to Max.

Both women stopped dead and stared at Simon like he had a second head popping out of his neck. It was a picture of a man holding a chocolate ice-cream cone and a leash that was attached to a little black dog. They stood next to a blue car and the sun was a mix of oranges and yellows all swirled together.

"Thanks, bud."

"He doesn't shed and isn't yippy," the boy said, pointing to the puppy.

"Perfect." Max felt this strange pull in the center of his chest. If only things could be this easy with Aidan. Maybe he only had to stick it out three more years and then his son would want to know him the way this child did. "Come back and visit when we have fewer chairs and more food, okay?"

Simon nodded and grabbed Lucy's hand, ready to go.

Max watched as Kendall and Lucy exchanged a watery look. Kendall turned back to him and touched his arm with none of the aggression she'd showed moments ago. "Thank you," she whispered.

He was never going to understand this woman.

CHAPTER SEVEN

KENDALL CHECKED HER watch one more time as the last chair exited the building. She was supposed to have been home an hour ago. She was going to owe Lucy big.

"Sorry for the error." The furniture vendor had sent a man the size of a football lineman to right their wrong. He handed Kendall a clipboard. "Can you sign here?"

She scribbled her name on the line and sent him on his way. All she needed was to get her coat and she could head home, too. It had been a long day.

Minus a hundred chairs, the restaurant looked more like it should. She still needed to paint the wall mural and the sushi bar needed to be installed, but Kendall felt more confident that this job would be finished on time.

"Thanks for coming in. I'll give you a call in a couple of days after I've finished with all my interviews," Max said as he shook hands with the last of his potential employees. The young woman thanked him for his time and the opportunity. She smiled at Kendall as she passed her on the way to the exit.

From the moment she met Max, Kendall had feared what would happen if Simon ever saw him again. The delivery problem compounded by a probable visit from Mr. Sato's son had left her without any options, however. Simon had to come to the restaurant. She'd tried to prepare him. Tried to warn him that he might see someone who looked like Trevor but who was not his father.

She never expected Simon to talk to him. Or for Max to be nice about it.

Kendall watched him jot something down in his notebook. Sometimes he looked so much like Trevor it gave her chills. Other times, like now, he seemed so different. He scratched the back of head and noticed her staring.

"Still here?"

"Just leaving," she said, retrieving her coat from one of the chairs by the door. "You're okay to lock up?"

"Yeah, no problem." Max stepped out from behind the bar. He made his way over to her.

Kendall tensed. The closer he got, the more she thought about Trevor. She felt like a spring wound too tight. The need to run from Max was equal to her desire to be close to Trevor. Her brain and heart were having a very difficult time working this all out.

"Let me help you with that," he said.

He reached for her coat and held it open so she could slip into it. He might have been difficult to work with at times, but the man knew how to be a gentleman, a crucial trait to possess in a service-oriented business.

"Thanks," she said, glancing at him over her shoulder as the scent of his cologne enveloped her. He always smelled good, making it easier to be around him when his mood was more than annoying.

He wasn't annoying her right now.

"Have a nice night," he said, taking a step back. "Tell Simon thanks again for the drawing. That kid is pretty talented for a six-year-old."

Kendall nodded. Her love for art had fortunately been passed down to her son. "Thanks for being understanding about him being here. I promise it won't be a regular thing."

Max shrugged. "I get it. Family comes first. My son doesn't go to school yet, but he could have a 'thing' happen someday, so I won't hold it against you."

His smirk made Kendall smile. His mention of a son made her eyebrows rise. "You have kids?"

"Kid." He held up one finger. "Singular.

He's why I relocated from L.A. I couldn't stand living a couple of thousand miles away anymore."

Well, that added a new layer to him she wasn't expecting. Kendall had assumed Max was driven by nothing but his own ambition, but maybe he was here to do more than impress Mr. Sato. She wondered if he was divorced or just separated. Was he here to win them both back?

"How long have you guys lived apart?"

"Pretty much his whole life. My ex moved back here to be close to her family when we split."

The child's whole life? How could he stand to be away from his son for that long? Of course, she'd often wondered that about her own husband. The military took Trevor away so much before it took him away completely. Maybe Max moved because he was tired of flying back and forth so much to visit. "I bet he's happy to have you closer."

Max grimaced. "He's three and all he wants is his mom. To tell the truth, I think Simon likes me better than my own son does."

Kendall's heart thudded with a mixture of emotion. It sounded so loud in her ears, she was sure Max could hear it, too. "You remind

Simon of his father. You kind of look like him."

She almost laughed at her gross understatement. It felt too strange to tell him the whole truth. Their working relationship was strained enough as it was. She didn't need to make it more awkward.

"Simon told me…" Max paused, shifting his gaze to his feet before peeking back at Kendall. "About his dad. I'm sorry for your loss."

It was shocking enough that Simon had spoken to Max, but for him to bring up Trevor was unbelievable. Kendall couldn't imagine how long their conversation had been or how Trevor's passing had become a topic. The strain of the day combined with the way Max's face messed with her head left her speechless and overcome with emotion.

"Oh, man, I'm sorry." His hand came up and his fingers gently wiped a tear from her cheek. The physical contact caught her off guard. It was so familiar, yet not. It made her want to cry harder. "I didn't mean to—"

Kendall shook her head and stepped back, out of reach. She couldn't let him get too close. He'd see her insecurity, all of her weakness. "I'm fine," she lied. She hadn't been fine in a long time. "I better get home to Simon. Have a good night."

He didn't stop her from going, but he looked like he wanted to. Sometimes he wasn't like Trevor at all.

LUCY WASN'T THE only sister waiting for Kendall when she got home that day. Emma greeted her at the door.

"This is serious. You do know how serious this is, right?"

The youngest of the Everhart girls was also the tallest. She almost never wore heels for fear she'd tower over everyone around her. She was thin like Lucy but had dark hair like Kendall. Her brown tresses were long again—she wouldn't cut her hair for a few more months. Ever since their mother got sick, Emma donated her hair once a year to Locks of Love.

Kendall shrugged out of her coat and opened the closet. "Please don't make this a big deal."

"He talked to this guy. He's been talking *about* this guy ever since he left the restaurant."

"He's been talking?"

Emma nodded. "To Lucy, to me, to Mom *and* Dad."

"Mom and Dad are here?" Kendall fumbled with the hanger.

"He talked to them on the phone." Emma waved a dismissive hand. "But still, this is amazing. This guy is the miracle you've been waiting for."

Kendall couldn't think in terms of miracles; she could only focus on the facts. Simon had been talking all afternoon. Talking like a normal kid. Talking to whoever would listen. Perhaps meeting Max had unlocked something inside him. She followed her sister down the hall and into the family room where Simon and Lucy were hanging out *and* talking.

"Do you think Max likes Halloween?" Simon asked, drawing on one of the many papers strewn all over the coffee table. Just hearing his voice made tears prick at the corner of Kendall's eyes.

"Probably. I mean, who doesn't like Halloween?" Lucy answered.

"Yeah, I bet he does." His tongue poked out between his lips as he focused his attention on the drawing.

Kendall tried to compose herself. She couldn't overreact or all would be lost. Psychologist #2 had been very clear about not showing too much excitement when Simon spoke to someone other than her. He had a hard enough time managing his own feelings—he couldn't deal with hers, as well.

"Hey guys," she said, stepping farther into the room.

Simon's head lifted and his eyes brightened. "Hi, Mommy. Does Max like Halloween?"

She let herself appreciate the sound of his voice, so clear and sure, then tried to swallow the lump in her throat. "I'll have to ask him tomorrow."

"Good idea." Simon returned to his picture. "But maybe I can ask. I want to go to work with you tomorrow." He didn't bother to check his mother's reaction.

Internally, Kendall cursed a couple of times. Of course he wanted to go to work instead of school. One step forward, two steps back. School was ready to kick him out because he couldn't talk or make it through the day there. Now he was talking, but only because of Max, who would be his new reason to avoid school.

Lucy shook her head ever so slightly. Her expression was one of support for being firm. Emma was the soft, overwhelmingly compassionate one. She seemed more sorry for them than anything. She'd tell Kendall to let Simon skip school if it meant getting him to open up more. Wasn't that what Kendall needed him to do more than anything? Maybe if he spent a little more time around Max, he'd really come out of his shell and none of the problems would exist any longer.

Lucy could see her crumbling. "What if Aunt Emma brings you over there tomorrow after school," she suggested. "But only if you make it through the whole day. That sounds like a good plan, right, K?"

Kendall nodded. "I'm sure Max would tell you anything you wanted to know if he hears you went to school for the whole day."

Simon didn't like this condition one bit. "My tummy hurts and everybody at school hates me. I don't want to go."

Emma sat down next to him on the floor and wrapped an arm around him. She would most definitely give in. "Aw, buddy, that's not true. Who could hate someone as awesome as you?"

Kendall made eye contact with Lucy, who gave her sister all the moral support she could without saying a word.

"That's the deal, take it or leave it," Kendall said. "Go to school and Aunt Emma will bring you by the restaurant. Don't go to school, you and Aunt Emma stay home all day." It was a risky offer. He could easily choose to stay home, and there was no guarantee that time with Max was a big enough reward.

The little boy contemplated his choices. He went back to his drawing and took his time, carefully coloring in the spaces he needed to fill. *Wait him out, wait him out,* Kendall told herself. She had to let him reason this out on his own.

The kitchen timer went off, breaking the silence. Lucy popped up. "That's me. Dinner's almost ready!"

As much as Kendall dreaded making dinner after such a long day, eating something Lucy cooked was hazardous to her taste buds. She glared at Emma, who would have none of it.

"Don't look at me like that. She was already whipping something up when I got here."

"When you say she was whipping up 'something,' can you be more specific? Did it resemble some kind of real food?"

"I was trying to figure it out when she dropped the you-know-what bomb on me. After that, I couldn't think straight."

Kendall could tell she was exhausted and stressed. Her sister was kind enough to make her and Simon dinner, and she was feeling nothing but ungrateful. She needed to suck it up. Dinner was likely some organic, non-dairy, gluten-free mystery concoction, but she was going to clean her plate.

"I can talk to Max if I go to school in the morning?" Simon asked, finally ready to make his choice.

"If you go to school all day," Kendall clarified. She had to be specific; he would take advantage of any loophole.

Simon's bottom lip jutted out at her catch. "Fine." He began to pick up his markers and place them in their bin.

"Dinner's ready!" Lucy shouted from the kitchen.

"Don't set a place for me. I'm not staying," Emma said as she stood up. "Wish I could, but I have that thing, so I need to get home."

Kendall mouthed the word liar.

"I'll see you tomorrow after school, bud." Emma ruffled Simon's hair. "I can't wait to meet Max." She smiled at her frowning sister as she grabbed her purse.

Kendall held out her hand to help Simon to his feet. She gave him a kiss on top of the head. "Let's go eat, huh?"

"I'll go to school, but I'm not eating Aunt Lulu's dinner," Simon said quietly but firmly.

Kendall smiled and shook her head. "*Et tu,* Simon? *Et tu?*" She couldn't really complain. He'd get peanut butter and jelly if it meant he'd go to school the next day. That was an easy deal to make.

KENDALL PULLED THE covers up under Simon's chin, making sure he was tucked in tight.

"Love you," she whispered before giving him a kiss good-night.

"I love you more," he replied quietly.

Switching off his bedside lamp, she smiled. "Impossible."

"No, it's not."

"Trust me, someday when you have kids, you'll know just how impossible it is. Now, get some sleep." She paused at his door and blew him one more kiss. When she was his age, she had no idea she could love someone as much as she loved him. Forget about to the moon and back. Kendall's love for Simon was infinite.

She padded down the stairs and found Lucy drying and putting away the dishes. The small kitchen was her favorite room in the house. It reminded her of the one in the house where she grew up.

The kitchen was where all the big and little events happened. Everyone used to crowd around the small table at dinnertime and talk about their day. Their dad would share funny stories about what happened on the construction site, Lucy would try to rally everyone to take up her latest cause, and Emma and their mom would discuss how they were going to save the world. It was at that same table that she told her parents she was engaged and, a few years later, that she was pregnant. Her mom was standing in the kitchen when she called Kendall to tell her they had found a lump, and they celebrated around the table when the news came back that the cancer was gone.

Life-changing moments could happen in a kitchen like this one.

Trevor would have hated it. He would have wanted granite countertops and stainless steel appliances. He liked an open floor plan so he could see the television in the family room from the kitchen table. They were so different in so many ways, she and Trevor. It had been the differences that drew her to him in the first place, but it had also been their differences that pushed him away and made him choose to go back to Afghanistan.

"You don't have to do that. The least I can do is the dishes." She took the damp dish rag out of her sister's hand, needing the distraction from her thoughts. Her heart felt as though it was being pinched.

"I'm used to cleaning up after myself, it's no big deal."

"Well, *I'm* used to cleaning up after myself, so let me finish. You've helped me enough today. At this rate, I'll never be able to pay you back."

Lucy knocked her hip against her sister's. "That isn't the way our family works and you know it. You don't owe me anything. You're my little sister and Simon's my only nephew until Emma marries a rich doctor and has those two perfect children she's sure will never fight, cry or ever do any wrong."

Kendall laughed. Emma had her entire life mapped out. She not only knew where she wanted to be in a year, she had a five-, ten-, even a twenty-year plan. "Emma usually gets what she wants."

"Our sister has been very lucky. I just hope when something finally doesn't go her way, she survives." Lucy was a realist. She'd been through enough to know life wasn't always easy and could be more than a little unfair.

"She's tough. And knowing her, she'll plan her way out of any setback."

Lucy smiled for the briefest of moments. "Speaking of setbacks…what are you going to do if using Max as a reward backfires and Simon has a major one?"

Kendall opened up the cabinet to put away the drinking glasses and sighed. "Seriously? You were the one who came up with this brilliant idea in the first place."

"I could see you were about to let him skip school. I had to think fast," Lucy said in her defense. "That doesn't change the fact that you need to consider this some more."

"Do I have to think about it tonight? Can I just enjoy the fact that he talked to you and Emma and Mom and Dad for one night?"

"What do you really know about him except that he looks like Trevor and works at the restaurant?"

"Not a lot." She tried to think as she put the last dish away. "He's originally from California. He's passionate about his work. He likes to be in control, and I'm guessing he's very good at what he does."

"He sounds like you," Lucy said with a chuckle. "What do you *really* know about him, though?"

"He has a son. He moved to Chicago to be closer to him. So, he can't be that bad."

"Right," Lucy drawled. "Because only decent, God-fearing people are allowed to have children." She began to pace around the small room. "Why does his kid live in Chicago if he was in California? Is he married? Was he married? If he's divorced, why? Did she leave him? Did he leave her? Did he cheat?"

"Stop!" Kendall shouted a little louder than she intended to. She threw the dish rag on the counter and pressed her hand against her forehead, hoping that would somehow hinder the headache she could feel coming from turning into a migraine. "Okay, I get it. Just stop."

Lucy stood still in front of her sister. "I'm not trying to make you mad. I'm trying to make you cautious. I know part of you thinks this is just me and my trust issues, and you would be right, but you *should* have trust issues. You have to be sure about this guy before you let him spend too much time around Simon. You're going to finish this job and never see the guy again. And then what?"

Kendall had more trust issues than Lucy would ever know. She had no plans to let Simon get too attached to Max. She hadn't expected Simon to respond this way to meeting him.

"The school wants to have a meeting to talk about sending Simon to a private school for kids with problems."

"What?" Lucy's green eyes went wide.

"When I picked him up at school, the principal said they don't think he can go there anymore if he doesn't start making some progress," she confessed as she leaned against the counter.

Lucy seemed shocked. "Do you think he needs to go to some special school?"

"I don't know. I don't want him to need to go to a special school. I want him to talk and not to be afraid."

Her sister placed a hand on her shoulder. "Of course you do."

"I'm going to be cautious when it comes to Max, but I have to see where this goes. I can't ignore what happened today."

Lucy nodded in agreement. If Max was the key to bringing Simon back to the world of the talking, then Kendall needed to get to know him—fast.

CHAPTER EIGHT

KENDALL AND OWEN were acting really weird. First, they'd invited Max to lunch. Then, they'd taken turns interrogating him. For some reason, the two of them were interested in his entire life history. They wanted to know what clique he belonged to when he was in high school, where he went to college, if he'd been in a fraternity, if he'd ever been arrested, if he owned or rented. It felt a little like he was applying for a mortgage or something.

"What about you two? How did you become business partners?" Max asked, trying to shift the conversation away from himself. He had nothing else to eat. He had taken huge bites of his sandwich in hopes that the questions would stop if he had food in his mouth. They hadn't.

"We met at design school," Owen answered, but quickly went back to his questions. "Do you have any hobbies or weird fetishes?"

"Owen!" Thankfully, it was Kendall who called him out on crossing the line.

"Too much?" he asked her. She pinched the bridge of her nose and nodded.

"What's with the twenty questions?" If they ever asked him to lunch again, he'd have to invite Wayne along.

Kendall jabbed her fork into the salad she'd been ignoring and took her first bite.

"We're just trying to get to know you," Owen said. Now Kendall was the one using food to avoid conversation.

Getting to know him. Yeah, right.

Owen's phone rang and when he answered it, he greeted the caller in another language. He stood up, excusing himself.

"Must be his mother. He only speaks Korean when he talks to his mom," Kendall explained, still picking at her lunch.

Max watched her. Now that it was just the two of them, he felt much less intimidated. She had really long eyelashes that weren't covered in black gunk. Kendall didn't hide behind a lot of makeup—she didn't need to. Max liked that she probably woke up looking the same as she did any other time of day. There was something refreshing about that.

"So, *you* got any hobbies or weird fetishes I should know about?" he asked.

Her smile made her cheekbones more pronounced. "Owen gets a little carried away, but he's harmless, I promise," she said instead of answering the question.

"You two met in design school and started KO Designs right after?"

"No. I ended up getting married and followed my husband out to Virginia where he started his Marine Corps training. That eventually led us to North Carolina, where I had Simon. Owen's the one who stuck with design. He got a job at a big firm in the city, learned so much more than we did in school, built an excellent reputation as an up-and-comer. Being a mother was my only job until…"

"Until?" As soon as the word came out of his mouth, Max felt like an idiot. "Until you lost your husband. Sorry. That was dumb of me."

"Don't worry about it." Kendall shook it off. "After Trevor died, I moved back here to Chicago to be near my family. I reconnected with Owen, who was already thinking about starting his own company. When he heard I was moving back, he offered to take me on as his partner. I actually tried to talk him out of it."

"Why?"

"Why in the world would he want to take on not only a grieving widow but a single mother who never got further than design school? Making me a partner was a huge risk, considering all he'd done to build his reputation."

"But here you are, a year later, doing great. He must have known something you didn't."

"I'm surviving," she said humbly. "Mostly thanks to my parents, my sisters and Owen. I certainly couldn't have done any of it alone. Plus, I've had to tell myself more than once that Simon needs a mother, not a basket case."

"You never come across like a basket case." Her ability to take control of her life after being widowed was impressive. Maybe she had some help, but something told him that it had more to do with who she was. She was the one who had to support the two of them and be present in Simon's life. She had been wise enough to know she had to come back here to give her son some needed stability. "You're a good mother."

Kendall shook her head as if she wasn't so sure. Her face flushed and she set down her fork. "Sometimes I wonder."

"I know a good one when I see one. I was raised by a single mom who didn't always make the best choices. Sometimes her desire to be whoever she wanted to be at the moment took a backseat to what I needed. You always put Simon first."

"Would you consider yourself a good father?" she asked, eyes wide with curiosity.

Of all the questions she could ask. Max would have rather answered the weird fetish question. Was he a good father? *No*. Did he want to be? *Yes*. That had to count for something. "I'm working on it. I think I could be."

"I appreciate your honesty," she said with an encouraging smile. "It takes a strong man to admit he's not perfect."

"Well, if that's the case, call me Superman."

Owen returned and slid back into the booth next to his partner. "Well, well. Sounds like things got interesting while I was away."

Both Kendall and Max fell into a fit of laughter. Max eased back into his seat. His shoulders relaxed and his smile remained. Maybe he was making some friends. Wayne would be happy.

"My sister is bringing Simon by the restaurant after school for a couple of minutes." Kendall's cheeks were still pink from laughing, but the color deepened as she spoke. Her eyes dropped to the food in front of her. "He wants to know if you like Halloween."

Simon was coming to find out Max's feelings on the upcoming holiday? For some unknown reason, this kid cared more about Max than his own son did. Of course, he had no one to blame but himself for that. Max had not been a good dad to Aidan. Far from it.

"I'm kind of indifferent to Halloween, but I have a feeling that answer won't impress a six-year-old."

"You don't like Halloween?" Kendall asked, her attention back on him.

"Doesn't do much for me."

"Did you like it when you were young?"

"A little," he said with a shrug.

"Too scary for you?" Owen asked, smirking.

"No," he said, refraining from throwing his napkin at Owen's head. "My mom was way too into it."

Kendall's eyes brightened. "Yeah? That's cute. Did she decorate the house or dress up?"

Max's mother was consistent about one thing while he was growing up. She loved Halloween. She always came up with elaborate costumes for herself and stayed in character all night long. As fun as that was when he was really little, it was horrifyingly embarrassing when he got into grade school.

"Both. One year, she was Mary Poppins

and spoke in this ridiculous English accent all day. I hoped she'd fly away with her umbrella when we got done trick-or-treating."

Owen and Kendall both laughed at his childhood pain. There were times he could find the humor in his mother's crazy. It was easier now that he was an adult and not under her roof.

"She doesn't sound so bad," Kendall said.

"She did the best she could, I suppose," Max relented. The check came and Owen insisted on paying.

"Simon wants to be a race-car driver this year. The only problem is he wants to be driving a car. I have no idea how to make that happen."

"My mom once went as my school bus driver. She made a bus out of a refrigerator box." He left out how humiliated he'd felt at the time. "I've got some boxes you could use. All you'd need is some paint and a little imagination."

Kendall's mouth fell open.

"That's a good idea," Owen said, chiming in and looking equally surprised.

"That's a *really* good idea." Kendall agreed.

Max's shoulders straightened a bit. Maybe his mother's quirkiness was good for something after all.

Two more interviews before Max called it a day. He had a visit with Aidan tonight, which meant he needed to go home, shower and change. He tried not to think about how the little boy couldn't care less if his father showed up smelling like sweat or not. He probably wished Max wouldn't show up at all.

The restaurant doors opened and a much easier to please boy scampered in. A woman trailed behind him. She was a brunette, like Kendall, but tall and thin like Lucy.

"Hey, buddy, you here to interview for the bartender job?" Max asked, folding his arms on top of the counter and leaning forward.

Simon laughed. He had a little smudge of blue paint on his cheek. "I'm just a kid. I can't work."

"You're just a kid? I heard you were a race-car driver." He gave Simon's aunt a wink and a crooked smile, but she just stood there gaping. She blinked three or four times. She did know he was kidding, didn't she?

The little boy found Max much more entertaining. "I'm not a race-car driver. I'm not even old enough to drive!"

"Well, then, we need to talk to your mother because she told me you were a race-car driver and I was going to get you a car and everything."

Kendall appeared out of nowhere. She'd spent most of the afternoon sketching the first part of her mural on the wall in the main dining area. Her hair was pulled up in a sloppy bun with three pencils sticking out of it. Dressed casually in jeans and a soft gray, long-sleeved T-shirt, Artist Kendall was much more relaxed than Designer Kendall. Max really did like this version of her.

She rubbed her hands on those long, jean-clad legs and smiled at Simon. "Hey, honey." She pulled him against her and kissed him on top of the head.

"Did you tell Max to buy me a car?"

A wrinkle appeared between her eyes. "I don't think I told him to buy you a car."

"You said he was a race-car driver," Max explained.

Her eyebrows lifted, as did the corners of her mouth. She had a lovely smile. Max found himself wishing he could see it more often.

"I told him you want to be a race-car driver for Halloween. He had a great idea for your costume." She turned her head and caught sight of her sister, who was still standing and staring with her mouth agape. Kendall's face fell. She let go of Simon and pushed her sister back a few steps. Max couldn't hear what they were saying, but the sister's eyes kept sliding back to him throughout their discussion. He thought he made out an "Oh, my God," but he couldn't be sure.

"Is your aunt feeling all right?" he asked Simon.

The boy glanced over his shoulder and shrugged. "Aunt Emma's a nurse. She never gets sick. Do you like Halloween?"

"Do you?" Max deflected. Simon nodded and grinned. Max decided to play along for the kid's sake. "It's pretty cool. My mom used to love it and make my costumes."

"My mommy just eats my candy."

Max chuckled, picturing Kendall poaching the best stuff out of her kid's plastic pumpkin. He leaned in closer. "Is that right? She's a thief, huh?"

Simon's head bobbed up and down. The two women rejoined them and Kendall made introductions.

Max straightened up and stretched out his hand. "It's nice to meet you, Emma."

Emma made eye contact and froze again. Kendall nudged her with an elbow until she managed to return the greeting. Max wondered what was up with this family. All three sisters stared at him like they couldn't believe he was real when they met him. Perhaps his resemblance to Simon's father had something to do with it. How much did he look like the guy?

"Max thinks Halloween is cool," Simon informed his mother.

"And Simon says you eat his candy," Max teased.

Kendall's eyes widened. "I do not eat your candy!" she said, tickling the boy's sides and making him squeal and squirm.

Max's chin dropped and he gave her a second to come clean. It was common knowledge that one of the perks of being a parent was raiding the Halloween candy after the little ones went to bed.

"Fine, maybe I eat the Milky Ways," she admitted. Max quirked a brow and waited. It didn't take long for her to add to her confession. "And the 3 Musketeers, but that's it!"

Letting her off the hook, Max turned his attention back to Simon. "I have some boxes at my place that I bet your mom could turn into the best race car ever."

"Where do you live?" Emma asked, earning her another jab from Kendall's elbow. "What?"

"I'm in Lincoln Park, a couple of blocks north of Oz Park."

Emma did the nudging this time. "That's right by you," she said to Kendall. "It's like… *fate.*"

"We live in the same neighborhood?" Max asked.

Kendall stopped scowling at her sister and nodded.

"Well, then, you guys should come over and pick out a box," he offered, even though Kendall looked mortified. There was no understanding this woman. Just when he thought they were on friendly terms, she clammed up and acted like there was something wrong with him.

"Let's go now!" Simon said, bouncing up and down and tugging on his mother's shirt-sleeve.

Max's next potential employee strolled through the door. "Can't right now, buddy." The disappointment put a quick damper on the kid's enthusiasm. Simon's shoulders slumped. Max couldn't bear it. "But maybe we can do it this weekend. You guys can stop by and find the perfect car."

A sparkle of hope came back as Simon gazed up at his mom. "Can we?"

She chewed on her bottom lip for a second. "Sure. Why not?"

"All right. I'll see you later, Simon. Nice to

meet you, Emma." Max made his way around the bar to greet his interviewee.

"Wait!" Simon called out. He ran over to Max and his eyes shifted to the man who had arrived for the interview. They stood there for a moment before Max realized Simon wasn't going to say anything in front of the new-comer.

"Can you wait right over there?" Max asked the potential bartender, pointing to a table a few feet away.

Simon watched and waited until the man was a safe distance away. He held out his hand. A shiny red Hot Wheels car sat on his palm. "I have two red Corvettes," he whispered so softly it was barely audible. He showed Max the identical car in his other hand. "Does Aidan like cars?"

Max felt his chest tighten as he stared dumbly at the toy. He was a terrible father. He didn't even know what his son liked. "I don't know."

"He can have this one."

"Thanks," Max choked out, taking the car and slipping it in his pants pocket.

Simon beamed at him. This kid lit up whenever they were together. He had to be-lieve he could do the same for Aidan someday. Simon gave him a boost of confidence that maybe he'd be good at this dad thing after all.

IF EVER THERE was a time when Max desperately wanted but didn't want to want a cigarette, it was before a visit with Aidan. A few years ago, he never would have believed he'd be antsy about hanging out with a three-year-old. Fear was a common friend nowadays. Max was afraid he might never connect with his son. He was scared all the conflict between him and Katie would negatively impact his relationship with Aidan in the long run. He had already underestimated the importance of his presence when Aidan was a baby. What else could he do wrong?

He rubbed his sweaty palms on his thighs as he sat in the office that doubled as a playroom for his visits. Laura Bishop was one of five counselors who worked as supervised visitation providers at this particular center. Redheaded and in her forties, she was nice enough but almost impossible to read. Max had no idea where he stood with her. For all he knew, she could have thought he was the world's worst father.

"I heard it's not usually this warm in October. Maybe I brought the California sunshine with me," he said in an attempt at making conversation while they waited for Katie to arrive with Aidan.

Laura glanced up from the paperwork that occupied her and gave him a smile that somewhat eased his nerves. "Next week, temperatures are sure to drop a good twenty degrees and it'll probably rain. Trust me, you'll get to miss that sunshine."

Max missed California, period. He certainly couldn't say that to the woman reporting back to the judge about his time with Aidan. Life was a lot less complicated out there, though. Max worked, he played, he was responsible for no one but himself. Here, he only saw his son twice a week during supervised visits, but he felt responsible to Aidan every day, all day.

The responsibility weighed heavy on him because he hadn't taken it seriously until now. He also had yet to experience any of the joys of parenthood. He hadn't heard "I love you" or been the reason his son smiled. Aidan hadn't hugged or kissed his dad or shown him any affection at all. Max hadn't earned any of that yet, but he wasn't giving up. California sometimes called his name, but the possibility of gaining Aidan's trust and love was worth staying put for. So every decision was made with Aidan in mind, from the neighborhood Max chose to live in to how hard he worked at Sato's. Aidan deserved a father who followed through on his responsibilities and was successful in his career. His father should be someone he could be proud of and look up to.

Max slipped his hand into his coat pocket and touched the toy car Simon had given him. He had avoided bringing Aidan gifts during their visits because he hadn't wanted Laura to think he was trying to buy his son's love. He figured this one was okay since it was small, and it was really from someone else.

There was a quiet knock on the door and the receptionist pushed it open. "Mrs. Michaels is here."

Max straightened up and ran a hand through his hair. These visits were worse than all the first dates he'd ever been on. Katie trudged in first, looking slightly harried. Her hair did not want to cooperate, falling from her ponytail as she wrestled with her bags and held tight to Aidan's hand.

As soon as they made it inside the room, Aidan latched on to his mother's leg. He was tall for his age, but skinny. The dark jeans he wore hung low on his hips. Paired with a blue-and-white-striped polo shirt, he looked like a kid straight out of a Gap ad. His light brown hair had a curl to it just like Max's did when he was that age.

"Momma, stay," he said with his hazel eyes locked on Max like he was some sort of villain.

With a bit of effort, Max was able to fake a smile. "Hey, buddy. I'm glad we get to hang out today."

Aidan ducked his head behind Katie's leg. "Momma, stay."

Katie dropped her bags on one of the chairs. "I wasn't able to get him down for a nap today, so he's a little cranky. He refused to eat anything at snack time. I packed a couple of things if he gets hungry. Can he have a juice box in here?" she asked Laura.

While the two women discussed what Aidan could and could not eat and drink in the office, Max tried to engage with the little boy. He crouched down so they would be eye to eye—that had seemed to help Simon earlier today. "No nap today, huh? I didn't like taking naps when I was little, either. Who wants to nap when there's so much fun stuff to do, right?"

Katie scooped their son up and frowned down on Max. "Aidan loves his naps. He *needs* a nap because he's three. We didn't get one today because we met Daddy for lunch and we had to run some errands." She gave Aidan a kiss on the cheek.

Max's blood began to boil. She probably had lunch with her husband so she could mention it at this visit. As much as he appreciated that this guy had stepped up and been willing to care for Aidan in his absence, Katie was fooling herself if she thought Max was going to roll over and continue to let someone else be the only father figure in Aidan's life. It had been a mistake to let them leave and not follow. He had no plans to be separated from his son again.

"Wow, lunch with your stepdad and playtime with your dad. What a day. Sounds like Mommy needs a nap." Max held out his arms so she could hand Aidan over.

Katie could dish it out, but obviously wasn't in the mood to take any of his gibes. "Jason is the only *dad* he knows, and that's no one's fault but yours."

"Well, I'm trying to change that if you'd let me."

"And when you lose interest? When being a dad gets too hard? Then what, Max?"

Her questions were like a slap across the face. He felt their burn on his cheek. Before he could respond, Laura jumped in. "Let's remember how many ears can hear you. This

is not the time or the place for this conversation."

Max dropped his arms and Katie pressed
her lips together in a thin line. The center had
strict rules about behavior during drop-off
and pickup for a reason. Max silently scolded
himself for the display of poor self-control in
front of his son.

As soon as Katie set Aidan down, he immediately began to whine and begged her to
pick him back up. It was painful to listen to
him protest as she told him he had to stay
and visit. How long would it take him to realize Max wasn't such a bad guy? What would
happen when the visits stretched longer than
a couple of hours?

When Aidan finally gave in, Katie's eyes
were wet with her own tears. She left the
room, and the little boy wandered over to the
play area. Laura's office had a wide array of
toys—trains, dolls, even a little stage for pup-
pet shows. She had a lot of puzzles and board
games for older kids, as well. Aidan pulled
out some building blocks and began putting
them together.

Max joined him on the floor and attempted
to summon the child within himself. That was
what his own mother would have done. If
Aidan was more interested in the toys than

his father, his father would be interested in them, too. Aidan built towers while Max made something resembling a house with an attached garage. He took the Corvette out of his pocket and rolled it into the garage.

Little fingers crossed the invisible line that had separated them and pulled the car out and pushed it back in. Hope bloomed.

"Do you like cars?" Max asked.

Aidan nodded and pulled the car out again. This time, he rolled it around the towers he built.

"You can have that one if you want. Someone gave it to me to give to you."

He didn't acknowledge the offer, but it made Max smile when he saw Aidan slide it into his pocket when they took a snack break. After the snack, they found more cars and trucks to play with and used the blocks to make roads. Max built a tall tower and let Aidan knock it over with the bulldozer, much to the boy's delight. His giggles filled the room, and Max realized it was the first time he'd ever heard his son's laughter.

Overcome, Max had to press his fingers against the corners of his eyes to keep from crying like a baby. It may not have been much, but to this father, it was everything.

CHAPTER NINE

THIS WAS A bad idea.

Max was a nice guy. He'd smiled a lot more this week and his smile was really nice. He smelled nice, better than nice. He was nice to Simon. But no matter how *nice* Max was, the thought of spending time with him outside of work had not been good for Kendall's heart.

The last few nights had been filled with dreams about Trevor. Nightmares that forced her to relive the last time they'd been together—the fight, the words she wished he would have taken back. Nightmares that ended with her in a cemetery, holding Simon's hand and a folded-up American flag.

Max's presence brought it all back no matter how nice he was or how positively Simon was responding to him. He was making it impossible to ignore the hurt she'd worked so hard to hide.

Emma thought it was a fabulous idea to spend more time with Max. She had talked to one of the child psychologists at the hospital, who said anything they could do to help "generalize Simon's communication behaviors into other speaking situations" was highly desirable. She thought Kendall and Simon should start spending as much time with Max as possible.

Lucy, on the other hand, was beginning to wonder what Kendall wasn't telling her, and it wouldn't be long before her older sister figured out there were secrets yet to be told. People believed Trevor was a good man who did no wrong, that he was a dedicated marine, an attentive father and a loving husband. There was no way Kendall wanted anyone to think any different. He had been a good father and an excellent marine. She was not about to speak ill of the dead.

"This is so close to your place," Emma said as they climbed the steps outside Max's three-flat. It was the only building on the street with a bright red door, making it easy to find.

"Too close," Lucy said, reading Kendall's mind.

Kendall had brought her sisters with her because she thought it was the best way to prevent them all from staying too long. The psychologist had also said the more people Simon spoke in front of, the better. Since meeting Max, Simon had taken to speaking in front of Lucy and Emma quite regularly. Kendall wanted that to continue.

"You want to press the button?" Emma asked Simon, who nodded gleefully. She helped him find the name Max Jordan and he rang the bell.

The yucks were having a field day in Kendall's stomach. They needed to get in and get out. Pick out a box that would work for a costume and go back home.

The door buzzed and Emma held it open for an eager Simon. There was no turning back. Kendall followed everyone up the stairs, her feet heavier with every step.

Max's neighbor stumbled out of his condo just as they hit the second floor. He was dressed in navy, and the Chicago Fire Department emblem on his jacket had a paramedic patch underneath it.

He said hello to Simon, who didn't reply. "You guys headed up to see Floor Three?" he asked.

Emma stepped up behind her nephew, placing her hands on his little shoulders. "The *guy* who lives on floor three."

Max's neighbor squinted and pointed at Emma. "You look familiar. Do you work—"

"At St. Joseph's? Yeah, I'm an ER nurse over there. What station are you from?"

"Twenty-two."

"Paramedic, I see," she said nodding at the patch on his jacket.

"Yep." His smile somehow widened. "I drive 43."

Emma bit her lip and tucked some hair behind her ear. "The triage nurses talk about you."

Tall, Dark and Enamored's eyes widened. "Good things, I hope."

"They like you a lot."

"Cool."

The two smiling fools stood on the landing with a restless Simon waiting in between. Lucy, rolling her eyes, huffed and gave her youngest sister a push. "We need to get up there."

"Oh yeah, of course. Sorry." The neighbor stepped back into his condo and made room for them to pass. "Maybe I'll see you around, Nightingale," he said, keeping his eyes on Emma as they all headed up. "Tell Floor Three I said hi."

Max was waiting in his doorway. A faint shadow of stubble darkened his jaw. His sights, unlike his neighbor's, were firmly set on Kendall.

"You guys met Charlie, I hear."

"He says hi, Floor Three," Kendall said, pushing her nerves aside.

Max had a dimple on his right cheek when he smiled big. "His nicknames for people need some work."

Kendall slipped into the apartment, holding her breath so she didn't smell him. He was bound to smell good, since his hair was slightly wet like he'd just showered. She was sticking to her plan of getting in and out fast. She couldn't give in to any pull he had over her.

"You ready to test-drive some vehicles, little man?" he asked, waving his hand toward a stack of boxes. Lucy and Emma helped Simon choose the perfect one for his costume.

"It's really nice of you to do this," Kendall said.

"No problem. I had a bunch of these lying around. Might as well put one of them to good use. I'm just going to toss the rest." He folded his arms across his chest, making the muscles in his forearms more defined.

Great. Now she could add nice arms to the list. Certainly there had to be some very not-nice things about him. Everyone had not-nice parts. Didn't they? A little voice in her head reminded her that people didn't always show their true selves until you were in too deep.

She didn't want to get too deep only to be disappointed. She certainly couldn't let that happen to Simon.

She turned her head away from Max and toward a console bookcase filled with record albums. He had quite a collection. A record player sat on top in between two enormous speakers that could probably cause some serious hearing damage.

Her grandmother used to play music on a turntable when the girls were little. The three of them would dance around her living room to "Dancing Queen" by ABBA and Neil Diamond's "Sweet Caroline."

"Does it work?" she asked.

"Like it's new. My music is the one thing I'm really good at taking care of."

Trevor didn't have much interest in music. When Kendall was in high school and throughout college, she went to dozens of concerts with her friends and sisters. When she met Trevor, that all stopped. He had a passion for fast cars and NASCAR races. Kendall had watched more cars drive around a track than she cared to admit.

She hadn't realized how much of herself she'd given up for Trevor until she moved back to Chicago. At the time, she had thought she'd been compromising. Marriage was about give and take. Somewhere along the line, though, Kendall had become the only one giving.

"What about this one?" Lucy said holding a large rectangular box around Simon's middle. "Not too big, not too small."

"Just right," Emma added.

"Let's paint it now!" Simon shouted. "Please, Mom."

This was better than she expected. In and out in under five minutes. She had needlessly worried about how difficult it would be to get him to leave.

"Okay, let's go. Tell Mr. Jordan thank you." Calling him Max was too comfortable. Simon shouldn't get too attached.

"Thank you, Mr. Jordan," he repeated, stepping out of the bottomless box. "Can you come paint the car with us?"

Max's face registered surprise. Feeling panicked, Kendall jumped in. "Let's not bother Mr. Jordan any more than we have."

"Please, Mom." He stood before them and tugged on his mother's arm.

"We were going to get some lunch with your aunts," she tried.

"Can you come get lunch with us?" Simon asked Max, his blue eyes full of hope.

Max looked unsure but unwilling to hurt a little boy's feelings. "I don't want to intrude."

Kendall felt the rug pulled out from under her. How could she not invite him without seeming like a jerk? Why couldn't he have said he'd already eaten or had other plans?

"You're more than welcome to join us, but I don't want you to feel like you have to come. Simon will get over it."

"No, I won't," Simon said.

She tipped her chin down and gave him a look. "Yes, you will."

"I won't, Mom. Please come, Max." Simon jumped up and down in front of them and grabbed both of their hands. "Please, please, please, please."

Max looked over at Kendall, who was sure she was bright red due to the extreme embarrassment mixed with her growing anger. "Only if you're sure," he said.

She was sure about a few things. She was sure this was a mistake, that she was going to regret this, and that Simon would now think jumping up and down, begging and whining was the best way to get what he wanted.

"I'm sure."

An awkward lunch ensued. Simon would only talk when the waitress wasn't in the general vicinity of their table and stopped altogether when another group of people were seated next to them. Max was great with him, though. When he picked up on Simon's silence, he switched to drawing pictures back and forth on his place mat with him.

Things got even more uncomfortable when they headed back to Kendall's house. She realized on the walk over that there were pictures of Trevor all over the place inside. Even though she had mentioned the resemblance, she hadn't been specific about the fact that he looked *exactly* like him.

It also didn't help that Emma had other plans and Lucy got a call from someone in her animal-rights group to go protest outside a pet store that bought puppies from a puppy mill. Kendall secretly wished Max would try to get out of painting the box.

When they got home, she had the boys wait outside. Box painting was an outdoor activity. Maybe she wouldn't have to invite Max in at all. While she gathered up all the necessary materials for costume construction, she spent a minute hiding the more obvious pictures of Trevor, just in case.

She was snagging the photo of him in his dress blues when Simon came bursting through the front door. "Mom! Don't forget the tinfoil for the bumper!"

Hiding the frame behind her back, she tried to act casual. "Got it. I'll be out in a minute. Stay out there with Mr. Jordan, okay?"

"He says I can call him Max. Can I call him Max?"

Of course he said that. Kendall was failing miserably at keeping this relationship from getting too personal. "You can call him Max if he's really all right with it. Now, get outside."

He smiled like she'd bought one of those puppies Lucy was worried about and shouted, "He's all right with it. Hurry, Mom!"

Simon closed the door behind him. It was a glimpse of the little boy she'd been missing since his father died, and it made her happy and terrified at the same time.

How long would Max want to hang out with some woman and her kid? There was no way there could be anything more than friendship between him and her. It seemed unlikely he'd stick around unless things went to another level, and that wasn't going to happen. Kendall had too much emotional baggage for any man, let alone one who looked like Trevor. Kendall's feelings for her husband were complicated at best. There was little hope of her ever resolving them now that he was gone. That left someone who looked like him up a creek without a paddle when it came to winning her affections.

Satisfied that Max would not see a picture of Trevor if he came in to use the bathroom, she grabbed the painting supplies and headed outside. Max and Simon were trying to decide where to attach the straps Simon would have to wear over his shoulders.

"What are you going to name your car?" Max asked.

Simon's face scrunched up. "I have to name it?"

"All the cool guys name their cars. It's a thing. I don't have a car anymore, but my last car was named Candy because she was red and so sweet."

"You had a girl car?" Simon's eyes were the size of quarters.

"All cars are girls."

"No way."

"Way."

Simon couldn't believe his ears. He needed his mother to verify this insanity. "Mom, did you know cars are girls?"

Kendall covered her mouth with her hand to stifle her laugh and nodded.

"I'm naming mine Lulu."

Kendall chuckled a little louder. Her sister would *love* having a car named after her, especially that name. "You might not want to tell Aunt Lucy that."

The three of them got busy painting and embellishing the costume. Their collective laughter created a lightness Kendall hadn't felt in a long time. Seeing Simon act like a normal six-year-old freed her from the year's worth of guilt and worry she'd been carrying around. This wasn't like having Trevor around. It was better.

Max came up with the idea of using a Frisbee as the steering wheel. He cut a hole in it and attached it to a paper towel tube that Simon had way too much fun unrolling. Max painted Simon's nose red and Max returned the favor by painting a white smiley face on Max's knee.

With the help of a lot of duct tape and some imagination, they created the coolest red sports car, complete with white flames on the sides. Kendall took pictures with her phone until Simon couldn't stand still another minute.

"We rocked that thing. My mother would be proud," Max said, grinning from ear to ear.

"It's pretty awesome," Kendall agreed as

they watched Simon run up and down the sidewalk, pretending he was in the Daytona 500.

Max looked at his paint-covered hands. "Can I use your bathroom to wash up?"

Although she'd been prepared for him to ask, the request still racked her nerves. Her shoulders stiffened. "Sure, we can all go in for a minute." She called Simon over and they left the car on the porch to finish drying.

Kendall let Simon show Max where he could clean up so she could scan the main floor for any other pictures of Trevor. Her heart raced. This was more stressful than presenting a design to a room full of her toughest clients. She climbed up on the couch and took down the photo collage that hung above it, hiding it behind the cushions. She sat down and held her head in her hands. Hiding all evidence of Trevor's existence was ridiculous and she knew it.

"Mom, can Max stay for dinner?" Simon skipped around the room, too excited for his own good.

"No, honey. Max probably needs to go home."

"He doesn't. His son lives with his mommy and Max doesn't have a wife. He's all alone. We should let him stay here for dinner. No one likes to eat dinner by themselves. I hate being by myself."

He was so sweet, and she appreciated his empathy, but there was no way she could ask Max to stay. She'd have a heart attack before the night was over from the stress of it all. Plus, Simon didn't need to get too attached. Once the job at Sato's was finished, it was unlikely they'd have anything to do with Max again. She had to protect her son from being disappointed later.

"Not tonight, Simon."

"But—"

"No buts. No. It's my final answer."

Simon glared at her. Her tenderhearted boy disappeared. "You're mean, Mommy."

"Hey, be nice to your mom. She helped make you the best costume in town." Max strolled down the hallway toward the family room. It felt strange to have him in this house. Trevor had never lived here, even though the ghost of his memory haunted it daily.

Max's eyes roamed the room. Kendall could only hope that as he scoped the place out he didn't notice things like the random nails sticking out of the wall or the unusual way the photographs on the mantel were spread out.

"Bye, Max. Mommy says you have to go home now." Simon sounded so dejected.

Max looked to Kendall and then patted Simon on the head. "I do have to head home, bud. But I'll see you around, right?"

Simon brightened. "Maybe you can come trick-or-treating with me."

Max paused. Kendall didn't know if she should hope for a yes or a no. Both had their pros and cons. He stared at her as if trying to read her mind. It almost made her laugh because everything in her head was one big jumbled mess. If he could figure out what she wanted, she'd be thankful.

"Sure, why not? If that's okay with your mom." He checked for her reaction, but she still didn't know how to feel about it. Part of her was relieved he didn't disappoint Simon and the other feared this only meant he'd let the kid down later, when he was completely attached.

"That's really nice of you," she said, getting to her feet.

Max rubbed his hands together and clapped once. "Great. I can't wait to see you and Lulu tear this neighborhood up."

"Yeah!" Simon pumped his fist in the air.

Kendall moved closer. "Thanks again for your help today."

"No problem," he said, turning and making his way back to the front door.

"Wait!" Simon headed for the stairs. "I need to show Max something. Don't go home yet."

They waited in the front hall for him. Kendall relaxed a bit. She was so close to successfully preventing any additional awkwardness. Max slid his hands in the front pockets of his jeans. The white paint on his right knee made her smile.

"I had a really good time today," he said, rocking back on his heels.

"Us, too." Kendall cleared her throat. It had been fun making the costume. They'd laughed and worked together. No one had bossed anyone around. "You are so good with him. He likes you a lot."

"I like him, too. He's a great kid, Kendall. Really great."

Simon came barreling down the stairs, jumping all the way to the bottom from three steps up. He was such a boy.

"Here's a picture of my dad's car. I don't know what her name was. My dad never told me." Simon handed Max a photo and the moment Max looked at it, Kendall knew which picture it was—Trevor and that obnoxious yellow Mustang.

Max paled and his hand began to shake ever so slightly. The resemblance was surely frightening. He handed the photo back to Simon. Kendall watched as his breathing became more labored. Finally, his eyes lifted to hers. She saw the shock and felt the questions begging to be asked.

"Baby, why don't you go take this back upstairs. I'm going to walk Max out."

"Bye, Max." Simon took off, oblivious to the bomb he had dropped on his new friend.

Max didn't return the farewell. She wasn't sure he would ever be able to speak again. She pulled open the door and stepped outside, hoping he'd follow.

"I told you when I first met you that you looked like him."

"Look like him?" Max's voice was loud enough that Kendall was glad they were on the porch. "Are you kidding me right now?"

"What did you want me to say? Hi, you're a dead ringer for my dead husband. Nice to meet you?"

Max wandered onto the front lawn and began to pace back and forth. "Is that why he talks to me? He talks to me because he thinks I'm his dad?"

"No!" Kendall said in a rush. "He doesn't think you're his dad. He knows you aren't his dad. His dad is in heaven. He understands that." She pressed her hand against her forehead. She had no idea how to rationalize this. "He talked to you because you look like him, yes, but he knows you're not him. He likes you. He likes Max Jordan, the guy who works at the restaurant his mom is remodeling."

Max linked his fingers behind his head as he continued to pace and put all the pieces together. "That's why you fainted the day we met. That's why both of your sisters gawked at me like I had three heads."

"There's a strong resemblance."

"I look exactly like him!" Max threw up his hands.

"At first glance, you look very much like him. But there are differences. I notice them more and more each time I'm around you."

Her words did not help stop him from freaking out. "This is weird. I mean, really weird."

"I know." There was nothing more she could say. She'd been coping with this for a couple of weeks and she was still reeling. He needed some time to process everything.

"You swear to me he doesn't think I'm his dad."

"He knows you are not his dad, I swear on my life," she said adamantly.

She could see his frantic need to believe her as he searched her face for an ounce of doubt. If there was one thing she was sure of, it was that Simon understood Max was not Trevor. The little boy probably understood and accepted that better than she did.

"I have to go," he said, pointing to the street. "I'm going." And he did.

CHAPTER TEN

THE WALK HOME wasn't long enough to help Max clear his head, so he kept walking until nothing was familiar. He wished the fresh air would help him sort out his feelings.

Confused. Freaked out. Curious. That was how he felt. What to do with that, he wasn't sure.

Kendall had told him he looked like her husband. She wasn't lying when she said she'd been up-front with him, but he had assumed it was a general likeness, not something out of the movie *The Parent Trap*.

People said everyone had a twin out there somewhere. Max never imagined he'd ever find that person. Or meet the guy's family. Or like his family so much. And he definitely couldn't have imagined the man would be dead.

Spending the day with Kendall and Simon had been fun. He hadn't just said it to her to be polite. They made him feel happy, and though Kendall's feelings were a mystery, he knew he made Simon feel the same. Now it all seemed tainted. Were they only enjoying being around him because he reminded them of Trevor? When they smiled at him, were they really thinking about the man they lost?

He wasn't about to try and replace someone like a creepy clone. He had a hard enough time living up to everyone's expectations as it was. He'd never be able to compete with a marine killed protecting the world from terrorists. That was more pressure than he could stand.

When he got back home, he looked up Trevor Montgomery on Google and read his obituary. The photo that accompanied the article made Max's head spin. If it wasn't for the short hair, he'd swear someone had put his picture in the paper. Trevor was born the same year as Max, but three months later. He had no siblings. His mother was deceased, but his father was still alive.

Max picked up his phone and dialed his mother. She answered on the second ring.

"Maxie!"

He didn't bother with the normal niceties. "Swear to me you didn't steal me out of some hospital in Chicago, change my birth date and tell me I had a deadbeat dad to cover your tracks."

"What?" she said with a laugh.

"Swear I'm your son."

"Of course you're my son! I have the C-section scar to prove it." She could have stopped there, but she didn't. "Did you know that nowadays the scars are so small, women can wear bikinis after one? That is amazing because my scar goes straight up and down my stomach. You weren't that big, but they cut me open like they were pulling out the Jolly Green Giant."

"Mom…" Max pretended to bang his head against the kitchen counter.

"What? You were barely six pounds. They didn't need to cut such a big opening. You know that's why I didn't have more kids. Can you imagine what my stomach would look like if they went in there more than once?"

"Okay, okay, I'm your son. I believe you. Any chance you had twins and sold one on the black market to pay the rent?" This theory made more sense. When he was little, there had been times he'd worried she was going to put him up as collateral.

"Maxwell James Jordan, what is going on with you? Why are you asking me all these questions?"

"I don't know." He moved to the couch and flopped down. "I'm having a weird day."

"What does that have to do with me giving birth to you?"

"Nothing." He was overreacting to this whole thing. It was a coincidence. A bizarre coincidence. "I just needed to be sure I'm blaming the right person for all my issues."

"What issues? You have my good skin, my amazing sense of humor, my excellent fashion sense. And you know you got your great hair thanks to me. They say baldness is inherited from the mother's side of the family."

"Really?" For all her quirks, she did know how to make him smile when he needed it most. "Aidan's in trouble, then, because Katie's dad is balder than Mr. Clean."

"How is my grandson?"

"He's good." Max rubbed his full head of hair. "I think there's a chance he might even like me someday."

"Someday? You're his father. He loves you." This was the most laughable thing she'd said in the entire conversation.

"Being someone's father doesn't automatically win you your child's affection. Trust me, no one knows that better than yours truly."

"Don't say that," she scolded.

Why she didn't have any resentment toward the man who'd left her alone and pregnant, he'd never understand. She never had a bad word to say about him. Truthfully, she never had *any* words to say about him. When Max had been old enough to question why he didn't have a mom *and* a dad, her only explanation was that sometimes love scares people, and that because his dad loved them, he had to leave.

That didn't make a lot of sense to a kid, and even less to the adult he'd become. His dad was a coward, and that wasn't the same as being scared. There was also no way he loved Max. He'd never met him. Never been part of his life. Certainly didn't care. How could she possibly think his father loved him?

"Mom, let's be real. He's nobody to me." All Max had was a first name and a picture of the guy from before he was born. "Even if I have to suffer through supervised visits the rest of his life, at least Aidan will grow up knowing I want to be his dad."

"Just because he wasn't there, doesn't mean your dad didn't want to be."

Max couldn't do this anymore. Listening to his mom defend his dad was worse than worrying about what to do about Kendall and Simon. "I have to go. I'll talk to you soon, okay?"

"I'll never regret loving him, Max. Without

him, there'd be no you. Without you, nothing would be right in my world."

He smiled again in spite of himself. She always did that. Maybe she was a better mom than he ever gave her credit for being.

MAX TRIED TO keep his distance from Kendall on Monday. She made it easy on him, working on her mural all day. Owen was there in the afternoon to deal with the installation of the new sushi bar. It was a stunning design, but Max was still convinced it would cause congestion in that area and make it more difficult for the waitstaff to get to and from the kitchen.

The stone Kendall had chosen for the countertop was gorgeous, a mix of black, gray and cream. The lighting above and around it was going to be chic and sophisticated. The placement of the bar was Max's main issue. They weren't taking into account the amount of traffic that would be flowing around that space.

Max stood with his arms crossed and sleeves rolled up, as the construction crew began installing the bases. He'd ditched his suit coat after lunch along with his tie. He'd hired his last employee this morning and would conduct the rest of his business on the phone today.

He glanced around the restaurant, trying to make the best of a bad situation. Maybe if they changed the number of tables in this room, they could make it work. There had to be something they could do differently if the bar had to go in here.

"It's going to look fantastic," Owen said, coming up from behind and startling him.

"It's going to look amazing, but it's still in the wrong spot."

"Trust Kendall."

That was a loaded request. He shifted his gaze from the bar to Owen to get a read on him. Had Kendall told him about what happened on Saturday?

"She tends to forget about certain details," Max said.

Owen frowned and tilted his head to the side. He had most definitely been told. "She's excessively focused on the details. Six-year-old details, to be exact."

Max didn't need a lecture on putting your kid first. Kendall had every right to do what she thought was best for her son. "Simon is a great kid. And I feel bad he lost his dad." Max let out a frustrated sigh "But I don't like being brought into a situation and not told all the facts."

"That's fair," Owen conceded. "And that being said, you should know that Simon hadn't spoken to anyone other than Kendall and her mother since his father died almost a year ago...until he met you."

A year without speaking to anyone but his mother and grandmother? That was simply unbelievable. "He talks to Lucy and Emma. I've heard him."

Owen shook his head. "Not until you. He would whisper to Kendall and she would relay the message. It's called selective mutism."

"Selective what?"

"It's an anxiety disorder. He can talk normally, like you've heard, but in most situations—at school, for example—he can't say anything."

Max had never heard of such a thing. He could tell Simon was shy, although not with him. But a mute? And what did that have to do with not telling Max he looked like Simon's father?

Owen gave him a pat on the back and answered his unspoken question. "A year of watching your son suffer in silence can make you question whether or not to tell someone, who makes his life easier, something that might make that person run for the hills."

Kendall dealt with much more than Max could have imagined. Compassion for her struggles quickly replaced the resentment he'd been feeling. He still wished she had told him, but now he understood why she hadn't.

Owen went to talk to the foreman, leaving Max to contemplate the next step he should take with Kendall and her son. It was still weird. Kendall had to be comparing him to her husband, and he was never going to live up to that. He wasn't even going to try. The kid was a different story, though. Kendall said he knew Max wasn't his dad, but Simon was searching for a father figure. If Max was somehow helping Simon by giving him a moment of his time, how could he justify walking away?

There was also a selfish part of Max that knew by helping Simon, he might earn himself another character witness in his custody battle. Kendall's story would pull at the heartstrings of even the most hardened judges. Like Kendall, Max was willing to do just about anything for his son.

He wished he could go back in time. If he had put Aidan first when he was born, Max could have saved himself all this trouble now.

He could have kept Aidan out of the middle and prevented the confusion the little boy surely felt. Aidan didn't deserve this mess, but there was no going back, only forward. Once Max proved himself to Katie, their son would have a new kind of stability.

MAX FOUND HIMSELF checking his watch more than usual. After what he considered a successful visit last week, hope burned in his chest. All he wanted was for Aidan to be happy to see him tonight. If Katie saw that he could be a good father, maybe she would back off and make it easier for him to be part of his son's life. A good mother should want that for her child.

The bases for the sushi bar were installed and the crew was working on the cabinets along the wall. Max had spent a large portion of the afternoon on the phone, and his cell was in desperate need of a charge. He'd left his charger in his office, which was located off the kitchen and was now fully functional.

As he crossed the main dining area, he considered offering Kendall an olive branch. Making peace with her would ease his mind some. She was washing her paintbrushes in the sink behind the drink bar. He wondered how the mural was coming along. Before he had the chance to approach her, the front doors opened. Mr. Sato glided in flanked by Jin and Chef Yamaguchi. Their unexpected visit created an unpleasant knot in his stomach.

"Mr. Sato, what a surprise," Max said.

Jin did the talking, as usual. Perhaps his father had the same anxiety disorder as Simon. "We came to plan the menu. Chef got into town this afternoon, and we didn't want to wait until tomorrow to get started. Opening day will be here before we know it."

Chef probably had the menu already planned. Max would simply see to it that he had the supplies he needed. The conversation should be short and sweet. He might not get out of here in an hour, but if he skipped his usual stop at home to change, he could make it to the visit with plenty of time to spare.

Kendall came over, wiping her hands on a towel. She had a streak of white paint in her hair and paintbrushes sticking out of her back pocket. This laid-back look reminded him of the fun they'd had painting Simon's car. When it wasn't so impossibly hard to get along with her, it was incredibly easy.

Max wasn't Kendall's only admirer. Jin's face softened when she was near. The tightness in his jaw relaxed and he smiled at her like she was the sun, the only thing capable of melting his usually icy exterior. The poor kid didn't have a chance with Kendall. Max might have felt a little sorry for him if he wasn't so annoying.

Jin introduced Kendall to Chef Yamaguchi, and she offered them a quick tour. Her smile was wide and her hands were in almost constant motion as she spoke. Her excitement in showing Mr. Sato the progress was contagious.

Her mural, though unfinished, was awe-inspiring. The layers and depth she created on a flat wall were unbelievable. The west room's sushi bar was saved for last. Mr. Sato moved around the room and took it in from all angles. Kendall described the way the counter would look and how the lighting would enhance the ambiance, seemingly unfazed by his silence. It drove Max nuts.

Jin was busy complimenting Kendall on a job well done when Mr. Sato spoke. "Too big," he said to everyone's surprise.

"Too what, sir?" Kendall asked.

Max, however, had heard him loud and clear. *Too big! Too big! Too big!* he wanted to shout. He'd said it from the very start, but no one had listened.

"Too big."

Kendall had to force her shoulders back. "I think it's hard to imagine it since it's unfinished, but—"

Mr. Sato cut her off. "Too big. Mr. Jordan, stand over there." He pointed to the doorway that led to the kitchen. "Jin, stand by the bar. Hisato, over there." He sent the chef to the spot where they had all entered the room. "Kendall, walk to the kitchen. Hisato, go to Jin. Max, come back into the room."

Everyone followed his directions and with all of them practically in the same space, Max and Kendall ended up chest to chest. He could see her shame the moment she felt it. It made gloating impossible.

"Too big for that side. Make it smaller or move it." With that, Sato exited the room, leaving the rest of them to untangle themselves. Jin chased after his father, claiming he had warned Kendall that the placement of the sushi bar was an issue.

Max hung back with Kendall, who pulled a paintbrush out of her pocket and slashed it through the air like a fencer with her foil.

"It'll work out," he said to reassure. "Shorten it a little or maybe flip the room, put it over on that side."

"Go ahead," she said, spinning to face him. "Say it. Tell me you told me so."

"I've worked in restaurants since I was sixteen. I had to learn how people move in each space or I ended up with food on the floor. And my shoes."

She pursed her lips to keep from smiling. "I'll figure it out. But first, I have to go cancel some deliveries." Her paintbrush went back into her pocket and she slipped out of the room.

Max found the other men sitting at one of the tables in the main dining area. He grabbed his laptop and joined them to work out the details of the menu. The discussion ran much longer than he imagined. The minutes seemed to tick off more like seconds. He was going to be late. He needed to call Laura and let her know, but there was no lull in the conversation for him to excuse himself.

Jin had big ideas, and they weren't in line with Chef's vision. This led to further debate and more discussion about the competition, their menus and how to be original. Max's leg bounced restlessly under the table. Finally, Mr. Sato leaned over and whispered something that quieted Jin as well. It was agreed that Chef's menu ideas were best.

Without a moment to spare, Max asked the chef to send him a complete list of his supplies and apologized for needing to be on his way when they invited him to join them for dinner. He was already late, and if the traffic didn't cooperate, he was going to miss the visit altogether.

In the back of the cab, he pulled out his phone to call Laura, only to find it had died. Katie was never going to let him live this down. The cab driver claimed not to have a phone, only his radio, so Max offered him an extra fifty if he could get him to his appointment before it was over.

When they pulled into the parking lot, Katie was there, loading Aidan into the car. Max jumped out and called to her. He jogged over to her car, hoping she'd let him have a minute or two with his son.

"I'm here. Sorry. Something came up at work, and then my phone died. I should have called from the restaurant. I forgot my battery was so low."

Katie pressed her lips together and closed the back door of her car.

"I know I'm late, but we can still have half a visit." Max bent down and waved at Aidan, who was all strapped into his car seat.

"Your visit was at six o'clock. You didn't show up. I have the right to leave after twenty minutes if you don't call."

"Come on, Katie. The owner came to the

restaurant without any warning. My phone died. Traffic was awful. Give me a break, please."

She opened her door. "You haven't changed. Work always comes first. I don't think arbitration is going to work, Max. I don't trust you. I'm asking for a judge. My lawyer will be contacting yours soon," she said before getting in her car.

Max wanted to pound on the window when she shut the door and started the engine. He wanted to scream at her for being so unreasonable and unforgiving as she started to back out. He wanted to throw something to break her taillight as she drove away. But he didn't do any of that because his son was in that car and Max had no one to blame for missing his visit other than himself.

CHAPTER ELEVEN

KENDALL HATED BEING WRONG. Not that she wasn't wrong lots of times about a lot of things, but she hated being wrong when she was so sure she had been right. How many times had she argued with Max about that sushi bar? How many times had he told her exactly what Mr. Sato said? Perhaps it wasn't being wrong that bugged her. Maybe it was her foolish stubbornness.

Trevor used that word because he knew it got under her skin. Just because she voiced an opposing opinion, he'd shake his head and tell her to stop being so stubborn. Sometimes he was right. She could admit that, on occasion, she could dig her heels in just to spite him. That was what she had done here. Max, in all his Trevorness, had repeatedly questioned her design, and in an attempt to prove to him she was smarter than he gave her credit for, she refused to listen to reason.

The worst of it was that Max hadn't even called her on it. He hadn't rubbed in the fact that he'd seen the same design flaw from the very beginning. That was notably un-Trevor-like and baffling given his recent realization. She was more confused than ever about how to handle his relationship with Simon.

Oh, Simon. Her son had left for school today after making the deal that if he went to school all week, he'd get to go trick-or-treating with Max on Friday. It was a lot to ask of him—it had been a long time since he'd made it an entire week without incident.

She watched him now as he ran in circles around the coffee table, pretending to make his red Corvette fly through the air. The letter Wilder had sent home with him lay open on the couch beside her. She had ten days to prepare for the meeting the school was requesting. Ten days to decide what she wanted for Simon and how to advocate for him properly.

This was not the time to let her stubbornness get in the way. The educational team wanted to discuss options, alternative schools that may or may not be a better fit for someone like Simon. Kendall wanted to be sure she was making her decisions based on facts, not on her stubborn need to be right.

"Mom, do you think cars can fly?" Simon asked, bringing his Corvette in for a landing on the armrest of the couch.

"Maybe they will someday. Planes fly, why not cars?"

"Do you think Max likes flying cars?" Max's likes and dislikes were still Simon's favorite subjects.

"I can ask him tomorrow."

Simon made a loud roar like an engine and lifted his Corvette back into the air. "Don't. I'll ask him on Friday."

"Okay." A tingle of excitement ran through her to hear him talk like he believed he'd make it through the week of school. She watched him run around the coffee table a few more times. "Do you like Max because he looks like Daddy?"

Simon came to a stop and shrugged. "He's not Daddy. He's different."

Kendall leaned forward, resting her elbows on her knees. "What makes him different?"

"His hair is funny. It grows on his face sometimes."

Laughter bubbled up and out of her. "His hair *is* different."

"And he's nice to you," he said as he went back to running in circles. "He makes you smile and laugh."

Kendall's heart sputtered and backfired. "Your dad was nice to me," she choked out, sitting back.

Her sweet boy climbed up on the couch and kissed her cheek. "Daddy made you cry, remember?"

She remembered, but it broke her heart to know Simon remembered, too.

THE EARLY MORNING light seeped through the rice-paper panels of the shoji screens that covered the street-side windows of Sato's. The quiet was a welcome change from the noisy construction that usually filled this space. This was the kind of silence Kendall could get used to. The crew was due later this morning to tear out the sushi bar bases they had installed the day before. Where they were going to put them was still a mystery. Kendall hoped the right answer would come to her while she worked on the mural.

Painting had always been therapeutic for her. When Kendall was little, she used painting to express her feelings. Like her son, talking about what was going on inside was a lot harder than putting it on paper or canvas. Art was also a needed release in a house with two sisters who never held back any of their emotions.

With the bristles dipped in the palest-of-pink paint, Kendall used the thin handle of the brush to scratch the itch on her nose. The mural was her favorite design element in the restaurant. She'd chosen a Japanese garden with cloudlike cherry blossoms and a bright red bridge crossing a lily-pad-spotted pond as her setting. A beautiful geisha holding her parasol would eventually be standing near the tall grasses beside the water.

There were still many layers of paint to apply before it would be finished, which was why Kendall had arrived so early. She was adding a bit more pink to the cherry blossoms when Max showed up.

The man was always dressed to the nines. His suits were impeccably tailored and his hair probably had more product in it than hers ever did. He was so handsome, good-looking in a much different way than Trevor had been. Max had an elegance about him, whereas Trevor's strength and power was what always stood out when you saw him.

"You may be the first person I've met who works harder than me." Max set a cup of coffee on the table nearest her. "I thought you might need this."

He certainly had this way of knowing what someone needed before they even knew they needed it. She thanked him and picked up the warm, delicious-smelling coffee. Owen, her usual caffeine dealer, was working on another one of KO Designs' projects today. His connections had landed them two more smaller projects, including a kitchen remodel in a gorgeous Queen Anne house on the north side of the city.

"How's Simon?" Max asked, turning out one of the chairs from a nearby dining table. He took a seat, sipping from his own cup of coffee.

"Good. He's hoping to come by on Friday. He has a new question for you."

Max tipped his head and smiled. "What is it this time? What time do I go to bed? How many marshmallows can I fit in my mouth? What's my favorite toothpaste?"

"I'm not allowed to tell," she replied with a laugh and shake of her head. "But that marshmallow one is good. It sounds like something he might need to know one of these days."

"He sure likes to get personal."

Kendall wondered if that bothered him or not. Simon did ask him a lot of personal questions, and she couldn't blame Max if he wanted to set some stricter boundaries.

"I can tell him he needs to cool it. I don't want things to get any weirder than they already are." She turned back to the mural, waiting for his response.

She heard him stand up, and the sound of

his footsteps warned her of his close proximity. "Simon's questions don't bother me. Not being up-front bothers me."

She swallowed hard before turning to face him. She focused on his eyes because they were the feature that never made her think of anyone but him. She expected them to be angrier than they were. "I'm really sorry I didn't tell you everything from the start. I wasn't sure how to even bring it up."

"I believe you." He lifted a hand to Kendall's cheek. His thumb swiped across it, applying the lightest pressure but still setting her skin on fire. "You had a little pink paint right there," he said.

She was sure the pink was quickly replaced by the traitorous red of her blush. "Thanks." She used her own hand to wipe the spot.

"Stop." He carefully grabbed her wrist to keep her from doing it again. The gentleness of his touch sent a tingle down her spine. "Now you really smeared it on there."

She hadn't noticed the paint on her fingers until he pointed it out. Feeling foolish, she stepped away and searched for the hand towel she used to take care of messes like these. She probably looked like some sort of clown. There was absolutely nothing fancy or elegant about her.

"I care about you, but I can't compete with someone who's dead," he said, still considerably close.

"You're not competing," she said, closing her eyes and holding her breath. Did he really care about her? Why did he have to smell so good? She cared about him, too.

He stepped away, putting some needed distance between them. "Sorry, I didn't mean it like that. I meant I care about you and Simon."

Of course he did. This was quickly becoming a sorry fest. Kendall had to fight the urge to apologize for being disappointed he wasn't having feelings for her. Ever since Simon had shared his thoughts on Max, Kendall's feelings were more muddled than ever.

"Simon told me last night that he doesn't even think you look that much like his dad. He said you have funnier hair."

Max's brows pinched together until Kendall's words had registered. His hands flew to his hair, patting and smoothing it down. "What's funny about my hair?"

Kendall snickered. "Nothing. He spends a lot of time with my dad, who's balding, and his dad always had a military cut. I think funny means fancy to a six-year-old."

Max gave his hair one more pat and returned to his coffee. "What about you? Do you look at me and see him?"

"Sometimes," she admitted. Truthfully, thoughts of Trevor weren't as haunting these days. Once Max found out about the two of them looking alike, the nightmares had stopped. Maybe it had been guilt over not being honest that had been driving them and not solely their resemblance.

"That's got to be confusing. It confuses me. Like when you smile at me, I don't know if you're smiling at me or at the thought of him."

Kendall set her paintbrush down and joined him at the table. The sound of the chair legs scraping against the wood floors filled the dining room. "I won't lie. It's been extremely weird." It was time to be honest with him and herself. Trevor hadn't given her a lot of reasons to smile before he died. "But I smile at you because of the things you say or do, not because of how you look. So, the smiles are yours."

His smirk told her he was pleased with that answer. He set his coffee on the table and propped his head up on his hand. "What was he like? If you don't mind me asking."

Kendall took a moment to consider what she should share. "Trevor was very confident. The first time we met, he introduced himself as the man I couldn't help but fall in love with."

"Confident?" Max arched a brow. "That sounds cocky."

She conceded with a nod and a shrug. "Maybe a little. He was…very sure of himself. He made decisions and never second-guessed them, even when he was wrong."

"Was he wrong very often?"

Kendall shook her head. "He didn't think so."

"Well, that settles it. Besides our good looks, we're nothing alike because I am often wrong about things."

"You weren't wrong about the sushi bar."

"Ah," Max said with a wink. "I was right about that, but I second-guess myself all the time. I'm always worried I'm not going to be good enough. Top that off with some incredibly bad trust issues and I'm a hot mess."

"Me, too." Kendall smiled. Max looked like Trevor but apparently had more in common with her.

"*You're* a hot mess? Please!" he shouted in disbelief. "You're a gorgeous woman who runs her own successful business and is raising an amazing kid by herself. You are the opposite of a mess."

She opted to ignore the comment about

being gorgeous. "The business is too new to be considered successful, but thank you. And Simon is amazing, but I could never say I'm raising him on my own. I have a lot of help from my family. And things still aren't easy. He took his dad's death real hard and every day is a challenge."

"Owen told me about the mutism. I hope that's all right."

She wondered what else Owen had told him. "Owen has a big mouth, but I love him, so it's okay."

"He doesn't talk to anyone outside of you, your mom and me?"

"Selective mutism is the oddest disorder. Everything about him is so normal when it's just him and me at home. But when we go out into the world, the anxiety takes over and makes it impossible for him to speak."

"Did he just stop talking when he heard his dad died?"

"No, it wasn't right away. I think the funeral was his trigger. It was so overwhelming and sad." She shuddered at the memory of it as well. "Imagine being five and everyone you love is crying and saying goodbye to your dad. I think that's when he realized Trevor really wasn't coming back."

"Then I came along, and he thought his dad *had* come back."

This was where things got even more confusing for Kendall. Simon had thought that, which explained why he'd spoken to Max the first time they met. What didn't make sense was that after he accepted Max wasn't Trevor, his desire to talk to him remained. There must be something about Max that reduced Simon's anxiety. What it was, Kendall didn't know.

"He absolutely thought his dad had come back the first time we saw you." She realized something else she hadn't told him. "We actually watched you get into a cab outside your house days before I met you here."

"You did?"

"The day I got this job, actually. I got called away in the middle of our meeting with Mr. Sato."

Max's eyes shut, then sprang open. "I remember that. I was late. A kid shouted at me and almost ran into the street. That was Simon. I saw you. I saw both of you."

"Crazy, huh?"

"You can say that again."

"He's aware you're someone else and he still wants to talk to you. That's about you, not his dad."

Max finished his coffee and let that sink in. Max was a thinker while Trevor was a doer, another clear distinction between the two men.

"That makes me feel better," he said, standing up and buttoning his suit coat. He nodded toward her mural. "I'll let you get back to work. That is going to be the restaurant's pièce de résistance."

He was full of compliments today. Praise wasn't always easy for Kendall to hear. Trevor had a way of focusing on her flaws, causing her to do the same. Max was certainly different. Kendall gave him another smile that was 100 percent his.

THE GEISHA'S KIMONO was coming along nicely. Kendall took a step back and squinted, tilting her head. She was relieved it still matched the drawing she'd first put down on paper. This was the most detailed mural she'd ever painted.

Max's compliment rang in her ears until it was her phone doing the ringing. The name on the caller ID filled her with dread. The school never called with good news.

"Hi, Mrs. Montgomery, it's Lisa." The rest of what the social worker had to say barely registered. Kendall heard the words "recess," "retard" and "no dad." She was already heading for the exit before the request to come to school was even out of Lisa's mouth.

"What's wrong?" Max surprised her, standing at the door like he'd seen her coming. He held it open for her and followed her out.

"I have to go get Simon," she explained, feeling more angry than anything else right now. "And I may have to spank someone else's first grader."

Max's eyes widened. "I think I better come with you," he said, hailing her a cab. Kendall was in too much of a hurry to argue. She knew kids could be thoughtless, but when had they become so cruel? She concentrated on her anger because being mad was easier than the alternative.

Lisa and Mrs. Nigel were waiting for them in the main office. Two little boys sat side by side in chairs outside the principal's office. Kendall wondered if they were the same two boys who'd told her son he couldn't go on the monkey bars because he was a retard with no dad.

They didn't look like the bullies she'd imagined on the drive over. In fact, one of the boys lived on their block. His mom had invited Kendall and Simon over for a play date when they'd first moved in. They weren't invited back after the woman realized Simon wouldn't speak to anyone but his mom. Like mother, like son. Someone had failed at teaching her kid some empathy.

Lisa took them out back to the playground where Simon was hiding inside the tunnel slide. The adults couldn't reach him from either end without getting in the tunnel with him. Everyone was afraid of Simon's reaction if they got too close, so they called Kendall instead.

Kendall knelt down and looked up the slide. Simon was tucked in sideways, his head buried between his knees. "Hey, baby, it's Mommy. Can you come out and talk to me?"

His little head lifted and his tear-stained cheeks were almost too much for Kendall's heart to handle. She wanted to go back in that school and shake those boys. Shake them until they were crying, too.

"Come on out, honey." She reached a hand up for him to grab. Simon shook his head. The fear not only silenced him but froze him in place as well. "Just slide down to me. I'm here."

She was so focused on Simon, she didn't notice Max had climbed to the top of the slide until she heard his voice at the other end of the tunnel. "Hey, dude." Simon's head turned away from his mom. Max had taken off his suit coat and was busy unbuttoning the cuffs of his shirt. "Mind if I try out this awesome slide? Maybe we can knock your mom over when we get to the bottom. Wanna try?"

Kendall bent back down and saw Simon nod ever so slightly. Max went in headfirst, reaching out to grab Simon as he slid on down. Kendall backed out the bottom and Simon's black gym shoes popped out first. A heartbeat later, he dove into Kendall's waiting arms.

How would she ever survive raising this child? The world was not always a nice place, and there was nothing she could do about that. It was the very worst thing about being a parent. You could love them and treat them right, but you couldn't make the rest of the world do the same.

"I love you so much. I am so sorry those boys said those things to you. They are in big trouble for using mean words."

"Take me home," he whispered in her ear. "Please, Mommy."

It was like a knife in the chest. She kissed his head, conflicted to say the least. Her heart demanded that she get him out of there, while her head said if he left now, he'd never come back.

"Don't let the mean words win, baby," she begged. She could feel him shaking his head no.

Behind him, Max had ungracefully gotten out of the slide and back on his feet. He had a piece of mulch stuck to his pant leg. He gave her a sad smile. He mouthed, "Should he stay?"

Kendall shrugged one shoulder. All the counselors she'd ever taken him to would say yes, but she wasn't feeling too confident in her ability to make that happen. He was holding on so tightly.

"So, Simon, you going to show me around?"

Surprisingly, Simon let go of his mom. He turned around to face Max but leaned against Kendall, needing the comfort the contact provided them both. He motioned for Max to come closer so he could whisper. Lisa was still standing nearby.

Max crouched in front of Simon, who proceeded to give him an earful. When the little boy was finished, Max nodded. "I get it. I'd want to go home, too. But you know what would be even better than that?" Simon shook his head. Nothing was better than going home to him. "Showing those kids you're brave like your dad and finishing your day."

Simon shook his head. Max was sweet for

trying, but it was highly unlikely Simon could recover from an episode like this. Far less traumatic situations had sent him into a tailspin. It also didn't help that Max brought up Trevor. The word "dad" in and of itself was a trigger.

"Your mom and I could stay for a little bit, make sure things are good. Then we could come back and get you after school. I think I would take a brave kid like that out for ice cream."

Simon didn't shake his head. It was almost as if he was considering Max's offer.

"Mommy, too?"

Kendall had to stop herself from gasping. The shock of hearing Simon's voice registered all over Lisa's face as well. It was the very first time the social worker had heard Simon speak.

"Yeah, Mommy, too. But you have to pay for her."

Simon smiled. "I can't pay for her. I have no money!"

"You have no money? What the heck?" Max stood up and looked around. "Don't they pay you around here? A dollar for every word you spell right or something like that? What kind of school is this?"

Simon *laughed* and Kendall wanted to cry.

"They don't pay the kids for school! They only pay the teachers."

"What? Only the teachers? But they have the easy job. You have to learn, that's tough." Max glanced at Lisa. "Seriously? Not even a quarter for saying the alphabet?"

"Sorry," Lisa said, shrugging and handing him his coat.

Max let out a dramatic sigh. He tossed his jacket over his shoulder. "Fine, I'll pay for your mom, too. But she can't have sprinkles. Only us guys get sprinkles."

Simon turned to Kendall. "Okay, Mommy?"

If ever there was a moment she wished she could bottle, it was this. Simon had never recovered this quickly. His bravery was worthy of the biggest ice cream sundae with sprinkles they could find. Max, on the other hand, deserved so much more.

"Okay," she managed to say without crying her eyes out. She kept the tears from falling until Simon took Max's hand and led him back into the building.

CHAPTER TWELVE

"THANK YOU," KENDALL said to Max as he held the door to Sato's open for her. She laughed at herself. "I feel like that's all I've said to you for the last twenty minutes."

It had been. She'd said it fifteen times once he started counting and probably said it fifteen times before then. She acted like he had rescued Simon from a burning building or something.

"You don't have to thank me. Especially for what happened back at the school."

Kendall spun around, her ponytail swinging from side to side. "I don't think I can ever thank you enough for that."

Making people happy by figuring out what they needed and getting it for them was basically in his job description. "You needed some help, and hanging out with Simon is hardly heroic."

Her brown eyes locked on his and drew him closer. She had this way of making him feel vulnerable by simply being that way herself. It was unnerving. "I will return the favor someday. Anything at all, I'm there for you."

"The only help I need is getting my ex to let me see my son as much as I'd like."

"Divorce is tough, huh?"

"Divorcing her was easy. The hard part is figuring out how to be divorced and still parent our son together."

Kendall seemed intrigued. "She's not letting you see him?"

"We haven't lived in the same state most of Aidan's life. She remarried and thinks her new husband is a better dad than me, so she's trying to get the courts to give her sole custody."

"That doesn't seem fair," she said with a frown. "What makes the new husband a better dad than you?"

Katie would say it was his presence in Aidan's life. Max didn't know Jason Michaels well enough to say what credit he deserved. He'd never admit it to his ex-wife, but Max was somewhat grateful Jason was so willing to take in another man's child. Having been raised by a single mother who had dated enough jerks, Max knew all about men who wanted nothing to do with somebody else's kid.

"I think her desire to get rid of me has more

to do with how little she thinks of me than how much she thinks of him."

"It's so hard to believe you aren't a great dad. The way you are with Simon…you're a natural."

Her confidence in him seemed a bit misguided. Simon was an amazing kid. Getting along with Simon was effortless.

"I have a custody hearing soon. My lawyer says I should be fine." An idea popped in his head, one that made him feel like he was taking advantage of Kendall. She would probably do anything for him in this moment. He couldn't believe it when the words came out of his mouth. "All I need is some people who will testify to the fact that I'm a decent guy."

Kendall took his hand and squeezed it between both of hers. "I could do that," she offered eagerly, like he knew she would.

Besides the guilt, fear niggled at the back of his mind. Max didn't ask for help. It wasn't in his nature. Other people tended to let him down. He also hated that relying on someone else made him vulnerable. Kendall already made him feel vulnerable enough. Opening up to her was too easy, and that scared him.

"You don't have to," he said, giving her an out.

"I'll tell any judge how good and kind you are, just tell me when and where."

Guilt and fear be damned, he'd take all the help he could get to win against Katie. "Thanks."

Her face broke into the most beautiful smile. "Maybe you'll let me get sprinkles on my sundae."

"Maybe," he said as she dropped his hand. "Probably...okay, fine. I was going to let you get them anyway."

"See, I knew you were a nice guy." She was being light and silly, but Max still felt that unease in the pit of his stomach. He hoped he was a nice guy and not some manipulator. The line was a fuzzy one.

KENDALL BIT HER lip and stood on tiptoe under the tree where they had promised Simon he could find them. Craning her neck, her eyes scoured the crowd of children exiting the elementary school. Max spotted Simon's shaggy-haired head first. The little boy hung back, a perfect imitation of his mother, scanning the sea of students as it merged with parents and caregivers. Kendall waved and his face lit up at the sight of her.

Simon dashed down the steps of the school, leaving the other children with their brightly colored backpacks in his dust. He jumped into his mother's arms, completely unashamed.

"You ready to get some ice cream?" Kendall asked, letting him go.

Simon nodded and smiled up at Max. "Can I get two scoops?" he asked, his voice much quieter than usual.

"Two scoops?"

"Let's just be grateful for one, mister," Kendall said, her tone firm.

"I was going to say why not?" Max said, to Simon's delight.

Kendall grinned, shaking her head as she grabbed Simon's hand. He was probably spoiling him, but Max figured Simon needed a little spoiling after the day he'd had.

Max still remembered how it felt when two boys had called him a bastard back in the sixth grade. They said his mom probably didn't even know who his father was. His mom had read the principal the riot act, even though Max had broken one kid's nose and given the other a fat lip when all was said and done. Sometimes she was cool like that.

Later that night, she gave him the only photograph she had of her and his dad. She said he was the most handsome man she'd ever met. Max still had that stupid picture, even though he hated the man in it. He kept it to prove his father did, in fact, exist. Of course, considering the man never cared about him, getting ice cream probably would have been better.

The Chi-town Chilly Cow was a little ice-cream shop nestled between the dry cleaner Max used and an upscale furniture store that sold couches and tables that looked like they were from the future. The Triple C—as Kendall called it—was decorated top to bottom, front to back in cows and cow print. It had been around for over twenty-five years and was where Kendall used to come after soccer games when she was young.

"My sister Lucy convinced the owners to go all organic a couple of years ago, before it was super trendy. I thought for sure they'd go out of business, but organic everything is all the rage now. The owners were able to retire early and handed over the business to their son last year."

"Do we get some sort of discount for knowing her?"

"Ha! No chance." Kendall lowered her voice and leaned closer. Max inhaled; she smelled sweet like vanilla. "But get this, they love her so much that my sister, who doesn't even eat ice cream because God forbid she put cow's milk in her body, can eat here for the rest of her life for free."

"I can tell you aren't bitter about that at all," Max said, stifling a laugh.

"At least extend the offer to her relatives who *do* eat ice cream," she complained. "Otherwise what's the point of the gesture?"

Given the passion in her tone, Max figured it was in his best interest to agree, even though he figured a little establishment like this couldn't afford to give away ice cream too often. "Absolutely. It's pointless otherwise."

"Right?" She seemed so pleased to be supported.

Simon tugged on his mother's jacket and whispered his order in her ear. Sprinkles, whipped cream and cherries were added to everyone's dish because they were celebrating and Max wanted Simon to know it. The young woman behind the counter was dressed in head-to-toe cow print, and she was slower than organic molasses. Poor service was Max's pet peeve, but anyone forced to wear a uniform that bad deserved a raise, so he tipped her the coins from his change.

The place was uncrowded this time of day. Simon still chose a secluded booth in the back with a checkerboard painted on the tabletop.

He simultaneously set up the board game and devoured his ice cream. Apparently this was the incentive to offer up. Perhaps his aunt Lucy should take note.

Mother and son played checkers while Max indulged in his salted-caramel-with-hot-fudge sundae. Organic or not, this stuff was amazing. He watched Simon double-jump two of Kendall's black checkers. She was carefully letting him win like any good mother should. For every one of his checkers she'd capture, she'd let him get two of hers.

Max would never discount how difficult Kendall's life was, but moments like this one made it look so easy. Kendall and Simon laughed and wore smiles Max wanted to capture and hold on to for when the two of them were both eaten up by the darkness. Kendall and Simon had lost a significant part of their family, but carried on side by side.

"I can't believe you beat me again," Kendall said when Simon jumped her last checker. Max smiled as she invited the winner over to her side of the booth to collect his prize—several kisses all over his face.

"Maybe you can beat Max," Simon said. His blue eyes fluttered but stayed firmly fixed on Max.

"I don't know. I'm pretty good at checkers

and your mom just got schooled by a first grader. No offense," he said to Simon.

Kendall's eyebrows shot up. "Seriously?"

"What?" Max laughed. "I'm just speaking the truth."

"Oh, it is so on." Kendall started setting up the board. Something told him she wasn't going to be so easy to beat.

Sure enough, she was a checkers master this time around. Every time Max thought he was setting her up to get jumped, she'd trap him in more ways than one. She almost had him, but he wasn't kidding when he said he was good. Kendall groaned when she could tell her defeat was imminent.

"Winner!" Max jumped her last checker and threw his hands up in the air, victorious.

"I'm pretty sure you cheated," Kendall mumbled.

"Don't be a sore loser."

"I'm not, but I was killing you. Your massive comeback is fishy, admit it."

Max's mouth dropped open. "That is a lie. There was nothing fishy about my comeback. You opened up that side for my guy to get through!"

"Are you going to give Max kisses because he won?" Simon asked, completely putting an end to their playful argument.

Kendall's cheeks turned petal-pink. What he wouldn't do to feel the heat of them under his lips. Max shook his head, shocked at his own thoughts. Why would he think about kissing Kendall? Romance between the two of them was a complication she'd certainly never welcome into her life. She'd been very clear about the fact that he might look like her husband but, aside from that, they were nothing alike. He wasn't her type.

But the way she looked at him told him maybe he was wrong.

"I'm not going to kiss Max," she said, her gaze shifting to the table. Her bottom lip caught between her teeth.

"Oh, she's got to win to kiss me, buddy," Max said to let her off the hook.

Her eyes lifted back to his. Suddenly, the idea wasn't so objectionable. "Kissing you is that great, is it?"

"I've been told I'm a very good kisser. The best by a few."

Her giggle was almost as cute as she was. "That sounds like a challenge," she said, setting the checkers back on the board.

Max had to throw this game. Letting her win was the only option now that the thought of her lips on his had settled in his mind.

"You have got to be kidding me." The voice

from the front of the parlor made all of their heads turn.

Katie and another woman stood in line with Aidan and a little boy about his age. She whispered something to her friend before making her way back to where Max sat. Simon practically climbed into Kendall's lap and his mouth seemed to be sealed shut.

"You can't leave work on time to make it to your visit with your child, but you can hang out with someone else's son in the middle of the day? Jason's going to love this." She pulled out her phone and started texting her husband, Max assumed.

"Kendall, this is my ex, Katie. Katie, this is Kendall, the interior designer for the restaurant."

Katie's laughter was mocking. "You're going to try to pass this off as work? Are you joking?" She gave Kendall a once-over. "He's not worth it, trust me. What's funny is this probably *is* work to him."

"That's enough." Max stood up and put himself between Katie and the booth.

"You're so predictable, Max. What's the angle with this one? What do you want from her? Just scratching an itch, or are you hoping she'll take some money off her final bill for the work she's doing at the restaurant?"

"I said that's enough," he repeated, his voice dropping lower.

Katie leaned around him to get Kendall's attention. "It's always something. Max only cares about two things—himself and his job."

"Can you not do this in front of Aidan?" he whispered near her ear.

"*Now* you care about Aidan?" Katie laughed again. "You don't even know him. What's his favorite color? What book does he like read to him at bedtime? What did he get for Christmas last year? What kind of birthday party did he have? Who's his pediatrician? What day and time does he have gymnastics? You know nothing about him. I hope the judge sees right through you."

Max had no answers for any of it. The worst part of this horrifying confrontation was that she was right about everything... except about not being able to care. He cared about Aidan. He took a deep breath and held it in his lungs until they burned enough to distract him from the humiliation he was feeling.

"I'm going to go say hello to my son and then I'm going to leave," he said to Katie as calmly as he could. "I hope you enjoy your ice cream."

Max swallowed his pride and turned to Kendall and Simon. They were both wide-eyed and shell-shocked, mother and son rendered mute by Katie's outburst.

"I'll see you back at the restaurant, Kendall," he said. "Simon, your dad would have been proud of you for being so brave today."

With that, he stepped around Katie and ignored the way her friend glowered at him. He held up his hand in front of Aidan for a high-five. "How's it going, little man?" Aidan slapped his hand, although his eyes kept shifting back to his mother as she came up behind Max. "How lucky we ended up getting ice cream at the same place, huh?"

Lucky, unlucky, whatever.

Aidan nodded and pulled the red Corvette out of his coat pocket, proudly displaying it for everyone to see. The hole Katie's words had punched through his chest healed instantly thanks to that simple gesture. Aidan didn't have to say anything. That car symbolized an attachment that hadn't been there before. Katie had given up on him, but Aidan hadn't.

Not yet.

CHAPTER THIRTEEN

CONFRONTATION MADE KENDALL sick to her stomach. Witnessing the one between Max and his ex-wife was no exception. Simon was even more uncomfortable than his mother. He had slid all the way across the seat and pressed up against her, each breath too short and fast.

They both watched as Max walked away, stopping to say hello to his little boy. She didn't miss the way all the tension eased out of him the moment his son pulled out the Hot Wheels car Simon had given him.

"Let's go to Nana and Papa's," she whispered to Simon, thankful her voice had returned. She gave him a gentle nudge out of the booth.

Simon's lips were sealed, his anxiety evident in the furrow of his brow and the tightness of his grip on Kendall's hand. They hurried to the door only to be followed out by Katie.

"I'm sure he makes you feel real special," she said. Kendall stopped but didn't turn around. "That's what Max does. He knows all the right things to say because it's good for business. But trust me, as one mother to another, he'll let you down. Max doesn't really care about anyone. It's all an act."

Kendall gave Simon's hand a squeeze and glanced back at Katie. "He cares about his son," Kendall said with conviction. She had to believe it. The alternative was that this woman was right and Max was a fake.

Katie's frown was sympathetic, as if she could see Kendall's need to believe. "I don't know what he's told you, but my son waited three long years for Max to care. The only reason he's trying now is because he can't stand it that someone else is doing the job better."

That was sort of what Max had told her. He'd left out the part where he hadn't attempted to be in his son's life until now. "We work together and he helped me out with something today. This isn't what you think it is."

Katie's phone beeped and she checked the message. "My husband is going to kill me for going off like that." She softened a bit and almost appeared remorseful. "I didn't mean to make a scene or assume anything was going on. You've got a kid, and I just thought you should know what you're getting into if you're thinking about getting into something with Max."

"Like I said, we work together. I barely know him." The thought caused the ice cream in Kendall's stomach to churn. She *barely* knew him and had let him into Simon's life like a fool.

What had she done?

KENDALL'S MOM GREETED them with arms wide open. Zoe barked and danced around their feet like a puppy.

"There's my handsome grandson." Maureen hugged Simon while she side-eyed her daughter. Kendall could tell she knew something was wrong.

Simon didn't say anything to his grandmother, and he had a death grip on Kendall's hand. There were big worries running through his little body.

Kendall crouched down in front of him. "Mommy has to go back to work for a little bit, but I'll be here to get you after dinner."

Simon shook his head.

"I was thinking we could take Zoe to visit that cockapoo down the street for a doggie play date. You know how much she likes it when you come to her play dates, Simon."

Kendall's mother played her best card first. Usually that would work like a charm, but given the day he'd had, it was possible that not even Zoe could pull Simon out of his yucks.

"Is there a kid in my house?" Kendall's father came out of the kitchen.

"What are you doing home so early?" she asked as he hugged some of the anxiety out of her.

"Ah, I went to check on a job nearby and decided to swing by and check on your mom. She said Simon was coming over, so I thought, there's no better reason to play hooky than to hang out with this guy." He picked Simon up, breaking the boy's hold on his mother. "Come see what Nana made and you and Papa are going to eat."

The smell of freshly baked cookies finally registered. "He just had ice cream," Kendall shouted after them as her dad rushed off with Simon to get some of those goodies. She was about to follow when her mom's arm shot out, blocking her path.

"What's wrong?"

"What's *not* wrong would take less time to explain."

Maureen let her arm drop to her side. "I

thought he made it through the day and you were celebrating."

Kendall leaned against the wall. She wanted to knock her head against it until all these jumbled thoughts made some sense. "He did, and we were. And we were having fun celebrating with Max. So much so that I think I forgot I don't really know anything about this guy other than what he's told me, and he could have told me anything. I'm relying on someone who has absolutely no obligation to help me out. Being around him helps Simon talk, but what happens when he doesn't have time for Simon anymore? What if he moves back to California? What if he's a bad person pretending to be good?"

"Whoa. Where did all that come from?" Maureen pulled her daughter into the small sitting room off the foyer. She sat her down and took a seat herself.

"We ran into Max's ex-wife."

Her mom's eyes widened and her head nodded with understanding. "Ah."

"Let's just say she had some choice words for him, and he took off without defending himself even a smidgen."

"Exes rarely have nice things to say about their former partners. Hence the ex in their title."

It was an excellent argument and one she was sure Max would use if confronted. Still, Max's ex had successfully created some doubt in Kendall's mind. Her decision to let Simon get close to Max was beginning to feel like a poor one.

"I think what's freaking me out is that I like him. I like him even though there are a million reasons why I shouldn't. But if I'm wrong about him and that ends up hurting Simon, I'll never forgive myself."

"Do you think the fact that he looks like Trevor is clouding your judgment? Maybe you only like him because he looks like the man you love."

Loved. Kendall's feelings for Trevor had definitely clouded her judgment in the beginning. But Max had won her over. Kendall and Trevor had a mountain of problems they'd kept hidden from everyone. She could relate to the anger and resentment Katie carried around. The only difference was that Kendall never got the title of ex-wife. Widow happened first.

"He's a lot different than Trevor, Mom. And I said I like him, not that I'm falling in love with him." But she had wanted to kiss him. That was dangerous territory. Much too dangerous now that she knew he might not be who she hoped he was.

Maureen held her hands up in surrender. "Okay, I was just asking. I wasn't sure what you meant and it has to be strange, that's all I'm saying."

Ever since Max walked into her life, everything was strange. Strange and confusing. Life was already hard enough. "I'm going to go before Simon notices I'm still here. Tell Dad I said thank you and goodbye."

"I will." Maureen stood up and gently grabbed Kendall's chin. Kendall relented and gave her the eye contact she sought. "You are a good mom," her mother said firmly. "You *always* put Simon first. You'll make the right choice. Trust yourself."

She let go and Kendall nodded. *Easier said than done.*

KENDALL SLIPPED INTO Sato's, her eyes scanning the room for Max. Luckily, he was nowhere to be seen. A rush of relief flowed through her body. She had hoped to have a moment to collect her thoughts before talking to him. Shrugging out of her coat, she decided to work first, deal with Max second. It was already after 4:30 p.m. and she had plenty to accomplish before she could go home for the night.

Paint therapy did wonders until she noticed the lily-pad green wasn't right. No matter how much she tweaked it, it wasn't what Kendall wanted. It needed some yellow and maybe a slightly darker shade of green. She grabbed the can labeled "Sun Shower" and searched for her paint-can opener.

"You're here." Max's voice carried with it a hint of surprise.

"I need to get this finished," she said without turning around. Looking at him would only make this harder.

"I wanted to apologize for what happened earlier. My ex-wife isn't much of a fan."

Kendall took a deep breath and reminded herself that Simon was her number-one priority. Max gave Simon confidence, but short-term gains were meaningless if the long-term effects were harmful to his emotional health. This man dropped out of his own son's life; what would stop him from doing the same to Simon? He had no stake in Simon's well-being, no reason to feel accountable.

She turned and faced him. "She made that very clear when she followed me and Simon out."

Max raked a hand through his hair. "Unbelievable," he mumbled under his breath. "Sorry about that. I promise no drama on Friday for trick-or-treating. I'm a big fan of no drama."

Kendall pushed away her nerves. "Listen, I really appreciate all you did for Simon today. You're good to him, and that means a lot to me."

"Why do I sense a 'but' coming?" Max rubbed his forehead and closed his eyes for a moment.

"It just sounds like things are a little more complicated than I thought."

Max stepped uncomfortably closer. Kendall had nowhere to go, however. He wasn't trying to intimidate her—it was like they were being pulled together by whatever it was that connected them. Her heart beat faster and her palms were sweating. There was no Trevor in his face. This was all Max.

"Earlier today, you were willing to go to court for me and tell anyone who would listen what a good guy I am. A couple of hours ago, you wanted to beat me at checkers so you could kiss me. Now things are too complicated?"

"I think it's best if I stay out of your business." Heat crept up her neck. "And I wasn't trying to kiss you." Her voice broke at the end.

"You feel nothing? I was imagining things?" he asked, somehow moving even closer. Their bodies were mere inches apart. He didn't touch her, but she felt *everything*.

"I feel like you should focus on making things right with your son while I work on making things right for mine."

He tipped his head down so they were nose to nose. His breathing was as unsteady as hers. "Is that what you think?"

Think? She was supposed to think right now? She could barely breathe. Her tongue darted out to wet her bottom lip, which was sore from her teeth digging into it. "Yes," she whispered.

They stood there until he backed down. "Tell Simon I'm sorry I couldn't take him trick-or-treating," Max said, slowly backing away. There was no denying the hurt emanating from his eyes. "Halloween was never my thing, anyway."

CHAPTER FOURTEEN

MAX HAD MADE MISTAKES. He wasn't a perfect person. He could take full responsibility for the mess he'd made of his relationship with Aidan. What he wouldn't do was accept that his past reflected his future. That was the way Katie made him feel today, like he couldn't change. Kendall apparently thought Katie was right.

He was surprised at how much Kendall's lack of faith stung. They didn't know each other very well. At the same time, he'd been more open with her than with anyone. She knew he wasn't as sure of himself as he wanted people to believe. He didn't think that would translate into him being a lost cause.

He wasn't, was he?

He couldn't stand his own doubt. It fueled his anger. Anger he didn't know where to place, other than on Katie. Maybe she thought what she was doing was best for Aidan. But how could keeping Max away be what was best for him? She was leaving him no choice but to fight back.

"Faraday and Associates, how may I help you?" Wayne's assistant was much too chipper for this late in the day.

"This is Max Jordan. Is Wayne around?"

"He's not, but I'll get a message to him and he can call you back."

"Yeah, thanks," Max grumbled and hung up. He tried to refocus on the purchase orders he'd been entering into the computer, but his thoughts kept going back to the way Katie attacked him at the ice-cream place. How small she made him feel. What was Aidan's favorite bedtime story? Max hadn't even gotten him a Christmas present last year. He'd sent money, figuring Katie could pick something good out since Max had no clue.

He shut down his laptop and packed up his stuff. He needed to get some dinner and be done with this day. Tomorrow, he had a visit with Aidan and he was going to make sure it was the best one yet. Avoiding Kendall, he hurried out of the restaurant and hailed a cab.

The October sky was dark early, but the city was full of lights. People filled the sidewalks, hurrying from here to there. Restaurants were busy—six to seven was always the busiest on a weekday. Max had noticed the trends in Chicago weren't too much different than in L.A.

His phone rang with Wayne's call. "Thanks for calling me back," Max said.

"Looks like Katie has the connections to get us in front of a judge ASAP," Wayne said. "We have an appearance on Monday."

The woman didn't mess around. What she didn't know was that Max was ready for her. "Great. I wanted to talk to you about the next step. Katie and I had a run-in today and I think we need to talk about it."

"A run-in? What kind of run-in?" Wayne's concern was evident in his tone.

"She made a scene in front of Aidan and an ice-cream store full of people."

"And what did you do?"

The accusation was another punch to the gut. "Nothing! I swear I didn't do anything to incite her at all."

"Where are you right now?" Wayne asked.

"Heading home."

"Why don't we meet for dinner somewhere out by you. You're right about needing to talk."

Max gave Wayne and the cab driver the name of the pub Charlie had taken him to for the best burger in town. He ordered a drink while he waited for Wayne to show up.

"Well, well. If it isn't Floor Three." Charlie took the empty seat at the bar next to Max. "How's it going, neighbor?"

"I've had better days. You?"

Charlie ordered a drink from the blond bartender. "I've also had better. There was a messy accident on Lake Shore earlier today. We brought one guy in, but I heard he didn't make it."

"Oh, man. Sorry."

"I guess we should be glad we aren't having as bad of a day as that guy." He held up his drink for a toast. "To being alive to live another bad day."

That was one way to look at it.

"Cheers," Max said, clinking his glass against Charlie's.

"What are we celebrating?" Wayne slipped into the seat on the other side of Max.

"Not being dead," Charlie answered. "Let's get you one, too. You look alive." He signaled for the bartender.

Charlie's attitude toward life made Max smile. What he wouldn't give to see the silver lining. Max's philosophy was to resent the clouds and convince everyone the sun was still shining.

"Wayne, this is my neighbor, Charlie. Charlie, this is my lawyer, Wayne."

"Oh, a legal eagle. Nice to meet you." Charlie stuck out his hand and the two men shook behind Max's back.

"Look at you," Wayne said to Max with a grin. "Making friends."

Max rolled his eyes. He was in no mood for being patronized. A half-dozen guys from the firehouse showed up and Charlie excused himself to join his buddies. Max and Wayne got a table and talked some business. Max gave him a play-by-play of what had happened with Katie.

"So, you said nothing inflammatory?"

Max shook his head. "She even harassed the people I was with after I left."

"You did the right thing by not engaging her in public. She could easily turn that around on you. Remember that any time you two have to interact."

"I've been nice up until now," Max said, leaning forward. "I accepted supervised visits and all the roadblocks she's put in my way. But I'm ready to give it as good as I've been taking it."

"What's that supposed to mean?"

"She has a history, too. I know who she was before she was this model citizen. She drank a lot and partied hard when we first met. I've noticed when she drops off Aidan for visits, she's sometimes disheveled and disorganized. Maybe we need to ask the judge—"

Wayne held up a hand to stop him. "Hold on. I want you to think long and hard about going this route. You could come across as very unsympathetic if you make a bunch of false accusations. Judges only want to know about the right now, not five years ago."

"How come the same's not true for her? She can talk about what I was like when we were together, but I can't? She can use everything I've done or not done against me and I just have to sit quiet?"

"Anything bad you say about her doesn't automatically make you look better. You're the one who let her be the sole caretaker of your son from day one. If you thought she was unfit or worried about her drinking and still left him in her care, you are just as negligible."

Max hadn't thought of it that way. It seemed all he did was make mistake after mistake. The last three years were filled with nothing but regret. His choices had left him with so few options at this point. If he wanted to be in his son's life, he saw no other way than to fight. "I need to do something, Wayne. She won't work with an arbitrator because she thinks she can win with a judge. I want to ask for full joint custody, legal and physical. I'll drag her through the mud to get it if I have to."

Wayne puffed out an exasperated breath. Leaning back in his seat, he rubbed the back of his neck. "I'll do whatever you want, but I'm going to warn you that taking the offensive on this might not be the way to go."

It might be a risk. It probably wouldn't work, and if it did, he would be turning his son's life upside down. How was their little boy going to come out of this fight unscathed? Max had no idea. He could only hope Aidan would be resilient enough. Max wanted Katie to know how it felt to be him. This seemed the only way to accomplish that.

THE NEXT DAY, Kendall was conveniently missing from Sato's. Owen was in charge and said she was working from home on another project. Max had to bite his tongue to stop himself from asking if Simon made it to school. He had to forget about Simon. That was the way Kendall wanted it. She wanted him to forget about both of them.

Maybe if she hadn't left her mark on everything in the restaurant, that would be a little easier. Kendall was in all the details—the artwork, the charming accessories, the quiet beauty of the space she'd created. Of course, there was also the mural. An undeniable showpiece, it was an obvious labor of love and left him in awe of her talent.

He couldn't afford to be infatuated with her, though. Feelings like that were the reason he tried to keep his relationships shallow at best. When he cared too much, he ran the risk of getting hurt. Aidan was the only one for whom he'd risk his heart.

The restaurant was opening in a little over two weeks. There wasn't time for anything but work and his son, anyway. Owen had given him the punch list and offered to walk around with him to make sure everything was getting fixed to his satisfaction. The waitstaff had orientation next week. Chef Yamaguchi would be working with the kitchen staff the week after.

Max was busy, which was good. He was much too busy to think about Kendall and the way her smile made him want to compliment her so she'd do it again. He couldn't waste time focusing on what she might have felt like in his arms. Or how he hoped Simon hadn't needed to be too brave today. His head fell on his desk.

"Everything okay?" Owen popped his head in the office.

Max sat up and ran a hand over his hair. "I'm fine. Everything out there going smoothly?"

"Smooth is my middle name," Owen joked. "There's no other way it could go."

"Good. I'm taking off soon to go see my son and I need to know everything's all right before I leave."

"Should be. I talked to Kendall and she said she's going to come in over the weekend and finish the mural."

"Did Simon go to school today?" he asked, unable to resist now that he was never going to see her again. She would make sure of that.

Owen seemed taken aback. "As far as I know."

"Don't look so surprised," Max grumbled. "Although the rumor around town is I don't care about anyone, I do care about *some* people."

Owen threw up his hands. "I've heard no such rumor. I'm sure you care about a lot of people. I just wasn't aware Simon and Kendall were two of them."

Max froze. Had he let something slip about Kendall?

"Don't worry. I won't tell anyone and ruin your reputation," Owen said. "I wanted to know if you want to take a look at the newly repaired bathroom tile before I let the guys leave for the day."

"Yeah, thanks." Max stood up, regaining his bearings. He followed Owen out and was unpleasantly surprised to find Jin talking with two men at one of the tables. "When did he get here?"

Owen casually glanced in Jin's direction. "A few minutes ago. He didn't want to talk to me or you, so I left him alone."

Max planned to do the same. He didn't need any trouble from Jin when he needed to get to his visit with Aidan. The bathroom tile was fixed as Kendall had promised it would be way back when. He'd given her such a hard time in the beginning. No wonder it was so easy to believe the worst about him.

"Max!" Jin called as he attempted to return to his office.

"How can I help you?" he asked with some effort.

"This is Harold James from the *Chicago Tribune*. He's here to interview you and Chef Yamaguchi, who should be here in…" he checked his watch "…a half hour."

He had to be kidding. Max felt his face warm. As much as he wanted to strangle his boss's son, he managed to keep his cool. He turned his attention to the reporter. "Well, there's nothing more I'd like to do than to promote Sato's opening. I wish Jin had given me a heads-up, though, because, unfortunately, I'm on my way out. Perhaps we could come up with another time that works for both of us?"

"There is no other time," Jin interrupted. "This is the time."

Taking a breath, Max looked at Jin and tried to deal with him like he would an unreasonable customer. "I hear what you're saying. I really do. Unfortunately, I have to go. How can I make this up to you?"

"Excuse us," Jin said to the reporter and photographer. Both men nodded then gave each other a look. Jin pulled Max over to the bar. "What exactly is so important that you can't do this interview, Mr. Jordan?"

"I have a visit with my son. I had one with him on Monday that I missed because you showed up unexpectedly then, too. You might want to try sending me an email or giving me a call the next time you want to schedule a meeting with me."

"The restaurant deserves a manager who puts it first, who is here when we need you to be here. If you don't think you're cut out for this job, I suppose I'm glad we found out now."

Max was finished being told what or who should take priority in his life. He was done being worried about not being good enough. No job was going to be his excuse for not being in Aidan's life. "My son comes first. If your father has a problem with that, I'd like to hear that from him."

Jin's glower created little creases on his forehead. "My father? My father listens to me."

"That's funny because I remember you telling me that you agreed with Kendall about the sushi bar, but your father agreed with me. I also remember you telling me I wasn't your first choice for this job, but your father told me I was his. Let's be clear about who's in charge here. Your father is my boss. Feel free to give the *Tribune* reporter my phone number and he can call me to reschedule my interview."

He didn't wait for Jin's reply. He went back to his office and packed up. On his way out, he wished all three men good-night. He hoped he'd still have a job in the morning.

MAX PULLED UP to the counseling center without a moment to spare. He got out of his cab and noticed Aidan entering the building in front of him. The little boy wasn't holding on to his mom's hand today. Instead his stepdad, Jason Michaels, was there to drop him off.

Hands on his hips, Max closed his eyes and asked God to give him a break. Wasn't Jin enough torture for one day? Now he had to deal with Katie's husband? Maybe it was a blessing in disguise. Dealing with Katie had to be worse.

They were waiting by the elevator. Max watched as Jason bent down and tied Aidan's shoe. While crouched down, he tickled Aidan's stomach and playfully pinched his nose. Aidan giggled with glee and gave his stepdad's nose a pinch back. Jason kissed Aidan's forehead before standing back up with the little boy in his arms.

Max's heart sank. All the rationalizing he'd done over the years seemed so ridiculous now. He had convinced himself that Aidan was too little to notice if his dad was around or not. He had told himself these were the years a kid needed his mom, not his dad. Dads weren't important until later. All the while, Jason was bonding with Aidan. Giving Aidan the attention he needed when Katie couldn't and stealing Aidan's heart.

He came up behind them just as the elevator arrived. Jason didn't recognize him immediately, but his smile faltered slightly when the connection was made.

"How's it going?" Jason asked, pressing the button to the correct floor.

"Not bad." Max nodded. "How are you guys?" He touched Aidan on the arm. His little head quickly burrowed in the crook of Jason's neck. Max's heart sank deeper.

"We're good. Right, buddy?" Jason tried to cajole Aidan to look up and say hello. When that failed, he tried to make conversation. "Katie's mom took a turn for the worse this morning, so she's been over there all day."

"I had no idea Katie's mom was sick," Max said, feeling stupid.

"Pancreatic cancer. We found out about three months ago."

"I'm sorry to hear that." That was around the same time she'd written to Max and asked him to give up his rights. Had her mother's illness been what prompted all of this? *You never know someone's story until you ask.* Max hadn't bothered to ask Katie what was going on in her life.

"It's been tough. Her dad is having a real hard time with it."

Silence filled the elevator as it continued up. Max patted his pocket for his phantom cigarettes while Jason tapped his foot and chewed on his bottom lip as Kendall did when she was nervous.

"I'm sorry about yesterday, by the way," Jason said as the elevator came to a stop on their floor. "Katie's under a lot of stress, but she shouldn't have lost her temper like that. Especially in front of this guy."

Max had no idea how to respond. He wasn't sure if Jason was for real or not. In Laura's office, Jason set Aidan on the ground.

"Have fun with your dad, okay? I'll be back to pick you up like Mommy usually does." He bent down and kissed the top of his head.

Aidan grabbed his leg. "Daddy, stay."

Max was pretty sure his heart dropped out of his chest. Jason tugged the little boy loose. "We talked about this. This is your dad's time with you. You were excited to play cars, remember?"

Aidan looked up at Max, then back up at Jason. "Bye, Daddy."

"Bye, bud." His eyes lifted to Max. "He wants to show you some of the cars he brought from home. They're in the bag."

"Thanks," Max said dumbly.

"No problem. He really was excited about coming. It sometimes takes him a minute to warm up. He doesn't talk around my parents until the last five minutes of any visit. Kids are so funny."

Maybe Jason wasn't the bad guy Max had made him out to be. The thought scared him as much as it created a little hope. As he pondered that, Aidan pulled out a rectangular box with Hot Wheels written across it.

"Let's have a race, Dad."

Max had been wrong. His heart hadn't fallen out of his chest because he could definitely feel it beating in there. In fact, it was almost as if it hadn't ever been there until now.

CHAPTER FIFTEEN

"HI, THIS IS KENDALL, Paul's daughter-in-law. Is he available?" Kendall was obviously desperate. She still hadn't told Simon that Max wouldn't be taking him trick-or-treating. Her plan was to have so much family there on Friday, he wouldn't be as disappointed when Max didn't show.

"Hi, Kendall," Paul's assistant replied. "Just one second."

Since she hadn't brought Simon out to Lake Forest in over a month, she figured inviting Paul for trick-or-treating would assuage her guilt. There was a distinct possibility he wouldn't be able to make it anyway.

"Kendall, is everything all right?" Paul wasn't accustomed to her calling him at work…or calling him at all, for that matter.

"Everything's great," she said, trying to sound upbeat. "Just wanted to invite you over tomorrow for Halloween. My parents and my sisters will be here and we're taking Simon trick-or-treating around four. Of course, you're welcome to stay for dinner afterward."

"Let me check my calendar." She was pretty sure he put her on hold to ask his assistant if he had any conflicts. The phone clicked. "Looks like I have a quiet afternoon. I can take off a little early."

Kendall cringed. "Great. Well, I'll let you get back to work."

"Wait," he said. "How's Simon doing?"

"He's okay. He hasn't missed any school in a couple of weeks. Hopefully, he keeps that up."

"With boys, you have to be firm. Trevor knew what the expectations were and met them. The moment you get soft, they'll take advantage. You baby him a little, Kendall. Trevor wouldn't want you to do that. He'd want Simon to be strong like he was."

If Trevor wanted Simon to be strong, he shouldn't have gone back to Afghanistan, she wanted to sass back. Trevor was perfect. He was raised by perfect parents. He went to the Naval Academy where he got perfect grades. He became a perfect Marine officer. He could do no wrong. Kendall could never say otherwise.

"We're working on it," she said instead.

"Being a parent is hard. It's the hardest job

around. You only get one chance to do it right. I did it right with Trevor. You've got to do it right with Simon."

No pressure.

"I have to let you go, Paul. I have another call coming in. We'll see you tomorrow." Her excuse was a lie, but it felt necessary. If she didn't hang up, she was going to go off, and then he'd probably evict her.

Luckily, he let her go and she set her phone on her desk. Today was her second day in hiding. She was pathetically avoiding Max. Thankfully, Owen didn't give her a hard time about it. Things were winding down at Sato's. The project would be complete sooner than later and Max Jordan would be nothing but a memory.

A sad memory.

She tried and failed not to think about the dejected look in his eyes the last time she saw him. The hurt that came off him in waves, waves that knocked her over and threatened to drown her in their sadness.

Kendall had to tell herself over and over it was the right thing to do. Better Max get hurt now rather than Simon getting hurt later. Her reasoning felt solid until Owen told her Max had asked about them yesterday. He didn't care. That was what she told herself to make all of this okay. But what if he did?

She couldn't think about that. She needed to finish the presentation boards for a potential new client and meet Owen for lunch. Worrying about hurting a grown man's feelings was pointless. Max Jordan was fine.

The phone rang and a breathless Owen was on the other end. "Drama at Sato's, K. You are missing *all* the action."

"What are you talking about?"

"So, last night Jin Sato showed up, throwing around his nonexistent weight, and Max basically told him to jump in the river. Today, Jin shows up again, goes back to Max's office and all hell breaks loose."

Kendall sat forward, her interest piqued. "What happened?"

Traffic noise came through Owen's end of the call. "There was some yelling. I heard Max say something like, 'If you think I'm going to explain everything I've done to get this restaurant up and running just so you can take it over, you are more delusional than I thought' and Jin told him to get out."

"Seriously? He fired him?"

"I don't know. I mean, his dad owns the place. I suppose he can fire people, right?"

"I don't know." Kendall leaned back in her

desk chair. "I don't think Mr. Sato is going to be too happy about this."

"I guess he's on a plane to California right now. Max tried to get him on the phone but couldn't." Owen's heavy breathing was distracting.

"Why are you running around outside?" she had to ask.

"I'm trying to find Max. He took off."

Of course he did. The going got tough and Max ran away. Wasn't that what his ex-wife said he did?

"I thought he could use a friend," Owen added.

Kendall's chest ached. A shot of guilt filled her veins. Owen was a good friend to have and it sounded like Max could use one of those. Even though she couldn't be in Max's life, she couldn't stop herself from feeling sorry for him.

"Any luck?"

"Nah, he's gone. Must have grabbed a cab. Poor guy," Owen said. He wasn't helping her not think about Max and his feelings. "Why don't we meet for an early lunch since I'm out."

"Fine, but no talk about anything or anyone from Sato's."

She got up and grabbed her coat. If anything, Max's firing meant there was even less chance they'd ever see each other again. That had to be a good thing. He didn't stick it out when things didn't go his way. He certainly wasn't someone she could trust to be there when things got rough, and all relationships went through rough spots. She had done the right thing by severing their ties.

Hadn't she?

HALLOWEEN WAS THANKFULLY sunny and not too chilly. When Simon was four, no one saw his costume because Kendall had him bundled up in a heavy winter jacket, hat and gloves. Today he'd be fine in his heavy sweatshirt and pants. They'd trick-or-treat after school before it got dark. She only had a couple of hours of work to do.

With no real reason to hide anymore, she had shown up at Sato's to finish the mural. There was a tiny part of her that hoped Max would come in so she could see if he was okay. The rest of her was relieved when he didn't.

Jin was there and slightly frantic. Supplies were being delivered and he wasn't sure what to do with everything. Kendall kept out of the way and to herself. She finished the mural shortly after lunch. That gave her time to stop at the office and make a few calls before heading to school to pick up Simon.

He had brought his costume to school for a Halloween parade. The kids walked the halls, showing off their costumes to the other classes. She wondered if he managed all right with a big box strapped to him. He was all smiles when she met him at the classroom door.

Mrs. Taylor reported that he had a great day. He had even volunteered to write some numbers on the board during math. Kendall was thankful for the positive feedback. The meeting to discuss his placement was looming heavily, like a dark storm cloud. She wanted Simon to give the school a million reasons between now and then to let him stay.

"Don't forget your picture, Simon," Mrs. Taylor reminded him on their way out. Simon ran back to his desk and grabbed the drawing. "Have fun trick-or-treating."

"Oh, we will," Kendall replied for him. She carried the red race-car costume down the hall as Simon tried to show her his picture. He had drawn a row of houses, and the one in the middle had a bright red door. On the sidewalk was a little boy in a race-car costume flanked by a man and a woman. It didn't take much to figure out who they were supposed to be.

She swallowed the lump in her throat. "You'll have to show that to Nana. She loves your drawings as much as I do."

Once they were away from the other walkers, Simon let go of her hand and bounced ahead of her. "Can we go to Max's house first?"

The dreaded question was, of course, the first thing to come out of his mouth. She was hoping to get home to the family before he had a chance to think about Max, but apparently he'd been thinking about Max all day long.

"I'm not sure Max is home, honey."

His eyebrows pinched together. "Is he at our house already? We have to hurry, Mom! Come on!" He grabbed her hand and pulled.

"He's not at our house," she said, halting his moving feet before he could cross the street without looking both ways first. With the crosswalk clear, they resumed their walk home. "But Nana and Papa are coming over. Aunt Lucy and Aunt Emma, too. Even Grandpa Montgomery is stopping by to see you."

"Uh-oh," Simon said.

"Uh-oh, what?" Kendall knew Paul could be overwhelming at times, but she'd figured it wouldn't be so bad with all the other family members around. Simon's attention was stolen by a squirrel that scurried up one of the trees lining the street. He bent down and picked up a large, yellow maple leaf. The edges were browning and beginning to curl.

"We better tell Grandpa that Max looks like Daddy so he doesn't get sad."

All of Kendall's emotion lodged in her throat. Her caring, compassionate boy was bound to be disappointed when she told him Max wasn't coming. Now she feared what would happen when he learned he would never be coming by again.

She waited until they were home, dropping his cardboard-box costume on the porch and opening the front door. Simon ditched his backpack and ran for the kitchen—to get his after-school snack, most likely.

Kendall followed him back there and sat at the kitchen table. This was the place for sharing news, good or bad.

"Come sit by me," she said, patting the chair next to her.

Simon sat and looked up at his mom with those eyes, Trevor's eyes. "Why are you sad, Mommy?"

"Well, I'm a little worried you're going to be sad. I know you're excited about Max coming over, but he's not going to make it."

Simon's bottom lip jutted out, and he shifted his gaze to his feet. "Doesn't he want to see me be a race-car driver?"

"I'm sure he wishes he could see you be a race-car driver."

"Then why isn't he coming?" His eyes came back to hers. "Does he have to go trick-or-treating with Aidan?"

She took a deep breath. "I don't know what he's doing. I asked him not to come, honey."

"Why?"

It was a fair question with a complicated answer. One she wasn't sure she could explain to a six-year-old. "Max and Mommy decided it was best if we didn't hang out anymore."

"Why? Don't you like him anymore?"

"Liking him or not liking him isn't the issue, honey."

"He's not Daddy." It wasn't what he said that made her pause, it was how he said it. Like he was trying to reassure her with tears in his eyes.

"I know he's not Daddy, Simon." She pressed her hand to his soft, little cheek. "Max is very nice, and I know you like him, but we decided that we can't be friends. That's all."

Simon thought about that for a moment, then stood up. "That's mean, Mommy. That's so mean!"

His footsteps sounded through the house as he ran up the stairs. His bedroom door slammed shut and Kendall let her head fall to the table. How far would this set him back? How quiet would he get? Trick-or-treating seemed pointless. She should probably call everyone and tell them not to bother coming over.

"Trick or treat!" Lucy's voice and a knock on the door kept Kendall from grabbing the phone.

"In here," she called out, lifting her head. Lucy might be able to rally him.

"Where's the little guy? I saw his race car parked out front." She laughed until she noticed the look on Kendall's face. "You told him Mr. Look-alike wasn't coming, didn't you?"

"And I am now, officially, the meanest mommy. Ever."

Lucy put a hand on her sister's head. "Oh boy. Just remember every mom has felt like that at one point in time. I know I crowned Mom the meanest when I was little. She was a repeat winner of the title for years."

Kendall let out a breathy laugh. "I remember you being much meaner to her than she ever was to you."

"Of course I was. I'm meaner than everyone," Lucy said, unashamed.

"I still love you, though." Kendall got up and grabbed a large bowl off the top of the refrigerator. From the pantry, she pulled out three bags of Halloween candy and tossed them on the kitchen table.

"You really shouldn't give out candy. I could have brought over a whole bushel of organic apples."

"We are not going to be *that* house." The two sisters opened and emptied the bags into the bowl. Lucy offered to help with dinner. Kendall had bought the ingredients for chili and no one chopped vegetables better than Lucy. Kendall set her up on the cutting board with an onion and some peppers.

"It's better that you rip the Max Band-Aid off now rather than later," Lucy said while they cooked. "Simon will get over it. So will you. It's always better to be the one who walked away instead of the one left behind."

"Which one were you again?" Kendall asked, recognizing that Lucy's guard was down.

"Ha-ha. I've been both. At the same time," she added. "Now, stop making this about me."

"You love when things are about you," Emma said, joining the conversation. Dressed in her nursing scrubs and a purple witch's hat on her head, she sat down at the table next to Lucy with a bag of cheese puffs.

Kendall held a hand over her heart. "Maybe knock next time and give a girl some warning. Isn't it against your nurse's training to give people heart attacks?"

"And isn't it against your nurse's training to put processed poison into your body?" Lucy added. She snatched the cheese puffs out of her sister's hands and walked them over to the garbage.

"Hey!" Emma sprung to her feet. "I was eating those! I haven't eaten all day."

"Another reason you shouldn't eat them. Your body needs fuel, not intestine-destroying acids."

"Uh-oh, who's eating junk food in front of Lucy?" Kendall's mom popped her head into the kitchen. "Girls, don't fight over food." She took the bag away from Lucy and handed it back to Emma, who scrunched up her face and pursed her lips at her sister.

"It's your body," Lucy relented. "Sorry for trying to protect it."

Their dad followed behind their mom and gave Lucy a hug. "You're a good big sister, but never throw away someone's cheese puffs."

"I'm coming over tomorrow and helping Mom throw away all your junk food. We're putting you on a diet."

"What?" He looked at his wife for confirmation.

Maureen's shoulders slumped and she glared at Lucy. "I wasn't going to tell him what we were doing. If you don't tell him, he doesn't miss it. When you tell him, he gets all worked up."

"We're headed into holiday season. How can I go on a diet before Thanksgiving and Christmas? You go on a diet *after* the holidays. It's a rule or something."

"Mom said your cholesterol was up again," Emma chimed in. "She's got to do something, Daddy."

"Says the girl licking fake powdered cheese off her fingers," Lucy said with a sneer.

"At least I don't have to color my hair," Emma said in retaliation. "How can you bear using all those horrible chemicals on your head?"

"I do not color my hair!"

"Yeah, right."

Kendall let them all fight it out. Her mom explained she'd be packing her dad's lunches from now on, which sent him into a tizzy. Emma and Lucy continued to exchange gibes.

Even as they roared, Kendall smiled. They were a loud and obnoxious bunch. They might not agree on everything, but they loved one another and she loved them.

"Where's Simon?" her dad finally asked.

"Probably hiding from Aunt Lulu, Chief of the Food Police," Emma teased.

"Don't call me that," Lucy said, her tone threatening.

"He's upstairs," Kendall said. Maybe she found their argument so entertaining because it distracted her from her own problems. "I'm not sure he's going to want to go trick-or-treating now that he knows Max isn't coming."

"He didn't take it well?" her mom asked.

Kendall shook her head.

"You want me to go talk to him?" her dad offered.

"You can try. Don't be surprised if he doesn't respond."

"I'll come, too," Lucy said. "He likes me best." She stuck her tongue out at Emma.

"Real mature!" Emma shouted after her. "Seriously, she should have been born last. I have way more firstborn traits than she does."

"Give me some of those cheese puffs," Kendall said, holding out her hand.

Emma shook a few onto it. "You waited until she left. You are such a chicken."

"I call it being smart." Kendall popped a cheese curl in her mouth and chewed it up. "No one can throw away your junk food if you don't tell them you have it."

"Don't tell your father that," her mother said.

Lucy ran into the kitchen, looking panicked. "He's not up there."

Confused, Kendall shook her head. "Of course he's up there."

"We checked everywhere. He's not in his room or your room. He's not in the bathroom."

Everyone moved at the same time and spread out in different directions. "Simon! Where are you?" Kendall shouted as she climbed the stairs two at a time.

Her dad came out of Simon's bedroom and shrugged. "He's not in any of the closets or under the beds. Maybe he's hiding downstairs."

Kendall flew back down the stairs, nearly knocking over Emma. "Simon!"

She scoured every room on the main level to no avail. He was nowhere to be found. Her heart raced as she ran outside. Families and costumed kids were beginning to fill the sidewalk on either side of the street. There were superheroes and princesses, but no Simon.

He wouldn't leave, she told herself. They must not have looked everywhere upstairs. Kendall went back inside and up to Simon's room. The sound of her family calling his name made her want to cry.

"Simon, you need to come out, honey. This isn't funny. Mommy is worried," she said, getting on her hands and knees and peering under his bed.

His cars weren't under there. On the other side of his bed, they were all spread out like he had been playing with them. Kendall knelt down and picked up the red Corvette. It was the only one he hadn't taken out of the container. That's when she noticed the picture. The one Simon had drawn at school. It was ripped down the middle.

She held the two pieces together and stared at the red door. Simon wasn't here. He was right where he wanted to be.

CHAPTER SIXTEEN

MAX BURIED HIS head under his pillow, hoping to block out the sound of his door buzzer. If those trick-or-treaters thought he'd throw candy out the window if they annoyed him enough, they were wrong. He was pouting. Life had kicked him when he was down and he wanted one day to pout about it.

Jin's audacity yesterday was beyond belief. He really thought Max would tell him everything and turn over the restaurant on a silver platter? The man was insane. If Max was being handed his walking papers, then he was walking out. He wouldn't graciously explain the entire operation. Let Jin figure it out for himself.

The door buzzer would not stop. Max threw his pillow across the room and marched to the intercom. "I have no candy. Go away." He headed back to his bedroom when the buzzing started again. Max growled in frustration. He pressed the intercom. "What part of no candy are you not understanding?" He pressed the other button to listen.

"Maxwell, open the gosh darn door!"

What in the world was his mother doing here? He buzzed her in and opened his door to the stairway. "Mom?"

Joanna raced up the steps. "There's no place like home, there's no place like home," she said as she climbed the last few stairs to his landing. "Happy Halloween, honey."

Joanna was dressed in a blue-and-white-checked dress with her hair in braids and ruby-red shoes on her feet. Her appearance in Chicago was surprising to say the least. He opened the door wider to let her in. "Welcome to Oz," he said. "I must have slept through the tornado."

She kissed his cheek and stepped into his condo, setting her bag down inside. Her hair was a new color, sort of a strawberry blond. If it weren't for the shoes, she might be mistaken for Pippi Longstocking or the face of Wendy's. She looked healthy, though. All that clean living in the Land of Granola was doing her some good.

"Why *do* you look like you just woke up? I thought you were working days until the restaurant opens."

"Unexpected day off," he replied, locking

the door. He decided he wasn't going to refer to what happened yesterday as being fired. Until he heard it from Mr. Sato, he was considering this an unpaid vacation.

"I was worried about you. The last time we talked, you were acting weird. I felt like I needed to check on you."

Max sank into his couch. "It's been a pretty brutal week. But you know me, I can take care of myself."

She frowned. "I know you like to think you can take care of everything by yourself."

"I've been doing it long enough."

His mom sat down next to him. "Oh boy, I didn't realize I invited myself to a pity party. Come on, kiddo, what's going on with you?"

He had no idea where to even begin. Nothing made sense and probably never would. He was fighting for custody of a child who already had two loving parents, and as much as he wanted to hate Jason Michaels, he couldn't. On top of that, his boss's son wanted his job, and for all intents and purposes, he'd fired him yesterday. Then, there was this woman and her son. A woman he couldn't stop thinking about and a little boy who made him feel like maybe he wasn't the bad guy everyone thought he was.

Max was a fool for thinking Kendall could

be interested in a relationship with him. She'd had the perfect husband. Max wouldn't automatically replace Trevor in her heart just because Max looked like Trevor. Trevor Montgomery fought for his country, and that was the only reason he would have been separated from his wife and child. Max's reasons were notably less noble. Kendall didn't want someone like that in her life, and Max couldn't blame her.

"Do you think people can change?"

Joanna stared at him for a second before falling into a fit of laughter. "Are you really asking *me* if people can change?"

Max rolled his eyes. It was kind of a ridiculous question to pose to someone who redefined herself all the time. "I mean really change. You might be infatuated with something different every time I see you, but you're still you. At the core, you're the mom I've always known. The one who dresses up in crazy Halloween costumes and shows up at my door without so much as a phone call."

Joanna wiped her eyes, her lips falling into a straight line. "I don't think it's a question of *can* you change, more so do you *want* to?"

"I want to. I want to be a good father. I want to be someone Aidan can look up to and trust." Trust being the most important. Aidan needed to believe Max was always going to be there for him.

"Then, you will be," she said simply.

He wanted to believe it could be that easy. He was afraid he wouldn't be able to let his guard down. That he wouldn't let Aidan in all the way and that would lead to real resentment. Or worse.

"What if I let people in and they're disappointed?"

"I've never been disappointed in who you are," she said, throwing her arm around his shoulders. "Nobody's perfect. We all make mistakes. If I've taught you anything in this life, it should be that."

It was Max's turn to laugh. She was right, but he'd been too hard on her lately. "You did the best you could, Mom."

"You have a good heart, Max. If you let people see it, *really* see it, there's no way they'll be disappointed."

A knock on the door brought their conversation to an end. Confusion creased Max's forehead. No one in the building had any kids who'd be trick-or-treating. Maybe someone snuck in. Max peered through the peephole and was greeted to a distorted view of Charlie's big head. It wasn't until he swung the door open that he could see Charlie wasn't alone.

"Hey, Floor Three. Speed Racer here was standing outside when I was heading out. He didn't say anything, but I got the sense he was looking for you."

Simon stood silently next to Charlie. His black sweatshirt was decorated with various NASCAR sponsors. His cheeks were red and so were his eyes.

"Hey, Simon. Does your mom know you're here?" Simon shook his head. That wasn't good. Max thanked Charlie and let Simon inside.

"Hi, there," Joanna said to Simon, who raised his hand and waved. "What's your name?"

"This is Simon, Mom. He's not the talkative type." He looked around for his phone. "I need my phone so we can call your mom and let her know you're here."

"No!" Simon shouted, startling both of them for different reasons.

"Buddy, your mom is going to be worried sick. We need to call her so she knows you're okay."

Simon looked at Joanna and bit his lip.

"You know what? I need to freshen up a bit before I go find the Wizard. Do you mind if I use your bathroom, Maxie?" she asked, somehow knowing exactly what Simon needed.

As soon as she was out of sight, Simon opened up. "Why don't you want to be my friend?"

Max's blood boiled. It was one thing for Kendall to tell him not to come around. It was another to blame the decision on him. "Is that what your mom told you?"

"No. She said she told you not to come with me trick-or-treating. She's mean."

That was a relief. He couldn't imagine Kendall throwing him under the bus. She took all the blame because that was who she was. Selfless, unlike him. He regretted his flash of anger. He would not put this child in the middle as he had with Aidan. "She's not mean. She loves you and wants to keep you safe, which is why we have to go back to your house."

"No!" the little boy pleaded and clung to Max's legs. "I promise I'll be good. I'll go to school. I'll talk to my teacher. I won't be bad."

Max pried the little guy loose and knelt down in front of him. This poor kid had been through so much. The last thing Max wanted was to add to his pain. "Listen to me. You are a great kid. You are not bad."

"Then why don't you like us anymore?"

"I do like you."

"Daddy left because he didn't like us anymore. I thought you were different."

Max felt completely unequipped to handle this. Explaining life and death to a kid was not something he'd learned in restaurant management. "Your dad dying doesn't mean he didn't love you guys. I'm sure he loved you so, so much."

"I heard him yelling," Simon whispered like it was a secret, tears welling in his eyes. "He told Mommy he didn't love her anymore. He made her cry and cry. She wanted him to stay here and be with us, but he said no. I heard him. He didn't love us and Mommy wasn't even mean to him."

Not knowing what to say, Max simply put his arms around Simon and hugged him tight. There was obviously much more going on than anyone, other than Kendall and Simon, knew. Perhaps Trevor hadn't been the perfect husband after all.

MAX TRIED KENDALL'S cell phone twice with no luck. It rang and went to voice mail the first time and was busy the second. Joanna had rented a car at the airport and offered to let Max drive them to Kendall's house. Max figured the faster he got Simon home, the better. He threw on some jeans and a clean shirt and convinced Simon they would talk to his mom together about all this.

Kendall's street was lined with cars on both sides. They had to make a few passes before a spot opened up nearby. Kendall's sisters stood on the front porch passing out candy to neighborhood kids. Instead of smiling, they looked quite anxious. Three other people stood out front, appearing equally distressed. Joanna and Max got out of the car, and Max opened the back door for Simon.

"Come on, buddy. I think you've got some worried people waiting for you to come home." He took Simon's hand and led him toward the house.

"Simon!" Lucy spotted them first. She came barreling down the sidewalk and scooped him up in her arms. "Don't you ever, ever, ever do that again. Do you have any idea how scared we were when we couldn't find you?"

Emma was next and basically said the same thing. They both looked at Max like he'd kidnapped the boy. "Where's Kendall?" Emma asked, as if he would know.

"What do you mean where's Kendall?"

"She went to your place to get him," Lucy explained.

Max patted his pockets. No phone. He'd forgotten it in his rush to get Simon home. "I never saw her. Can you call her and let her know he's okay?"

Lucy pulled out her phone and sent off a text.

"Simon, honey." A woman with short gray hair and a gentle voice joined them on the sidewalk. Max assumed she was Kendall's mother. They had similar smiles. "Thank you for bringing him home, Max."

"No problem," he said. He always felt a bit like a freak show around people who knew Trevor. Every time he met someone from Kendall's life, he had to remember they had to get over the initial shock of him looking like her husband. The two men on the porch were definitely gawking.

One of them appeared to be Kendall's father. He was the taller of the two. His round face and balding head were a dead giveaway. The other man had a death grip on the porch railing. He was staring at Max as if he had seen a ghost.

Kendall's dad steadied the other man and sat him down on the porch steps.

"How?" the man croaked, overwhelmed with emotion.

Simon wiggled out of Lucy's arms and ran

over. He gave the man a hug before sitting next to him. With a reassuring hand on the old man's knee, Simon smiled up at Max. "It's okay, Grandpa. That's Max. He's not Daddy. Don't be sad."

Simon's grandfather became completely overcome. His eyes glistened with tears and his hands were shaking something fierce. Max figured this guy had to be Trevor's dad. This was more than awkward, it was downright depressing.

"Simon!" Max turned to see Kendall sprinting toward them, dodging the trick-or-treaters. He could only imagine the panic she'd been feeling all this time. She didn't stop running until she had her arms wrapped around her son. Out of breath, she hugged him and told him over and over that she loved him and that he couldn't run away ever again.

Max heard his own mother, her ruby slippers click-clacking on the sidewalk pavement behind him. As he watched Kendall and Simon reunite, he realized how grateful he was for her presence today. She came when he needed her, without even being asked.

Joanna stopped cold. "Monty?"

Monty? But that... Max's head swung around to see his mom bug-eyed and slack-jawed. He looked back at Mr. Montgomery, sitting on the steps. He was much older than the man in the photo Max had hiding inside the Pearl Jam album back at home, but there was a definite resemblance, now that he thought about it.

"Joanna? Is that really you?" he asked, rising to his feet. Kendall's dad offered his hand again for support. Max wasn't confident in his own legs' ability to hold him up. He suddenly felt like the Cowardly Lion standing next to Dorothy when they faced the Great and Powerful Oz.

Joanna put her hand on his shoulder. "Max, this is Monty. Monty, meet Max." There was an eerie silence, then, "Our son."

CHAPTER SEVENTEEN

THERE ARE MOMENTS in your life that seem surreal. Moments that make you believe that if you closed your eyes tight enough, they would simply unravel and be exposed as nothing more than a dream. Kendall had experienced a few of those in her lifetime. The last one being the day she found out Trevor was dead. Today, she watched as Max had one of those moments.

"Our son? Max." Paul said his name the same way it sounded in Kendall's head when she'd first met him. It took a minute for it to feel right.

Max's mother stepped forward in her Dorothy costume. She had Max's eyes, big and brown. "What are you doing here?"

"What am I doing here? What in the world are *you* doing here?" Paul asked.

In Kendall's mind, this made perfect sense and no sense at all. Max was Paul's son. That was why he looked like Trevor. On the other hand, how was it possible? Paul and Nancy had been married for over thirty years when she died. He was also the most overinvolved parent she knew. If he had another son out there in the world, wouldn't he be just as possessive?

"I guess Max knows your grandson. Is this your daughter?" Max's mom nodded her head at Kendall.

"Daughter-in-law," Kendall clarified for him.

Max's mom smiled, the sad kind that didn't reach her eyes. "You had a son. I always wondered."

Kendall's attention was drawn back to Max, whose blank stare was beginning to become worrisome. On the run back home, she was planning to strangle him for not calling her or answering her frantic calls while she stood outside his building, imagining the worst. Now she wanted to go to him, offer him some comfort. Whatever was going on here was blowing his mind, and not in a good way.

Paul moved in Max's direction and that did the trick. Max took a step back, his eyes widening with alarm. Paul stopped. "You look exactly like your brother."

"My brother?" Max scoffed. "Trevor wasn't my brother and you…you are nothing to me."

Sensing the increased tension, Kendall's mother took Simon's hand. "Why don't we go inside and get you ready for trick-or-treating. Everyone with the last name Everhart should probably join us," she said pointedly to Lucy and Emma who were watching this awkward family reunion with rapt interest.

As her family retreated into the house, Kendall sought some answers. "I don't understand, Paul. Did you know Max existed?"

"This is none of your business, Kendall. Go inside with your family," Paul snapped at her, earning him more of Max's ire.

"Don't you dare talk to her like that. Answer her question. Better yet, *Paul,* tell her how you cheated on your wife and got my mom pregnant. Tell her how you lied about who you were and not being ready to be a father, when apparently you did just fine being Trevor's. Go on, tell her."

Paul said nothing, shaking his head and wringing his hands.

"Your name isn't Monty?" Max's mother seemed baffled.

"His last name is Montgomery, Mom. He's nothing but a liar. I don't have time for this. Not now. Not ever." With that, Max took off for the car.

Max's mom didn't move. She looked at

Paul with new eyes. Her sad smile was gone. "I knew you were married," she said. "We both made so many mistakes back then. But I believed you loved me. Was I wrong?"

Paul shook his head. "My life was never the same after I met you, Joanna. I've thought about you every day since."

She reached up and touched his cheek. "In another life," she said wistfully. His hand covered hers, holding it against his face.

Kendall had to look away from such a private moment. This was not the Paul she knew. Her father-in-law never showed much affection toward his wife unless Kendall counted Paul buying his wife things. He saved all his care and concern for Trevor. Now she wondered what part guilt had played in all the things Paul ever said and did with regards to his son.

Max had pulled the car out of its spot and honked the horn for his mom.

"He's a good man, my Maxie. Give him some time. He doesn't let people in very easily, but he wants to be loved, just like the rest of us."

The words were meant for Paul, but Kendall felt them obliterate all of her defenses. She glanced up as Joanna walked away and Lucy came outside with Simon.

Joanna got in the car and Simon yelled, "Bye, Max!"

Max gave a wave but drove away as soon as his mom closed the car door.

"We're going trick-or-treating. You coming, K?" Lucy asked.

Kendall nodded and touched Paul's shoulder to get his attention. "We need to talk when I get back."

Ever since Trevor's passing, this man had made her doubt herself. He questioned her decisions and made her feel like the only one who ever stumbled through life. Truth was, he was far from perfect.

Simon looked so adorable in his race-car costume. He had Lucy hold his bag so he could "drive" the car. He got enough candy to keep his sugar levels high for the next few days.

Candy wasn't the first thing on Simon's mind, however. He wanted to know why Grandpa said Max was his dad's brother and why Max was so mad about it. In fact, he chattered on and on about it the entire time, oblivious to the other people around who might hear him talking.

Kendall had to tread carefully. She didn't know how to explain this situation to a six-year-old. She tried to steer the conversation in another direction, but Simon kept returning to it.

"How come Max didn't know Daddy if they were brothers?" he asked as they headed home.

"It's complicated, Simon."

"Do I have a brother?"

Kendall didn't answer immediately. She looked over his head at Lucy, who narrowed her eyes as if to ask why she'd paused. "Not that I know of," Kendall answered. Lucy's right eyebrow quirked up.

"We're going to talk about that answer later," Lucy warned.

Simon's questions rolled on. "If Max is Daddy's brother, is he my brother?"

"I guess he'd be your uncle." She hadn't thought about that until he mentioned it. It really didn't matter if Max acknowledged Paul as his father or not; he was Simon's family. She couldn't be sure how this connection would impact Max's desire to be in Simon's life. It changed everything for Kendall.

"I never had an uncle before!" Simon bounced excitedly.

"Uncles smell," Lucy deadpanned.

"Smell like what?" Simon asked innocently.

"Never mind." Kendall ruffled his hair. "Don't listen to Aunt Lucy."

Without missing a beat, Simon changed the subject back. "Now you have to let me be friends with Max, Mommy. He's my uncle."

She couldn't argue with that. Family was one thing Kendall would never keep from Simon.

Back at home, Paul was noticeably missing. Emma informed them he left but promised to talk to Kendall soon. *Coward,* Kendall thought. Apparently he wasn't going to give her any answers tonight.

The family ate dinner and avoided all conversation about what had happened until Simon was in bed. Kendall's dad offered to tuck his grandson in so the women could start their discussion in the kitchen while they cleaned up.

"At least that explains why he looks so much like Trevor," Emma said to get things rolling.

"I feel bad Max had to find out that way. The poor man looked like he was coming undone." Maureen handed Kendall a dry dish to put away.

"I was more worried about Paul," Emma said, her hands deep in the soapy dishwater. "I thought I was going to have to give him CPR when he heard that woman say, 'our son.'"

Lucy didn't say anything as she leaned against the counter on the other side of Emma; she just eyed Kendall. Her gaze made Kendall's face warm and her stomach uneasy. She could tell her older sister was waiting to see if she would talk or would need to be confronted. She didn't want Lucy to confront her, nor did she want to open any more cans of worms tonight.

"I wonder how many affairs he had. You know it had to be more than one," Emma continued. "His wife always seemed so cold to me. I bet that's why he cheated. Men will go looking for affection when they don't get it at home."

"Is that what you think?" Kendall's temper suddenly flared. "His cheating was somehow Nancy's fault? If he had issues in his marriage, he should have been man enough to say something before he cheated."

"You sound like someone who's speaking from experience," Lucy said like a challenge.

Maureen and Emma's eyes shifted from Lucy to Kendall and back again. "Why would you say that?" their mother asked.

"I don't know." Lucy pushed off the counter she was leaning against. "I just get a feeling that Kendall has been keeping something from all of us for a long time now. Something that's been eating her up inside, but that she's been too afraid to bring up because it's about Trevor. Trevor's dead, K. What are you so afraid of?"

She wasn't afraid. It simply didn't seem right to speak ill of the dead. Plus, the truth made her feel like a failure.

"What are you talking about? What is she talking about?" Maureen asked her daughters.

Kendall shut her eyes and pressed the heels of her hands over them to keep from crying. She'd cried too many tears over this. She dropped her hands and focused on the concerned and confused faces of her mom and sisters.

"I guess you can say Trevor and his father had more in common than we knew."

"What does that mean?" her mom asked. Lucy nodded like she'd known it all along. Emma's eyes bulged from her head.

"He was cheating on you?" Emma asked, shaking her hands off and casting around for a towel.

Kendall sat down at the kitchen table. She'd held on to this secret for so long she didn't know where to begin telling it. "When he came back from Afghanistan after the second tour, I could tell something was different. I chalked it up to him being at war. He'd had a hard time adjusting after his first deployment, but after a couple of months, he went back to normal. But this time, it didn't get better, it got worse. He would start fights with me for no reason. He'd pick on every little thing I did wrong. He was just plain mean."

Her sisters and mother joined her at the table. Her mom took hold of Kendall's hand. "I had no idea."

"I didn't want anyone to know, Mom. I mean, it was embarrassing. I felt like it was my fault. Then he told me he was going back, he *had* to go back." Kendall remembered that day so clearly. She'd actually been relieved. "Part of me wanted him to go, but Simon was so happy to have his dad around, I begged him not to. That's when he told me he wasn't in love with me anymore."

"Did he tell you there was someone else?" Emma asked.

"No, he didn't mention anyone else, so I thought I could fix things. I thought maybe if he went away and we had a little space, we could work on things when he came back. He didn't come back, though."

"So how do you know he was cheating?" Emma pressed.

"She came to the funeral, didn't she?" Lucy was always more perceptive than anyone other than Kendall gave her credit for.

Kendall nodded, unable to answer with words.

"What? How do you know this?" Emma asked Lucy. "How do I not know this?"

"She was the only other woman crying her eyes out. I saw her approach Kendall. I also noticed when Kendall ran after her and pulled her aside for a private chat."

"She worked with him as a translator," Kendall said. "I knew the moment she offered her condolences and told me all the amazing things she was going to miss about him that she was the reason he didn't love me anymore." Kendall shook her head. "I confronted her like a fool. I shouldn't have. She didn't come to cause drama. She came to say goodbye to someone she loved. But I had to know if I was right. And I was."

"Kendall Marie, how could you keep all this from us?" Her mother's arms folded around her. Now that Kendall knew how good telling the truth felt, she, too, questioned why she hadn't done it sooner.

"Oh, my gosh, what do you do when you

want to kill someone who's already dead?" Emma asked, holding her head in her hands.

"This is why I am never getting married," Lucy said, causing her mother to sigh.

"Can you two keep the focus where it belongs?" their mother scolded. She placed her hands on Kendall's shoulders and looked her in the eye. "Do you have any idea how hard it was for me, as your mother, to call you up and tell you I needed your help when I got sick? The last thing I ever wanted to do was burden you girls. But I did it because I needed you. You came home and you held my hand and sat through treatments with me. You were there for Lucy, too. She needed all of us when she got sick. And should things ever not go as planned for Emma, I know you'll be there for her. That's what our family does. Don't deny us the chance to do the same for you. No matter what it is that knocks you down, we'll be there to pick you up and dust you off."

Deep down, Kendall had always known that. She wouldn't forget again.

"I don't want to interrupt mother-daughter bonding, but there's a little boy who wants his mom to give him one more kiss good-night," her dad said, returning from bedtime duty.

Kendall gave her mom a kiss on the cheek.

"Thank you," she whispered before going upstairs.

She found Simon in his bed, buried under every blanket they owned. Her father had even pulled out the baby blankets from his closet.

"Did you tell Papa you were cold?"

He giggled and nodded. Kendall smiled at her own memory of being tucked in by her dad when she was little. He'd ask if she was cold and she'd say yes just so he'd go hunting for another blanket. It was a game they'd play until she was covered in dozens of quilts, blankets and even oversized beach towels from the linen closet.

She kissed Simon's forehead, the only part of him uncovered. He'd scared her half to death today. She needed him as much as he needed her. They were going to have a very long talk in the morning about not leaving the house without permission. Right now, she was going to enjoy this moment and focus on how Simon spent the evening talking and playing as if his selective mutism didn't exist.

"Do you think Max likes Thanksgiving?" Simon asked, already moving on to the next holiday. She was happy he hadn't skipped straight to Christmas.

"I don't know. You'll have to ask him the next time you see him."

"Can we see him tomorrow?"

Like most of his questions today, she wasn't sure how to answer this one. She had no idea how long Max would need before he'd talk to anyone related to Paul. Kendall also had to make amends for the way she'd treated him.

"I don't know, buddy. His mom is visiting him. We should let him spend some time with her before we ask him any more questions."

Simon was too tired to argue. His eyes shut as he yawned.

"Get some sleep, Blanket Boy. I love you."

"I love you more."

"Impossible," she said, shutting off his light.

When Kendall got back downstairs, she picked up her phone and scrolled through her contacts until she got to Paul's name. She tapped the call button and listened to the phone ring. She had no idea what she was going to say if he answered, but something had to be said.

It went to voice mail. She tried again with the same result. He was avoiding her, she was sure of it. Kendall asked her parents if they'd stay with Simon so she could have it out with

Paul, face-to-face. She needed some answers and she needed them now.

The drive north to Lake Forest was long but uneventful. It was late enough at night that the traffic was light. Kendall rarely drove her red Honda Civic except when she took Simon to visit his grandfather. Trevor most definitely rolled over in his grave the day she traded his yellow Mustang in for it. First, it wasn't made by an American car company, and second, it was a boring sedan. It was a safe and reliable car, just right for her and Simon. But there was part of her that knew her motivation to purchase this particular vehicle had had a little to do with spite.

She pulled into Paul's driveway just before ten. His enormous, all-brick estate sat on over an acre and a half of land. Trevor had come from a home where he always got what he wanted. She rang the doorbell twice and knocked on the door to be sure Paul knew she wasn't leaving without seeing his face.

He swung the door open with a frown on his face. "What in the world are you doing here this time of night?" He stepped out to look behind her as if she might have brought someone else along. Whether he wondered if that someone was Simon or Max, she couldn't tell.

"We should talk," she said, letting herself in without an invitation.

"It's late. It's been a long day. Can we do this later?"

Kendall shook her head and kept moving deeper into the house. Every room was like something out of a museum. It looked like a model home rather than a place where someone actually lived. She made her way to the gourmet kitchen, which featured a huge center island that wouldn't fit in any room in her house.

Paul said nothing. Like an old, familiar friend, Kendall welcomed the silence. She needed a minute to gather her own thoughts. She was angry with him and she wasn't exactly sure why. Maybe it was because Paul was always so full of himself. He knew best. Nothing Kendall did was ever good enough. Trevor had been perfect because he had the perfect parents. All of Simon's weaknesses were obviously Kendall's fault.

"Did you know? Did you know Max existed?" When he didn't answer, she pushed harder. "I need to know, Paul. Max is important to Simon." Important to her, too, if she was being completely honest.

"Are you in a relationship with him? How could you when he looks so much like

Trevor?" His tone reeked of judgment. For a moment, she allowed him to make her feel guilty. Like being attracted to Max was somehow a betrayal of Trevor's memory.

Then the anger resurfaced. There was only one person who deserved to feel guilty. "Did you know he existed, or not? Because he seems to think you did and chose to have nothing to do with him. That's pretty unbelievable."

"I don't need to explain myself to you," he said, sitting down on one of the stools that lined the island.

"Wrong," she snapped, surprising herself. "Simon wants Max to be in his life, so I need to know if what Max said is true. If you did that, if you left his mother to raise him alone…" Kendall struggled to believe he could have done that. It went against everything she knew about him. "Max may not want anything to do with us now that he knows you're Simon's grandfather."

Paul held his head in his hands and spoke to the granite countertop instead of her. "You could never understand."

Maybe that was true. Kendall certainly couldn't understand how someone could take no responsibility for his child. She couldn't imagine walking away and never looking back. "Try me."

He sighed and sat upright, rolling his head around to ease some of the tension he surely felt. "I knew Joanna was pregnant."

"But she was just someone you slept with, so you just left?"

His back straightened and his cheeks flushed. "I was in love with her! She was like no one I had ever met. Certainly not like Nancy, who I was going to leave. But I needed to have a plan before I gave up everything and made a new life with Joanna. Things like that take time."

Kendall didn't have any trouble picturing Paul doing exactly what his son—Trevor—had done, pushing his wife away until he worked up the courage to tell her he was leaving her for someone else. Trevor had been too much of a coward to admit he'd been in love with another woman, though. Not that it would have made his leaving any easier.

"Then Nancy announced she was expecting a baby, too. I couldn't leave my wife when she was carrying my child. My parents, her parents, they never would have accepted that."

"So you abandoned Max and Joanna instead."

"I did what I had to," he said defensively. "I offered Joanna money. I promised to help her if she needed it, but she refused. She said she didn't want my money. She wanted me or nothing. She left me with no choice."

Kendall's emotions were all over the place. She felt sad for Max and heartbroken for his mother, who had undoubtedly thought Paul was going to start a life with her only to have that dream ripped away a couple of months later. At the same time, she could sympathize with Nancy. She knew what it was like to be in a failing marriage and clinging to any shred of hope that it could be saved. Nancy probably thought the baby would fix all their problems, and in some ways Trevor had, but it still didn't change the fact that Paul was in love with someone else for the rest of their marriage.

"I thought about them all the time, though. Wondered where they were, if he liked the same things Trevor liked. Every time Trevor did something new, my thoughts returned to the child I didn't know. I couldn't be there for both of my kids, so I poured everything I had into Trevor."

She would have felt bad for him if he hadn't brought all of this on himself. His choices, his consequences. The problem was, he wasn't the only one who paid the price for those choices. Max and his mother had suffered unfairly.

"I don't know what to say." How would Max ever be able to forgive Paul? If he couldn't forgive Paul, would he want anything to do with her or Simon?

"I never wanted him to hate me. He hates me, doesn't he?"

There was no reason Max shouldn't hate him, but she had no idea how he felt about any of this. "I don't know for sure, but you have a lot of work to do if you hope to change that."

"He must be a good man if you let him around Simon."

The twinge of guilt was back. She had asked Max to stay away for no reason except that she was afraid he was too much like the picture his ex-wife painted of him. The man she knew, though, was caring and kind. He was funny and polite. He knew how to make others feel comfortable and how to lighten the mood when it was needed the most. He admitted his wrongs and tried to make up for his mistakes.

"He is."

Paul's lips curved upwards for the briefest of moments. Max was a good man. He deserved good things. Kendall realized Paul wasn't the only one who had some making up to do.

CHAPTER EIGHTEEN

As much as Joanna had wanted to process the events of the day, Max refused to discuss anything that happened on Halloween with his mother. Part of that was due to the fact that she was clearly happy about this predicament, while Max's feelings were quite the opposite.

For Max's entire life, he'd pictured his father as a guy who never settled down. Someone who didn't have time for a family because he was too self-centered for that kind of thing. His leaving was more about him than about Max and his mom. He couldn't be there for *anyone,* not only them.

Paul Montgomery, on the other hand, had chosen to raise another son. The better son. The son he wanted.

Not talking about it didn't stop Max from perseverating on it, though. It crept up on him every time his mind got quiet. It didn't help that he had no job to fill his time and occupy his thoughts. He only had his mother, who was getting on his last nerve after sharing space with him for two days, and his plot against Katie.

"Did you know that kale can not only lower your cholesterol and reduce the risk of heart disease, it has so much Vitamin K that it can help prevent cancer? It's the miracle vegetable." She dumped a glob of plain yogurt into the blender.

The small breakfast bar that broke up his kitchen from his living room was covered in notes he'd written for Wayne. Making a case against Katie wasn't as easy as he thought, and every attack he jotted down made him feel more and more like the bad guy.

"I was never much of a vegetable lover... or did you forget?" he asked, crossing off the notation to have Wayne look into a DUI Katie got before she was pregnant.

"You used to love celery. I'd make you ants on a log after school. You'd gobble up a plate full."

"Ants on a log? That sounds less appetizing than that kale concoction you're making."

"It was celery, peanut butter and raisins. You loved it. I remember." She switched on the blender and all her ingredients mixed together into a dark green sludge.

She was respecting his wishes with regards to Paul Montgomery, but he knew her well enough to know that she desperately wanted to talk about him. His mother had been very much in love with Paul and probably still was to some extent. There hadn't been any real closure for her. Every time she looked at or talked to Max, she had to think about him. Trevor and Max had both inherited many of their father's features, hence the creepy resemblance to one another. Perhaps it was less creepy knowing they were related.

Max had mixed feelings about the brother thing. On the one hand, it would have been nice to know he had a sibling. Maybe they would have had some sort of a relationship. Trevor had been married to Kendall, and he was Simon's father—he couldn't have been a bad guy. Of course, according to Simon, things between husband and wife hadn't been going so well before he died. Maybe he wasn't a *great* guy, either.

It didn't matter what kind of man Trevor was because he was dead, and Max was never going to know him personally. He could add that to the long list of things to hold against Paul Montgomery. Because of him and his lies, Max would never know his half brother.

Thinking about Trevor always led to thinking about Kendall and Simon. Simon was his nephew. Aidan had a cousin. These were family ties, ones Max would not let Paul's lies destroy. The only obstacle he worried about was Kendall. She hadn't wanted Max in Simon's life when he was just some guy she knew. Would her feelings change now that he was Simon's uncle?

Joanna set a glass of the kale "power smoothie" in front of him, a bright pink straw sticking out of it. She had her own that she was already sucking down like it was the tastiest milkshake she'd ever had.

"Does cancer or heart disease even run in our family?" he asked, hoping the answer was no. His grandparents were both still alive and in their eighties. He couldn't remember either one of them having heart trouble or ever facing the evil "C" word.

"Not on my side," she said, taking the seat next to him. "Just think—if it wasn't against your rules, I could ask he-who-I-cannot-name about his side, and you could have a complete family medical history. But since you refuse to talk to him or about him, I guess you'd better drink up to be safe." She nudged the glass in his direction and grinned like the brat she knew she was being.

Max picked up the smoothie and pulled the straw out. He downed the entire thing in a matter of seconds. It tasted as terrible as it looked, and he prayed it would stay down because he did not want to taste it twice. The glass made a loud thud as Max slammed it down on the counter. He went back to his notes.

"Don't you wonder if all of this was some divine intervention? Maybe you were meant to meet your brother's family. Maybe this is your chance to get to know him. I mean, even you have to admit, what are the chances?"

Max gathered his papers into a pile and rubbed his eyes. "I don't want to talk about this."

"Not talking about it doesn't make it go away. Your father is here. He's the grandfather of a little boy who ran away from home just to see you. Your paths are going to cross again. You can't avoid him forever."

The door buzzer rang and offered an escape from this discussion. Max hit the talk button. "Hello?"

He pressed the listen button, hoping it wasn't the man he wasn't talking about with his mother. "Mr. Jordan, this is Jin. My father and I are here to speak with you. May we come in?"

Max buzzed them in, more than a little surprised by their visit. In a mad rush, he attempted to make the place presentable. He picked up some pillows off the floor and tossed them back on the couch, his temporary bed while his mom was here. He grabbed some garbage off the coffee table and shoved the pile of mail into one of his kitchen drawers.

"Who's Jin?" his mom asked. "And why did he bring his dad?"

"Jin's dad is my boss." Is. Was. He wasn't sure, but he was about to find out.

He ran a hand through his hair and caught a whiff of his unshowered self. Deodorant and a clean shirt were a must. His face needed a shave, but there was no time for that. The knock on the door came as soon as he finished checking his teeth in the mirror for green bits of kale.

Jin slunk in after his father, looking awfully abashed when Max welcomed them in. That had to be a good sign. He ushered them into the living room and offered them a seat on his couch. Snatching up the television remote before Mr. Sato sat down, Max introduced them to his mother. Thankfully, she excused herself to the other room.

Mr. Sato got right to business. His stern expression and deep voice always made Max feel like a child. "My son has something to tell you."

This appeared to be the last place on earth Jin wanted to be. He reminded Max of a kid standing on his neighbor's front porch, forced to admit he was the one who threw the baseball that broke a window. He bowed his head when he spoke. "Mr. Jordan, I am here to apologize. I was wrong to tell you you were not welcome back at Sato's. It was a grave error and I hope you will accept my sincerest apology."

Sincerest? Max doubted it. Coerced was more like it. "Of course."

Mr. Sato may have been pleased but his face didn't show it. "Wait for me downstairs, Jin. I want to speak to Mr. Jordan alone."

Jin did as he was told, scurrying out the door without so much as a goodbye. Mr. Sato's head slowly shook side to side. "My son very much wants to prove himself to me."

"Your son wants my job, sir. I need to know what that means for me in the long run."

"Sato's is yours to manage. My hope is you will mentor Jin so he can run his own restaurant someday. He thinks I'm the only one who can teach him something, but this is not wise. Life offers us many people. We can learn from them all."

Max was surprised by Mr. Sato's perspective. He seemed to be a man who liked being the authority on all things.

Mr. Sato stood, ready to leave. "I will explain to Jin that he is the student, and you are the teacher. If you and I work together, we can send him off on his own sooner than later. I expect you back to work Monday morning."

Monday. "I have a conflict on Monday. My ex-wife and I are ironing out a few details regarding the custody of our son. I need to be in court that morning, but I can come in later."

"No problem. A good father puts his child's needs first," Mr. Sato said, making his way to the door. "We must be careful not to put the child's wants or even our own desires above what is needed. But that's not always easy."

"No, sir. It's not." So not easy it made Max's stomach hurt. He'd been spending a lot of time focusing on what he wanted and not what Aidan needed.

Mr. Sato left and Max sat back down at the breakfast bar. Joanna rejoined him and gently rubbed his back. He stared at his notes for Wayne. If he threatened Katie with all this, it would only make her hate him more than she already did. The more she hated him, the harder she'd fight to keep him out of Aidan's life. The more she pushed, the more Max would push back. Aidan would grow up caught in the middle of a war. How was that what his son needed?

Max turned his whole body in his mother's direction. "Why don't you hate him?"

He didn't need to say his name for her to know who he was talking about. "Because what good does it do to hate him?"

"He left you. He left us. He took no responsibility for me and you had to do everything on your own. How is that fair?"

Joanna laughed lightly. "Oh, honey. When is anything fair?"

"I know, but still, there had to be times when you hated him."

"Were there times I was angry? Sure. Were there days I didn't want to face the world and wished I could curl in a ball and cry all day? Absolutely. I had dark days just like everyone else does. But I can't carry that all around with me forever. It wouldn't have done me any good and it certainly wouldn't have been what was best for you."

"If he had come for me, when I was little, would you have let him have me?"

"Have you all to himself? No way. I would have shared you, though. Just like I'll share you now, if you want to get to know him."

That was *not* happening. There was too much on Max's plate right now. Sorting out his daddy issues was at the very bottom of the list.

"This isn't really about him. It's about Aidan."

Joanna's eyebrows disappeared into her bangs. "I see. So, why do you think Katie hates you?"

"Because I wasn't present. I was barely around when he was born and not at all when they left."

"So why would she hate you now that you want to be around?"

Max rested his elbows on the counter and held his head in his hands. That was the real question. Was it her or was it him? Why was she so mad at him for wanting to be here?

Joanna grabbed the stack of papers off the counter. She flipped through them with her thumb. "Something tells me all the things you've written down here aren't going to make her hate you less."

"Definitely not."

"Is that what you want? Or maybe I should ask, is that what Aidan needs?"

Max scrubbed his face. Since when was his mother so insightful? "Probably not."

"I'm not going to tell you what to do," she said, giving his back another rub. "You've always made your own decisions, and you're a very smart guy. I'm here to support you, whatever you decide. Be someone you'd want me to support."

He turned his head and narrowed his eyes at her. "When did you get so wise, exactly?"

She shrugged and smiled. "Kale is a magical vegetable. I'm telling you."

She certainly had.

WAYNE WAITED OUTSIDE the courtroom on Monday. Dressed to kill and looking more like a million-dollar attorney than someone Max could actually afford, Wayne was ready to go. Appearances were important, he'd said, and he meant it.

Katie and her lawyer, a woman from the same firm as Jason, were sitting on a nearby bench. Max snuck a glance in their direction. Katie seemed tired. She was a beautiful woman, but he could tell she spent less time on herself now than she did when they were together. Ever since Jason had told him her mother was sick, Max wondered how often Katie was not only taking care of Aidan, but her mother as well.

"You ready?" Wayne asked.

"As ready as I can be."

"I got everything you faxed over to me yesterday. I think things are going to go exactly the way you want them to." His confidence was encouraging.

Wayne went to check how much longer it would be until they were up. Katie's lawyer got a phone call and stepped away to take it down the hall. Katie was glued to her own phone, staring at the screen and sending off text after text. Max walked over.

"Can I sit down for a second?"

She sighed and refused to look up from her phone. "It's a free country where you're free to do all sorts of things. You know that better than anyone."

He sat on the bench beside her. "I don't want to fight with you, Katie."

"And yet that's all you ever do, Max." Her phone beeped and whatever the text said made her somehow look more unhappy.

"How's your mom doing?"

Her head snapped up and her eyes narrowed. "How do you know about my mom?"

"Jason might have mentioned that was why he was the one dropping off Aidan the other day."

"You talked to Jason?"

Max was surprised she didn't know. "He's a nice guy," he admitted.

She went back to her phone, running her finger over the picture of Jason and Aidan that acted as the wallpaper. "He's an amazing guy. And an even more amazing father."

Max nodded, glancing back at his mom. He understood where Katie's digs came from and somehow that made them easier to take. "He's really good with Aidan. I see that."

Katie studied him with wary eyes. She had pushed and he didn't push back. She didn't seem to know what to do next.

"So, how's your mom?" Max asked again.

Katie stared at her phone. "She's having some tests done today."

Her lawyer was headed back their way. Max put his hand on Katie's knee and gave it a squeeze. "I'm sorry. I hope she doesn't get more bad news. You guys have probably had enough of that."

He stood up and her eyes followed him. Her eyebrows were pinched together. "Yeah… thanks."

Max walked back over to his mom as Katie's lawyer sat back down, giving him an equally confused look. Joanna smiled at him and gave his cheek a soft pat. Over her shoulder, Max watched as Kendall appeared in the hallway. He almost asked his mom to smack him harder. *What was she doing here?*

She was almost too pretty to look at. Her hair was down, cascading over her shoulders

in long, brown waves. She carried her coat
in her arms and wore a green dress the color
of clover. He wondered if she could be his
lucky charm.

She approached them cautiously. "Hi."

"Hey," he replied dumbly. Those warm
brown eyes and soft pink lips turned him
into a fool.

"You made it," his mom said.

That got his attention. "You knew she was
coming?"

Joanna shrugged, and Kendall's smile was
apologetic. "Word to the wise, your mom
answers your cell phone when you're in the
shower."

Nice. He'd be taking his phone with him
everywhere from now on. "What are you—"
Before he could finish asking her what she
was doing there, Wayne reappeared to an-
nounce it was time to start.

"You are?" Wayne asked Kendall.

"Kendall Montgomery. Friend of Max. I'm
here for moral support or to testify to Max's
character. Whatever he needs," Kendall explained.

"Thanks," Max said with all the sincerity he felt in that moment. Showing up here
meant maybe there was a chance she was

willing to give him a shot. At the very least, she'd let him be in Simon's life.

"I don't think we'll need to call any character witnesses," Wayne said. "But it's good for him to have some people on his side." He held the courtroom door open and let the ladies go first.

Everyone took their seats. Laura from the counseling center was there. She gave Max a polite smile when they made eye contact. Judge Keller shuffled through some papers, then he got started. He announced they were there due to Katie's petition for sole custody without visitation. He was disappointed in them for not being able to work things out in arbitration.

Katie's lawyer spoke first. She did a great job of spinning one missed visit into the perfect example of Max's past behavior. Luckily for him, Laura testified that the visits Max had shown up for had gone well. Her recommendation was that visits should continue and could be unsupervised.

"I see that a motion for joint physical and legal custody was filed by Mr. Jordan, but my understanding is that has been withdrawn? Is that correct?" Judge Keller asked Wayne.

Katie leaned forward so she could see around her lawyer. Her disbelief was clear in her eyes. He knew she'd assume he had come to do war.

"Correct, your honor," Wayne replied. "My client agrees with Mrs. Michaels that it's best for Aidan to reside with his mother and stepfather. He also agrees that it's best for her to continue to make the decisions regarding his educational and medical needs. We're simply here to ask that Mr. Jordan's visitation continue. We would be willing to go back to arbitration to settle the terms."

"That's quite a change of heart," the judge noted. "Mr. Jordan, care to explain?"

Max cleared his throat and rubbed his sweaty palms on his thighs. "I've been absent from my son's life. Distance played a part, but I could have put forth more of an effort to be there for him."

"Your honesty is appreciated. So you withdrew the motion because you knew you wouldn't win," Judge Keller assumed.

"No, I withdrew because what my son needs, what my son deserves, is parents who care more about him than their hurt feelings. I've made too many decisions based on my anger and frustration."

"This is a trick," Katie said from her side of the room. Her lawyer quickly shushed her.

Max leaned forward to speak to Katie instead of the judge. "You have every right to be mad at me and I completely understand why you don't trust me. I'm not trying to trick you, though. I just want a chance to prove it to you."

"You're three years too late, Max."

"Since when is there a time limit on being someone's father? I messed up. You helped me see that. Please give me a chance."

Katie eyes welled with tears. She looked emotionally spent, but he hoped she would listen to reason. Max readdressed the judge. "Katie and Jason provide Aidan with a good home. I can't deny that. I certainly don't want to take any of that away from Aidan. That's why I asked the motion to be withdrawn. All I want is a chance to spend some time with him. I think he needs that, too."

"Mrs. Michaels, it's very hard to argue with that, but I'm going to let you try," Judge Keller said.

Katie and her lawyer whispered back and forth. Max took deep breaths to keep the anxiety at bay. She had to agree. He was done fighting with her. It wasn't healthy for any of them, Aidan most of all. It was time they started working together. Time to fight *for* Aidan rather than over him.

"My client agrees to arbitration."

Max felt all the tension leave his body.

Judge Keller handed some papers to the clerk. "All right. Mrs. Michaels maintains custodial rights as well as all medical and educational rights, and the terms of Mr. Jordan's unsupervised visitation will be determined in arbitration."

The gavel struck the sounding block. The weight on Max's shoulders lifted and disappeared. Doing the right thing had paid off. He was tired of being angry and was ready to start fresh with Katie. If he made good on his promises, they might be able to pull this coparenting thing off.

He shook hands with Wayne and hugged his mother. Behind her stood Kendall, smiling like she was truly happy for him. Before he could thank her for coming, even though they hadn't needed to call any witnesses, she wrapped her arms around him. She smelled like vanilla and felt like warm sunshine. Letting go was going to be very, very difficult.

CHAPTER NINETEEN

MAX'S MOM WAS INTERESTING, to say the very least. From the sound of it, she and Lucy would be instant friends. No one had ever been interested in how often Kendall consumed kale before.

"I think it was that smoothie I made you the other day that helped you see things more clearly," she said to Max as they walked out of the courthouse.

"I agree I have you to thank for changing my mind, but the kale had nothing to do with it." Max stuck out his tongue and scrunched up his nose, making Kendall laugh.

Wayne gave Max a pat on the back. "I won't try to guess what it was, but I think you did the right thing. We could have dragged this thing out forever and Aidan would have been the one who lost in the end."

"I think so, too."

"Well, I have another client to meet back at the office," Wayne said. "Max, I'll see you at arbitration. Joanna and Kendall, it was nice to meet you."

Max pulled out a key ring and handed it to his mom. "I need to head over to Sato's for a few hours, clean up the mess Jin made."

She dropped the keys into her purse. "Time for some retail therapy."

"State Street is just a couple of blocks east of here. There's lots of shopping," Kendall suggested.

"Excellent," his mom said. She kissed her son on the cheek and gave Kendall a hug. "Hopefully we'll see each other again."

"I hope so." Max and Kendall stood outside the Daley Center, both unsure of what to say now that they were alone. His cheeks pinked up a little and he scratched the back of his head. "Do you want to share a cab with me?"

"Sure." She'd made it this far. Talking to him was the logical next step. Of course, in the back of a cab, there wasn't much to say. Max thanked her again for taking time out of her day to come support him. She relayed the story of talking to his mother instead of him when she had finally mustered up the courage to call.

It was a quick drive to Sato's. Max held the door open and they stood in the dining room, once again at a loss for words. Kendall had thought about what she wanted to say for days. Max was Trevor's brother, Simon's uncle. She wanted to see how he felt about that. How would that change things between them?

Kendall got the impression on Halloween that Max did not want to have any part in Paul's life. Her fear was that that would extend to the whole Montgomery family.

"Simon has lots of new questions."

Max let out a puff of laughter. "I bet. Something tells me they all have to do with our newly discovered blood ties." He pointed to a booth by the window and they both sat down.

"Good guess. I'm pretty sure I've answered more questions about how people are related than I ever thought possible."

"This is crazy, right? I'm not the only one who thinks this is a little nuts?"

Kendall found it more than a little strange. "What's weird is that I never really considered the possibility you could be related to Trevor, even though there aren't too many brothers out there who look more alike than you two." She took a deep breath, fearful of what kind of reaction bringing up Max's father would elicit. "I never imagined Paul as the kind of man who would—"

"Cheat on his wife? Lie to everyone? Abandon his child?" His hurt was still very raw.

"All of those things," she said softly.

"I don't want to talk about Paul Montgomery. Not now, maybe not ever."

"He's Simon's grandfather. I'm not sure how to not talk about him."

Max ran a hand over his hair, smoothing it down unnecessarily. "Let's talk about why you showed up for me today. A few days ago, you didn't want me to have anything to do with Simon. Or you, for that matter. I'm still the same guy I was back then. What changed?"

"I showed up because you deserved it. You've never been anything but good to me and Simon," Kendall explained. "You are the man who rescued my son from a tunnel slide and always helped me with my coat. You're also Simon's uncle."

"So because Simon and I are related, all is forgiven? You aren't afraid my life is too complicated?"

"Oh, I'm scared to death." There were still no guarantees. Kendall was as convinced as Katie that Max meant what he said today. He wanted to stick around and make a life here. That was great news for his son's life, but what did it mean for Kendall's? "You could choose not to be a part of our lives because of Paul."

"I want to be in your life," Max said. His hand reached across the table and rested on top of hers. Those words made her heart soar.

"That makes me happy. The truth is, *you* make us happy. Me and Simon. It's been so long since I've felt that way, I didn't know what to do with it." The tears began to well up in her eyes. She had promised herself she wasn't going to cry when she talked to him.

"Simon told me about the fight you and Trevor had when he told you he was leaving. The poor kid thinks he could have done something to make his dad stay."

The tears spilled over. Her sweet boy. "That's what he told you on Halloween?"

"He came to tell me he would be a good boy if I would still be his friend."

Kendall covered her face with her hands and sobbed. She had no idea how badly Simon was hurting. Max slid out of his side of the booth and into hers. He put his arm around her and pulled her into his chest.

"I brought him back home with every intention of telling you that it doesn't matter if you're afraid, I'm not going anywhere. And now that Simon is my family, you can't get rid of me, Kendall. I'm here for both of you."

His declaration made her cry harder. She wanted to believe that, but things were so much more complicated. He held her close and consoled her until she regained her composure.

Wiping her wet cheeks, she looked up into those eyes that made her feel safe. Eyes that she'd trusted from the very start. "We want you. *I* want you."

Max's gaze fell from her eyes to her lips. They were so close, they were breathing each other in. As wrong as Max should have been for her, Kendall couldn't help feeling like he was the most right thing in her life. He wet his bottom lip with his tongue and she was sure he was going to kiss her when there was a crash from the kitchen.

Max jumped up and Kendall followed. A string of Japanese words accompanied the loud crash. Chef Yamaguchi was in the kitchen along with two of his sous chefs. There was a plate of food on the floor and several things cooking. Chef continued to chastise the underlings.

Kendall let Max sort things out. There was more to discuss, and work wasn't the place to do it. Paul Montgomery couldn't be a forbidden topic forever. Not if what Max said was true. For their lives to meld together, Max had to come to terms with who his father was.

"So, I saw Max today." Kendall dished out some peas onto Simon's dinner plate.

"You did? Was he taller?"

Kendall laughed lightly. "I don't think so. He looked the same to me." Smelled the same, too. So good.

Simon pushed the peas to the far side of the plate. Something told her he wasn't going to eat those. "Does he still want to be friends?"

"He does. But he's more than a friend, he's your family."

"He's your family, too," Simon said before shoveling in a mouthful of mashed potatoes.

"Well, he's not really my family. He's Daddy's family like Aunt Emma and Aunt Lucy are my family. Max is Mommy's friend. How do you feel about Max being Mommy's friend?"

"I like him being your friend. I want him to always be your friend, like Ava and Riley."

"Who's Ava and Riley?"

"In my class. They're best friends. They *always* play together." He set his fork down and rested his cheek on his hand. "Nobody wants to be my friend at school. They think I can't talk and I'm a baby. But I'm not a baby and I *can* talk. You can hear me. The yucks just steal my sounds at school."

It was the first time Simon had ever spoken about the other kids at school. It broke her heart. "What if you pretended the kids at school were like Max? Maybe you could pick someone to try to talk to."

Simon's head shook back and forth so fast she had to stop him before he made himself sick. "What if it wasn't in the classroom? Maybe at recess where no one else would hear."

"The yucks hate school."

"What about you? Do you hate school?"

His little shoulders lifted up and fell down.

"Why do you think you hate school?"

He shrugged again.

"Can you think about it? Think about what makes the yucks really mad about school."

Simon finished his dinner, except for the peas. Kendall let him be quiet and hoped he was truly thinking about it. When she took his plate to the sink, he finally had an answer. "There's so many kids at school. It makes the yucks go crazy. Mrs. Taylor can't help me when I need her. Everybody wants her. Grant is always raising his hand and making her come by him and Gianna always says, 'Mrs. Taylor! Mrs. Taylor! Look! Look!'" Simon waved his arms around and raised his voice in imitation.

"Mommy has a meeting at school this week to talk about how Mrs. Taylor, Mrs. Warner and even Mrs. Nigel can make things easier for you, so talking will be no big deal someday."

"I like Mrs. Warner. She has funny toys in her room."

"Would you like it if you could see her more? She's really nice like Max. Maybe you could start by talking to Mrs. Warner."

Simon shook his head. Kendall was grasping at straws. Nothing about Wilder made Simon feel safe enough to talk to someone there. How was she going to prove to the school that he belonged there when he didn't even feel like he did?

"Can Max come to school? I'll talk to Max at school."

"Max can't be there with you every day." But he could come with him the day of the meeting. Maybe if Simon spoke to Max at school, he'd start talking to other people there like he did with Kendall's family now. It was a plan. Not a very good plan, but still more than she had a few hours ago.

ASKING MAX TO come was easier than she thought. Getting him to school at eight in the morning was the hard part. Kendall and Simon stood in his living room, waiting while he threw on a shirt and tie. The couch was currently occupied by a pile of blankets and a pillow. He'd overslept. Mornings weren't his "thing," evidently.

"I swear I set my alarm," he said, coming out of his room with his shirt half-buttoned. "I should have warned you I tend to be useless before ten."

"It's fine," Kendall said, resisting the urge to check her watch. Maybe with Max there, Simon wouldn't freak out about not being the first person in the classroom.

His mom came out of the bedroom, pulling her hair up in a ponytail. "I would have gotten him up, but I think I'm still on West Coast time."

"Yeah, I've used that excuse before," Max said as he slipped on his shoes.

"You have funny hair," Simon said, pointing at Max's head. His hair was sticking up in all directions.

Kendall gave Simon a stern look. "Manners," she whispered.

"It's true," he mumbled back.

Max smoothed his hair down and flashed

them both a toothy grin. "He's just looking out for me. Right, Simon?"

"Right."

Kendall found herself unable to do anything but smile back. They headed down the stairs of his three-flat while Max tied his tie and asked Simon the names of all the cute girls in his class.

To Kendall's surprise, Simon didn't blush or fuss that he didn't like girls. He rattled off two names.

"Cute girls were the only thing that got me through school, buddy," Max said. "Whenever I was having a bad day or felt nervous, I'd look at the prettiest girl in class and all the bad thoughts went away."

"That works?" Simon was skeptical.

"Sure it does! As a matter of fact, I had a big meeting this week with lawyers and a judge. I was really nervous. So, I looked at your mom and boom, I felt better." One corner of Max's mouth curled up as Kendall glanced at him over Simon's head. Her face quickly heated.

"You think Mom is pretty?"

"Yeah, I do," Max said like that was the craziest question ever. She could feel his eyes on her now, and it was doing the complete opposite of calming her nerves.

"Are you encouraging my son to ogle girls in his class? That could cause more problems than it would solve."

Max laughed as they stepped outside. "I didn't say he should *ogle* anyone." He put a hand on Simon's head. "Remember, it's not a staring contest. You gotta be subtle, dude."

"What's subtle?" Simon asked innocently.

"Be cool about it. It's quicker than a look. Like this." Max demonstrated the art of being subtle. His warm, brown eyes stole a glance in Kendall's direction, meeting hers just long enough to cause her heart to skip a beat.

"Got it." Simon grabbed his mom's hand. "I'm going to be subtle at Lauren."

Kendall was still a little worried this strategy would backfire. But if it worked, she'd let Max subtly ogle her anytime he needed to feel better.

The trees outside Wilder Elementary were almost bare, their leaves blanketing the ground underneath them. Buses filled with sleepy-eyed children pulled into a circle drive on the side of the building. Simon stopped talking as soon as the school came into view.

Kendall and Max checked into the main office before walking Simon to his classroom. Max held his backpack for him while Simon took off his jacket and hung it on the hook by his name. Mrs. Taylor welcomed them warmly. Kendall introduced Max as Simon's uncle. It sounded better than anything else she could call him.

"He's nervous about recess but excited to show his uncle around today," Kendall told Mrs. Taylor so she'd have the usual heads-up.

Simon gave Max a silent tour of his classroom. They looked through his desk and Simon showed off the class pet, a fat black-and-white hamster named Oreo.

The hallway began to fill with students. As the sound of their chatter and laughter got louder, Kendall could see Simon begin to stiffen. The yucks were in full effect.

Mrs. Taylor was attending their meeting, so she was there only to prepare the substitute. Kendall watched her hand the gray-haired sub some notes and wondered what they said about Simon. She noticed Mrs. Taylor nod in his direction, and the sub's eyes followed him around for a minute.

Simon was one of *those* kids. The one about whom the teacher had to make special notes. The one the substitute had to know about ahead of time…or else. As much as she knew he needed it to be that way, she wished her son could be like everyone else, not in need of any extra attention.

"Have a good day, buddy," she said to him as other kids began to trickle in. "Nana will pick you up from school, okay?"

He nodded and Max held a hand up for a high-five. A trio of girls walked in and ran up to Mrs. Taylor for a hug. Max leaned down and whispered to Simon, "Which one is Lauren?"

Simon whispered something back that Kendall couldn't hear. Max looked up at the girls by Mrs. Taylor, then gave Simon a thumbs-up. Kendall was used to being Simon's only confidante. Jealous about not being in on the secret, she nudged Max.

"Which one?"

"Pink flower."

Lauren was an adorable blonde with dimples and a huge flower barrette in her hair. Simon had chosen wisely. Kendall wanted to pull Lauren aside and beg her to be Simon's friend. Max pulled Kendall out of the room.

"Leave Lauren alone. Let's get you to your meeting."

Sometimes Kendall wondered if Simon would have developed the same issues even if Trevor had lived. She had her own issues with anxiety. Maybe he was this way because of her, not because of what happened to his father. Her stomach ached as they walked back to the main office.

Max didn't say anything. He made no promises that everything would be fine. He didn't try to convince her not to worry. He simply grabbed her hand, interlocking their fingers. It was exactly what she needed.

Lisa met them in the office and brought them back to the conference room. Several people were already seated around the table. Kendall recognized most of them—the speech and language pathologist, the principal, one of the special-education teachers. The woman at the head of the table introduced herself as a special-education coordinator and the man next to her said he was from the alternative day school.

Kendall was overwhelmed and felt outnumbered. It was her against all of them. Max's presence helped, but she kicked herself for not asking Lucy to come. Lucy had a law degree, and even though it wasn't in educational law, it was better than nothing.

Kendall tried to stay calm and focus on what was being said. They went over Simon's current performance in the classroom. Mrs. Taylor talked about his excellent handwriting and artistic ability. She often let Simon communicate through his drawings. His reading level was difficult to assess because he would not read aloud. Kendall assured them he was reading age-appropriate books at home.

Lisa was up next. She discussed Simon's difficulties with socializing and making friends. Simon's anxiety was a huge concern for the school, and he was not making any significant progress in developing coping strategies during his social-work sessions. Kendall knew this all to be true, but it hurt to hear it all laid out this way.

Kendall shared that Simon was making progress at home. He was speaking in front of more family members. He spoke in public as long as no one around them was paying him any attention. The school might not see a change, but she did.

Regardless, the team was recommending a new placement. They felt Simon would better be served in a therapeutic setting. Smaller class size, more than one adult per classroom and more intensive counseling services. Transportation would be provided and Kendall would get weekly feedback.

This was it. They wanted to kick him out. Kendall felt her shoulders tense and the pain in her stomach returned. "Why couldn't he get more counseling here? Or what if I took him back to one of the psychologists we've gone to outside of school? Maybe we could build off the gains he's been making at home."

The special-education coordinator was the only one doing the talking for the rest of the group. "Having him see Mrs. Warner more is a possibility, but Simon really requires more attention than she can give him. At the therapeutic school, he'd have group sessions every day and the social workers stop by the classrooms all the time."

"What if changing schools causes him to regress? He likes Mrs. Taylor and seems to be connecting to her. What if he doesn't get along with the new teacher? That could do more damage, right?"

The man from the therapeutic school took over. "Our teachers are all very good at working with students like Simon. He wouldn't be the only selective mute we've had. We have had a lot of success in working with this and other anxiety disorders."

Kendall felt like the room was shrinking. The table seemed too big for the space. Everyone was sitting too close. The air was thick and too hard to breathe. It felt like nothing she said was going to change their minds.

Max spoke for the first time since he'd introduced himself. "Can I have a minute to talk to Kendall privately?"

Lisa jumped up. "You can use my office."

She led them down a short hall to her room and left them alone. Kendall shut the door and paced around. The tears she'd been fighting flowed freely. "I'm failing Simon. They won't listen to me."

Max shook his head. "You aren't failing Simon. I think they hear what you're saying, but are you hearing them?"

"They want to kick him out of school."

"They want to help him."

"They think I screwed him up. They think I baby him. They think I'm a bad mom."

In the middle of her complete meltdown, Max grabbed her and kissed her. His lips gently caressed hers as his hands released her arms and slipped around her waist. Pulling her closer against him, she felt her own arms wrap around his neck.

When it came to an end, he continued to hold her in a tight embrace. Their noses still touched. Kendall had to remember to breathe. That was the best first kiss she'd ever had. Her entire body felt like it was filled with jelly.

"You are the best mom for Simon. No one loves him more than you do. Those people in there would never argue with that. You know what he wants and needs better than anyone."

"He wants a smaller class. And more time with the social worker," she said, remembering their conversation from the other night.

Max smiled. "See."

"You kissed me," she said, still a little light-headed from it.

"You looked like you needed it."

Kendall busted out laughing. He'd rid her of her nerves, that was for sure. One hand cradled her face as his thumb gently caressed her cheek. He kissed her once more, a short and sweet peck.

"That one was for me. Come on, let's finish up this meeting and get some food. I didn't eat breakfast this morning." He held out his hand. Their fingers threaded together and she wanted to believe she wasn't going to end up alone.

CHAPTER TWENTY

"WHY ARE YOU smiling like that?" Joanna asked as she mixed another disgusting kale smoothie in Max's blender.

Max had been smiling a lot. He couldn't stop. There was a lot to be happy about lately. The restaurant opened tonight, he had a very successful arbitration meeting with Katie, and a few pleasantly unsupervised visits with Aidan. Father and son had had a dinner date at the Rainforest Cafe with Grandma Jordan, a play date with Simon and Simon's car collection, and a visit to Lincoln Park Zoo for a couple of hours. Not once did Aidan cry for his mom to stay when she dropped him off.

Kendall, however, was the reason for this particular smile. She had texted him a picture of her and Simon holding a sign that said, "Every time you eat at Sato's, an angel gets its wings!" They had drawn angels flying around the words and the address at the bottom. Kendall promised to post a copy of it on every street corner between their house and the restaurant.

The blender stopped whirling.

"When are you going back to Portland?" As much as he appreciated his mother's support, especially when she'd first gotten here, he was ready for her to go home. He was tired of sleeping on the couch and having no room in his refrigerator because of her fruits and vegetables.

"I kind of like it here. I have several reasons to stay."

"I have several reasons why you should go."

She narrowed her eyes. "Be nice to me. I don't have to stay *here*. I mean, I like it here in Chicago. You're here. My grandson is here. I like Kendall and her family."

The last one gave him pause. "Her family?"

Joanna took a drink of her smoothie instead of clarifying. Kendall's family included a lot of people. One Montgomery, in particular. Max couldn't be bothered with that today. He had a lot to do to make sure the restaurant was going to be ready to go this evening when they opened for business.

"Well, if you're moving here, you'll have to start looking for your own place. No one is ever going to marry me if I live with my mother."

"Marry?" His mother perked right up. "You'd consider getting married again?"

"Not anytime soon, but yes. I'd like to get married again. To the right person this time."

"You know that makes me want to move here even more, don't you?"

Max shook his head. He couldn't figure out what version of herself she'd be if she moved here. Doting mother and grandmother? That would be…interesting.

"Chicago is a great city. Move here if you want to, but I want my bed back."

"I can sleep on the couch, you big baby."

"Right, like I'm going to be the guy that makes his mom sleep on the couch."

"You're the guy who kicks her out of your house," she teased.

Max rolled his eyes and headed for the bathroom to get ready for the day. Today was hopefully the day many, many angels would be getting their wings.

SATO'S WAS READY for business. No detail had been overlooked. The bar was properly stocked. The chef was a madman but a genius in the kitchen. The handpicked staff was pumped up for opening night. Max was proud of what he had helped accomplish. Sato's was going to be the most talked about restaurant in the city after tonight. He'd done a ton of promotion via social media and in the local newspapers. The reservations had been coming in all week. It was going to be an amazing opening.

Kendall and her family were due in around seven. He'd reserved the very best table for them. They were close to her mural and he made sure his best waiter was working that section. Kendall and Owen had a lot to be proud of, as well. From the fabric on the banquette to the chandelier that hung in the reception area, their design helped make Sato's the chic, contemporary restaurant Mr. Sato had envisioned. Celebrating with Kendall would be the perfect ending to the first day of this new beginning.

Twenty minutes before the doors opened, Jin arrived, dressed to the nines and ready to work the room. Max had been trying to do as Mr. Sato asked. Of course, mentoring would be a lot easier if the mentee wanted it. Jin still had a hard time admitting he didn't know it all. Every time Max took a moment out of his busy schedule to explain something, young Mr. Sato would roll his eyes and make some snide comment. Kendall's wise suggestion had been to think of mentoring Jin as good practice for parenting teenagers.

"Did you want to say anything to the staff when I get them all together before we open?" Max asked him as he jotted down some last-minute notes.

"What would I need to say? Shouldn't they be ready?" He didn't even look up from his phone, which always held his interest better than anything Max had to say.

"It would be your chance to thank them and to build a positive morale."

"Why would I thank them *before* they do their job?"

"Many of them have been working all week getting this place ready to go. All of them have put in several hours of training and learning the menu. Thanking them before we open encourages them to continue working hard and makes you look like a good guy." And Jin needed all the help he could get to look like a good guy.

"Fine."

"I also moved your father's table to the west room and will make sure we have space for him and your mom at the sushi bar if he wants."

"Well, aren't you going to be my father's

favorite. Congratulations," Jin said sarcastically.

Max set his pen down. Resting his elbows on his desk, he folded his hands together in front of him. "All right, I've had enough of your attitude. You don't like me. You also think you're ready to run a restaurant like this all on your own. Well, it doesn't matter if you like me or not. I don't care. I can also tell you that you aren't ready to manage a restaurant of this caliber by yourself. If you want to run a successful restaurant someday, I suggest you get over your hurt feelings and listen to the things I tell you."

"I graduated from one of the most prestigious business schools in the country. I don't think there's anything someone who didn't even go to college can teach me."

Jin thought that slam would hurt, but Max had heard it all before. He didn't need a college degree. He had learned how to run a restaurant by working in one since he was a kid. He'd been in the business longer than he hadn't. Business school didn't teach you how to estimate the weekly supply needs or how to smooth-talk an unhappy customer. Those things had to be learned outside the classroom.

This wasn't about who was smarter. This

was about Jin thinking his father didn't believe in him. Max knew all about daddy issues.

"Your dad asked me to help you so he could give you your own restaurant someday. If you don't want my help, that's fine by me. Can you go ignore me somewhere else, though? I have some work to do."

"He said that?"

Finally, something struck a chord with this kid. "He said all of it."

"He wants to give me my own restaurant?"

"When he thinks you're ready, yes."

"All I have to do is listen to you?"

Max sighed, exasperated. "Yes. All you have to do is listen to me. Knock that chip off your shoulder and listen to me. Then you'll get what you want."

"Why didn't my father just say that? He acts like I should know what he wants from me. He says, 'You have much to learn,' but he doesn't say, 'Listen to Max and I'll give you a restaurant to run.' I thought he was punishing me."

"I'm no expert on fathers. But yours has done nothing but give you opportunity after opportunity. Take advantage of them and learn something instead of simply taking advantage."

Jin put his phone away and smirked. "I do hate you, Mr. Jordan. But I'll listen to what you say. Then I'll run my own restaurant that will make more money than yours, and all will be right with the world."

Max chuckled. Jin could believe anything he wanted if it meant he wouldn't be such a thorn in Max's side. "Good luck with that." He rose to his feet. "But let's go get this one up and running first."

SMOOTH WAS THE word of the day. Everything was running smoothly. People were coming in the door, food was getting to the tables, money was filling the register. Max worked the room the best he could, spending a little extra time at one table in particular.

"How's the sushi?" Max asked Simon, who was busy putting a whole piece in his mouth.

"It's very good," Kendall's dad replied.

"The shrimp avocado is to die for," Emma said, picking up another piece with her chopsticks.

"Do you know where you get your edamame from? Our waiter wasn't sure." Jon, their waiter, had told Max all about Lucy and her questions. She apparently had a thousand of them.

"All our produce is purchased from a local

wholesaler. I can get you more information if you'd like."

"You should consider having some organic options," Lucy suggested.

"I love that idea." He glanced at Kendall who was trying not to laugh. "So, what's Simon's favorite?"

Owen pointed at the half-empty plate. "He's been eating the California rolls like they're going out of style."

"You like crab, huh?"

Simon's eyes bugged out and he immediately spit out what was in his mouth.

Kendall grimaced, handing him a napkin. "We didn't tell him what was in them for a reason."

"Sorry." Max failed to hold in his laughter. "How about I get him a chicken kabob since I ruined sushi for him?"

Simon nodded, grabbing for his water. "Yes please!"

He found their waiter and had him add a complimentary kabob. When Max turned to go back to talk to Kendall some more, two patrons seated by the window caught his attention. The image of his mother sitting with Paul Montgomery made his blood boil. He stormed over there, unable to control his rage.

"What in the world are you doing here with him?"

Joanna set down her menu and smiled up at her son. "We came to see what you've done with the restaurant."

Max refused to even look at her companion. He couldn't believe the nerve of this man. "He can't eat here. He's not welcome."

"Max."

"I'm serious. We have the right to refuse service. I want him to leave."

"Maxwell."

"I can't believe you would even sit with him."

"Your father is going to have dinner with me at your restaurant, or we're both leaving."

Paul set his napkin on his plate and raked a hand through his hair. "Joanna, I don't want to make a scene."

Max's blood pressure skyrocketed. "You don't want to make a scene? You abandoned her when she needed you the most and now you're going to sit here thirty-four years later and eat sushi with her?"

"He's your father, like it or not," Joanna argued. "He's here to support you."

"He's not my father."

She cocked an eyebrow and lowered her

voice. "Since when does being a father have a time limit?"

Max wanted to scream at her for using his own words against him like that. It wasn't the same. What happened with Max, Katie and Aidan was not the same as when Paul chose his family over him and Joanna. He had to get out of there before he did something stupid. He ran for the kitchen and the safety of his office. He picked up his stapler and threw it against the wall.

A knock on the door stopped him from doing the same with his pen holder. "Hey." Kendall poked her head in.

He sat on the edge of his desk and scrubbed his face with his hands. What in the world was his mother trying to do to him?

Kendall shut the door. She stood in front of him and pulled his hands away. "That didn't go well."

He took a deep breath and tried to focus on Kendall's face and nothing else. "Did you know he was coming here tonight?"

"No clue. If you hadn't confronted them so loudly, I'm not sure I would have known he was here at all."

It was a little comforting to know he wasn't the only one who'd been blindsided. She placed her hands on his face and gently placed her lips against his. The kiss was so soft, his whole body relaxed.

"What was that for?" he asked when she pulled away.

She shrugged one shoulder. "You make me nervous when you're so upset. Kissing you is my thing, remember?"

Her answer made him half smile. He stood up and retrieved his stapler, setting it back on his desk. There was a nice indentation in the wall where it had hit. "How loud was I?"

Those kissable lips twisted up while she thought about it. "Loud enough."

Max dug his fingers through his hair. "Great." Thank goodness Mr. Sato was in the west dining room and hopefully not in earshot of his outburst. "I just can't understand how she can share a meal with him. And I can't believe she thought I would be okay with them being here tonight."

Kendall frowned. "Your mom is a big girl. She gets to choose who to forgive. She also said she knew he was married when she got involved with him, which means she didn't go into their relationship blindly. She was taking a risk and she knew it."

"So, you're siding with him?" Max took a step back. "He told her he was married, so it was okay to leave me behind?"

Kendall shook her head. "I am not taking anyone's side. I also don't condone anything Paul did."

"I can't forgive him," Max said, reaching for her again. Having her close made him feel better.

"You also get to choose who you forgive. Or not forgive, in this case."

"I choose not."

"But," Kendall began.

He let go of her. He didn't want to hear what was coming next. "No buts."

She held up one finger. "One but, and it's a big one." Max shook his head. There was nothing in this world that would make him forgive Paul for deserting him. Kendall continued anyway. "He is Simon's grandfather. He will always be part of Simon's life, of my life. You haven't wanted to talk about it, but now I think I need to know if you can handle that."

"His relationship with Simon means nothing to me."

"So, when Simon has his birthday party in a couple of months and Paul's invited, should I not bother sending you an invite?"

This wasn't easy to answer. There was no doubt in his mind that he wanted to be in Kendall's life. That was indisputable. Simon was a nonnegotiable bonus. Max couldn't have one without the other. Paul was something altogether different. Could Max accept that Kendall and Simon had to have a relationship with him? Probably. If there was ever a Max, Kendall and Simon, could he accept Paul as part of his family? That answer was less certain.

Letting out a breathy sigh, he said, "Simon and I could celebrate separately."

"What about Thanksgiving? Christmas? Paul has no one. I have to invite him. Simon's going to want his Uncle Max there, too. What about that?"

Suddenly, his mother having one meal with the guy seemed like much less of a problem. Historically, Max had spent his holidays working. Work allowed him to keep everyone from getting too close. That all changed when he moved to Chicago. Kendall opened him up, and being vulnerable was more than uncomfortable. He pushed back a little. "I feel like you're telling me I have to forgive him."

"I'm not telling you anything," she said, holding her hands up. "This is the reality of our situation. You can be mad. You can hate him. But he is eating dinner with your mother tonight. He will be sitting at my dining room table at Thanksgiving. He'll be at Simon's birthday party this year and the next and the next. You can't refuse to deal with him without removing yourself from key parts of my life, of Simon's life."

She was right and it made him crave a cigarette. Old habits had a way of refusing to die. Hating his father had become somewhat of a habit. A destructive habit like smoking. One he feared he'd always struggle to overcome if he tried to quit it.

"I want nothing to do with him, Kendall. I can't handle it."

Kendall's forehead creased. "That scares me."

"It shouldn't. This doesn't change the way I feel about you."

She crossed her arms and closed her eyes. When she opened them, the way she looked at Max terrified him. "It changes the way I have to feel about you, for Simon's sake."

Kendall gave him a chaste kiss on the cheek and went back out into the dining room, leaving Max alone with his thoughts and doubts. He couldn't lose her because of his father. But how could he make this work?

BY THE END of the night, Max and his staff had successfully fed every customer who had walked through the door of Sato's. There hadn't been one single complaint and several patrons had shared their positive experience with Max before leaving. Mr. Sato was thrilled. Jin took notes. Max counted tonight as a win, even if his mother and Paul's date night had ruffled his feathers.

He rubbed his eyes. The clock in his office said it was a little after eleven o'clock. The kitchen was closed and cleaned. The day's receipts had been counted, the credit-card report sent and daily sales information recorded. All Max had to do was set the alarm and lock up. He shut off the lights and headed out.

The city was quite tranquil this time of night. There were still cars on the roads, but the sidewalks were almost empty. It made him feel alone, something he was just beginning to think he'd never have to feel again. He pulled out his phone and searched for an address. There was only one thing he could do to avoid the lonely road ahead. He asked the driver to change his destination.

Kendall's street was quiet. Her house was dark except for the porch light she'd left on. Max texted his arrival so he didn't wake Simon.

She pulled the door open, wearing flannel pajamas and glasses. She was beautiful. "Hey there," she said, taking in his somber expression. "What's wrong?"

Lucy appeared from behind her. "Kind of late, isn't it?" she asked, ever the ferocious guard dog.

He kept his focus on Kendall. "Can I borrow your car?"

"Sure, but where are you going?" She looked worried, as if she thought he might say back to California. Her concern gave him a little hope.

"I need to talk to my dad and I can only imagine how much a cab would cost to Lake Forest."

Her lips curled up into the sweetest smile. He wanted to kiss her so it would never fade. She disappeared from the doorway before he could do just that. When she reappeared she had shoes on and keys in her hand. "Want some company?"

His nerves kicked in as soon as they exited the highway. He almost asked Kendall to pull over at the first gas station they came upon so he could buy some cigarettes, although he doubted smoking a whole pack would help, given his level of anxiety.

Kendall's hand moved from the steering wheel to his leg. "It's going to be okay."

He placed his hand over hers and squeezed. "Thanks for coming with me."

"I lean on you, you lean on me. That seems to be our new thing."

The next breath went in a little easier after she said that. He liked the thought of having someone he could count on and being that someone for Kendall.

It wasn't too long before they drove up to what appeared to be a mansion. Landscaping lights illuminated the trees and shrubs that surrounded the house. Red brick covered the entire exterior. This place was so humongous, it looked like it could take up an entire city block.

"This is where he lives?" Max bent forward to get a better view through the windshield.

"This is it. This is where Trevor grew up."

The knot of anger that had taken up a permanent home in his stomach since he found out his father was alive and well grew larger. Paul Montgomery had enough money to support ten families. Max almost asked Kendall to drive away.

"He told me he offered your mother money, but she said she wanted him or nothing," Kendall said as if reading his mind.

Max pulled his eyes away from the house

and set them on Kendall, his reason for being here. "Of course he said that."

"Does that sound like something your mom would do?"

It did. Max let his head fall back against the headrest. That didn't mean it was true. He'd have to ask his mother before he'd believe it.

"Do you want me to call him so he knows we're here?" Kendall asked, taking her phone out of her purse. He nodded and she dialed.

Paul opened the front door before Max mustered up the courage to get out of the car. Kendall waited for him to make the first move. It was now or never. He pulled the handle and pushed the door open. He wasn't going to go inside the house, he had decided. He didn't need to see any more of Paul Montgomery's wealth.

"Is everything all right?" Paul asked as Max made his way up the brick paved walkway with Kendall at his side.

"As all right as it can be," Kendall answered since Max didn't.

"Come on in out of the cold," he said, stepping back inside.

Max shook his head. "We're not staying."

"Oh," Paul said, coming back out. He wore a navy blue robe over his pajamas. Max hadn't worn real pajamas since he was a little kid.

"I came here to get a couple of things straight." Max reached out in search of Kendall's hand. Her fingers were cold when they found his. "My mother is important to me. Kendall and Simon are important to me. I want them to be in my life. I understand that means there are going to be times when our lives intersect."

"I don't want to cause you any trouble. I know I don't deserve anything from you."

"You don't, and I'm not really offering you anything. Let's be clear. This isn't me forgiving you or welcoming you into my life. This is me setting some ground rules I can live with because I refuse to give up Kendall and Simon."

Kendall squeezed his hand a little tighter.

"What kind of ground rules?" The air was cold enough that they could see their breath. Paul wrapped his arms around himself.

Max had thought about nothing but the rules on the way over here. Now his heart was beating so fast, he couldn't think straight. He took a deep breath and stole a glance in Kendall's direction. "I'm not ready to talk about what happened between you and my mother. I'm not sure I'll ever want to know. Do not offer up stories or things you remember about my mom when you two were…together."

Paul nodded.

"What happens between me and Kendall is between me and Kendall. You do not get an opinion. I don't care that you're one of the reasons I'm alive, or who else was your son. You have no say in this relationship."

"Kendall makes her own decisions. Always has."

"That's true," Kendall said. "But you have a way of letting me know when you think I've made the wrong one."

"I've been trying to look out for you and Simon," he said in his defense. "Without Trevor, I thought you needed some help."

"She doesn't need help unless she asks for it. I hope she won't need your help with me." He turned to Kendall. "Can you handle that?"

She nodded and smiled. He was glad she had offered to come along.

"I'll keep my opinions to myself, then," Paul said, sounding slightly wounded. He stared at his feet. "Can you two come inside so we don't freeze out here?"

"We're almost done. My mom doesn't get to decide who I choose to be around, and I don't get to choose who she lets into her life. But know this—if you hurt her again, I will show you no mercy."

Paul actually laughed. Not in a mocking

way, but as if the threat filled him with pride. "I wouldn't expect anything else."

"Last one and you can get back to bed," Max said, wishing he wasn't so proud and had taken Paul up on his offer to go inside. "I don't like you. I don't forgive you. I don't know that I ever will. The way you'll show me you care about that is by keeping your distance and respecting my wishes."

"Understood."

"Good." A feeling of calm came over him, and Max held his hand out, the only peace offering he was willing to give. Paul stared at it for a second, perhaps wondering if this was some sort of test, a trick maybe. He reached out slowly and took Max's hand, shaking it firmly when it wasn't pulled away. "See you around," Max said, backing away.

He and Kendall jogged back to the car, which was thankfully still warm from the drive over.

"You did great," she said as she backed out of the driveway. "I'm proud of you for finding a way to make this work."

Max suddenly felt exhausted. His adrenaline was no longer flowing and his whole body ached for his bed. He held her hand and closed his eyes. "Anything for you."

Kendall drove him home and double-parked outside his building.

"Thanks for coming with me," he said. "Having you there helped a lot."

She twisted in her seat to face him and gave him her crooked smile. "I saw you subtly ogling me when you got nervous. It really is your thing."

"Pretty girls—helping me out since 1987," he said, making her laugh. "I hope you know how serious I am about you. I want this. I want you."

"Good," she said, reaching for his tie and pulling him closer.

"Good." He initiated the kiss this time. Sweet and soft. She tasted like toothpaste and felt like true love.

He pulled back, then kissed her one more time on the cheek. "You better go home before Lucy comes looking for you. And me." Smiling like a fool, he grabbed the door handle and slipped out of the car. They had all the time in the world to feed this flame. He wasn't going anywhere. Well, he was going home, but that was as far apart as they'd ever be.

CHAPTER TWENTY-ONE

KENDALL STOOD IN the doorway to get a full view of the bedroom as Max came up behind her. She could hear Simon counting in the living room. The two of them were in the midst of an intense game of hide-and-seek.

"All finished?" he whispered.

"I think so. What do you think?"

Max took a look over her shoulder. "Kendall," he gasped, pushing past her and standing in the center of Aidan's new room. "This is incredible."

Once it was decided that Max would get his son every other weekend, he enlisted Kendall's help in setting up a room for him in the condo. There was a race-car bed and checkered-flag curtains. Colorful grandstands filled with cheering fans and race cars crossing the finish line were painted on the wall behind the bed. Kendall had found a dresser that looked like a mechanic's tool chest and a traffic-light lamp for the nightstand.

She'd managed to keep Max out of this room until today, although she wondered if he hadn't taken a peek when she wasn't around. He seemed genuinely surprised, so maybe not.

"Ready or not, here I come!" Simon yelled from the other room.

Max put his finger to his lips and slipped into the closet.

"Mommy, where did Max go?" Simon asked as he meandered down the hall.

"If I told you, that would be cheating. You have to look for him."

"Whoa! This is Aidan's room?" The mural was similar to the one in Simon's room. The accessories and fancy bed were not. Simon's look of jealousy was something Kendall hadn't seen before. "I want a race-car bed!"

"Don't you have an uncle to look for?"

"But how come he got this?" Simon asked, picking up a pillow in the shape of a red race car.

"You act like Santa didn't bring you five hundred presents earlier this week. Stop whining and find Max before he's lost forever."

Simon scowled and tossed the pillow back on the bed. He opened the closet and Max came tumbling out. "You found me," he said, trying to sound disappointed.

"Let's play with Aidan's toys," Simon suggested, tugging on Max's arm.

Max looked at his watch. "He should be here any minute. Why don't we wait for him? Your mom did such a nice job getting everything perfect, let's not mess it up."

"Fine." Simon's bottom lip jutted out and the sulking began.

So much had changed over the last six weeks. Simon had started at his new school, and he was thriving. The smaller setting and more individual attention were exactly what he needed to chase away the yucks. Just before winter break, he'd actually spoken to one little boy in his class. It was a major breakthrough, and something Kendall hoped would happen more often and with a variety of peers when he went back after the holidays.

Simon wasn't the only one overcoming obstacles. Max survived Thanksgiving and Christmas with his father in the picture. He opted to work on Thanksgiving Day to avoid any confrontation, but he had been there Christmas Eve when Kendall's entire family, including Paul, gathered to celebrate.

The two men exchanged little, other than meaningless pleasantries, but it was a start. Max had a tough road ahead, especially since his mother was moving to Chicago and had every intention of welcoming Paul into her life. The whole thing flabbergasted Kendall as much as it did Max, but who were they to judge? Their relationship could easily raise a few eyebrows.

Kendall had fallen in love with the man who looked like her dead husband. A man who was her husband's half brother, a secret love child. Max didn't think it was too funny when she'd called him that once. She hoped if he believed he was created out of love, he'd be more accepting of all the love that was being offered to him now.

Love was hard enough without all these extenuating circumstances. Kendall and Max both had to overcome their trust issues and be willing to drop their defenses. That meant fighting their instinct to hide their feelings. Only time would tell if they could make it work. The good news was they both wanted to try and neither one was willing to walk away.

The door buzzer sounded and Simon sprinted to the intercom. "He's here!"

Max planted a kiss on Kendall's forehead. "Thank you for this. He's going to love it."

She took his hand and led him to the front door. Simon nearly tackled his cousin when he walked in. Aidan didn't mind. He was a big fan of Simon. Katie and Jason carried in so much stuff, it looked like the little guy was moving in permanently. Katie had three pages of notes and reminded Max five times to call her if he had any questions.

"He's got it, honey," Jason said, taking the notes she'd written and handing them to Max. "Let's go."

Katie's eyes were wet and Kendall couldn't help but feel for her. Had Trevor survived his last tour of duty, they would have gotten divorced and Kendall would have been where Katie was right now. How could someone ever take care of your child better than you could? It would have been very difficult to relinquish control.

"He needs a night-light at bedtime. I packed one in case you don't have one. There's also a humidifier in that bag because I wasn't sure how dry it was in here. Our place is so dry in the winter."

She'd literally thought of everything. No wonder there was so much stuff.

"He'll be fine. I promise to return him on Sunday in the same condition he's in now," Max assured her. "I have Kendall one block away if I need help. Plus, I'll call you if I have any questions."

Jason gave him a thumbs-up behind his

wife's back. "All right. Let's say goodbye to Aidan."

The two boys came running out of Aidan's new room with cars in both hands. "Mommy, come see my room!"

Kendall and Max hung back while the rest of them went to check it out. Max frowned and motioned to the pile of stuff that now littered his living room floor.

"Be nice," she whispered back. "I would probably be the same way."

"No, you wouldn't. That's why I'm dating you and divorced from her."

"Cool room," Jason said, leading the pack back into the living room. "Did you paint that?"

Max gave all the credit to Kendall. Katie carried Aidan in her arms. She told him to be good for his dad and was failing miserably at not getting emotional.

"He's going to have a blast with Dad, right Aidan?" Jason said, taking the boy from his mother. Kendall was certain the guy was afraid he was never going to get out of Max's condo. He handed Aidan to Max. "We'll see you on Sunday, and we'll call you tonight before bed."

"And don't forget to have him brush his teeth with the toothpaste I packed," Katie said as her husband pulled her toward the door. "He can't use adult toothpaste. It's in the notes."

"Got it," Max said.

"He's got it," Jason echoed.

She shook loose and gave Aidan one more kiss goodbye. There was no doubt in Kendall's mind that Katie would be calling more than once at bedtime. They all waved as Max shut the door. He set Aidan down so he could run off with Simon. Pressing his back against the door, he let out an exasperated sigh.

"Do I really have to brush his teeth with special toothpaste?"

Kendall laughed and nodded. He had so much to learn. "You better read your notes. There will be a quiz later."

Max pulled an album from his shelf and slid the record out of the sleeve. There was always music playing at Max's house. Kendall loved it. Being with Max allowed her to rediscover some of the things she'd given up during her marriage to Trevor—music, art, little pieces of herself she'd forgotten. Max appreciated her talents and respected her need for independence.

He carefully set the needle in place and held out his hand to her as the song began to play. Smiling, she took it and let him pull her close. His other arm snaked around her waist while hers wrapped around his shoulder. Her fingers scratched the hair at the nape of his neck as they began to dance in a small circle.

"Thanks again for helping with his room. I think he likes it." His lips pressed against her temple.

"You don't have to thank me. I loved doing it." She rested her head on his shoulder. He was her warm, safe place. It didn't scare her as much as it used to that she felt at home in his arms.

They swayed back and forth, enjoying the soft music as it mixed with the sound of their sons' giggles coming from the bedroom. Kendall smiled, knowing Simon found the same sense of security when they were all together. It was that feeling that helped him fight the yucks. For that, she would be the one eternally grateful.

"I love you," he whispered. It was the first time he'd said it. She let it sink in as the sentiment overfilled her already full heart. She held on to him tighter, smiled bigger, fell deeper. He stopped moving. "That doesn't scare you, does it?"

She pulled back so he could see her. Kendall placed both hands on his face. His brown eyes searched for confirmation that it wasn't too soon, that he wasn't pushing too hard. Shaking her head, she reassured him, "The only thing that scares me is how much I love you back."

Max let out a relieved breath. "Let's try not to second-guess this even though we're both scared, okay?"

"Okay," she agreed before kissing him soundly on the lips. He held her face like she held his. Lost in the moment, they didn't even notice the song change, but the groans of disgust coming from the hall were another story.

The two boys ran back to the bedroom, both in agreement that kissing was so gross and weird. "Someday you won't think it's so gross!" Max shouted after them.

Kendall laughed and planted one more kiss on his cheek. "Let's get all this stuff moved into his bedroom."

It was Max's turn to groan. "Ten bucks says we don't even unpack half of this."

She grabbed two bags and headed back to the room. "Come on, you big baby."

AFTER MOVING AIDAN'S stuff into his room, Kendall and Max got the boys dressed to play in the snow. Emma had called, hoping for a distraction. Yesterday's shift at the hospital had been emotionally draining, and she needed to be around family. Kendall invited her over to Max's to build a snowman.

They all trudged downstairs in their snow pants and boots, mittens and hats. Emma met them outside. Whatever had happened was clearly weighing heavy on her shoulders. Kendall wrapped her arms around her little sister. "Sorry for your rough day."

"Thank you for not making me sit in an empty apartment all day."

A snowball smacked the back of Kendall's head. She turned around slowly to face her attacker. Simon and Aidan were both holding snowballs, while Max was suspiciously empty-handed.

"Are you three really prepared for what will happen to you if you start a snowball fight with the Everhart sisters?"

Max's smile slipped a little. Simon hopped up and down, the smile on his face hidden by his scarf. He tossed his snowball at her, but it fell short. Aidan giggled and tossed his, which basically landed at his feet. It was clear who had hit her with the first snowball.

She bent down and packed her own ball of revenge. "We both played softball. I was the pitcher."

Before Max could run for cover, she unleashed a fastball that hit him right in the center of his chest. The little boys screamed and laughed, quickly gathering up more snow. Emma and Kendall took turns assaulting Max with snowballs. He managed to throw a couple himself. One whizzed past Kendall's head.

"Hey!" a voice sounded over her shoulder.

She turned around to find Max's neighbor wiping snow out of his eyes.

"Nice aim, Floor Three. But now, you're going down."

Charlie joined the fight, making it three against three. Kendall didn't feel bad about the fact that her team had the clear advantage. Simon and Aidan weren't much of an offense. Max realized his only strategy was to use the boys as a shield rather than as weapons. He picked them up and used them to block the flying snow.

Kendall and her team had no choice but to surrender. "I thought we were making a snowman," she said, ending the fight.

The boys got to work rolling the snow into a giant base. Emma and Charlie helped while Max crossed enemy lines to make peace.

"You have a wicked fastball."

"You have no shame. Using children as a shield? That's not right."

"You had Charlie and Emma trying to kill me, what was I supposed to do?"

"You should have taken it like a man," Kendall said, shaking her head.

"Is that what you think?" He pulled her into his arms and rubbed his cold nose against hers. His cheeks were red from the cold and from the snowball he took square in the face from Charlie.

"I think we kicked your butt."

He laughed and gave her a quick peck on the lips. "That you did. I deserved it. I'll admit it."

"Mom, stop kissing and come help us!" Simon and Aidan were trying to lift one snowball onto the other. Charlie came over to offer his muscle.

They added a head and went to work finding some arms. Emma untied the scarf around her neck and wrapped it around the snowman. Kendall watched as Charlie wiped some snow off Emma's hat. Her sister smiled and tucked some hair behind her ear.

"I saw you yesterday, Nightingale. You looked busy."

"Yesterday was not my favorite."

Charlie nodded. "I brought in the girl from the house fire. Makes me wish I had a delete button on my brain so I could unsee things, you know?"

"That's why I needed to hang out with my nephew." Emma pointed at Simon.

"Speed Racer is your nephew? Speed Racer and I go way back. I helped him out on Halloween."

"He and I go way back, too. All the way back to the day he was born."

"We have *so* much in common," Charlie mused.

Kendall butted in, linking arms with Emma. "Let's go see if Max has any carrots," she said, pulling Emma inside.

She unlocked Max's door and headed to the kitchen.

"Wow, this is serious. You have keys to his place and know your way around his kitchen. I think my sister is in love."

"He gave me his key so I could work on the mural for Aidan's room while he was at work." No carrots. Since his mother had gone back to Portland, Max had refused to buy anything that could be considered healthy.

Emma sat down at the breakfast bar. "I'm happy for you."

"What?" Kendall gave up on the carrots and began searching the cupboards for some hot chocolate.

"I'm happy for you. I think Max is a nice guy. As weird as it is that he's related to Trevor, I think you guys are good together."

"Thanks." Kendall's sisters hadn't shared their opinion with her and she hadn't asked, for fear they would tell her she was crazy. "I think we could be good together, too."

"So you aren't hanging out with him to get to the hot paramedic that lives below him?" Emma teased.

Kendall pushed her off the stool. She grabbed the only thing she could think of to use for a nose. "You're hilarious. Let's go talk them into taking us out for some cocoa."

The guys and boys had finished the snowman. He had sticks for arms and Max's hat on his head. Kendall stuck the orange pencil in for a nose. It wasn't perfect but would have to do. Perfect was overrated, anyway.

"Who wants Max to take us to get hot chocolate?" Emma asked like she was trying to incite a riot.

"Me!" both Aidan and Simon screamed.

"Charlie, you want to come with us?" Max asked. He glanced at Emma, who was was already on her way to Starbucks, hand in hand with the two little boys.

"Nah, you guys have fun. I'll see you around."

Kendall held on to Max's arm, snuggling against him for some warmth. He pressed a kiss to the top of her head.

For over a year, she'd been mourning the loss of what she had convinced herself was the best life she could ever have. As she walked the wintry streets with this man at her side and their sons' giggles in the air, she realized that that life had been far from the best. After all the hardship, this was the better life with the better man.

Kendall couldn't ask for more.

* * * * *

LARGER-PRINT BOOKS!

GET 2 FREE LARGER-PRINT NOVELS PLUS 2 FREE MYSTERY GIFTS

Love Inspired®

Larger-print novels are now available...

LILPDIR13R

ReaderService.com

Manage your account online!

- Review your order history
- Manage your payments
- Update your address

---

*We've designed
the Harlequin® Reader Service
website just for you.*

Enjoy all the features!

- Reader excerpts from any series
- Respond to mailings and
  special monthly offers
- Discover new series available to you
- Browse the Bonus Bucks catalog
- Share your feedback

Visit us at:
ReaderService.com